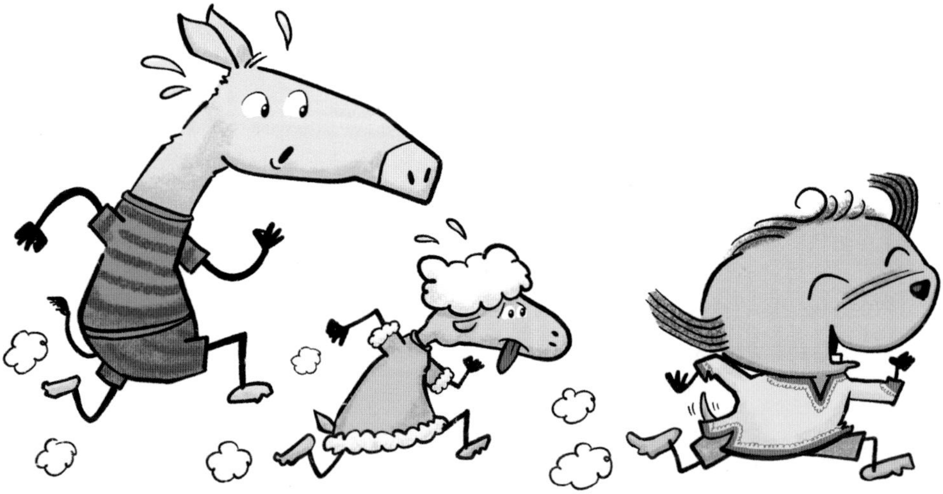

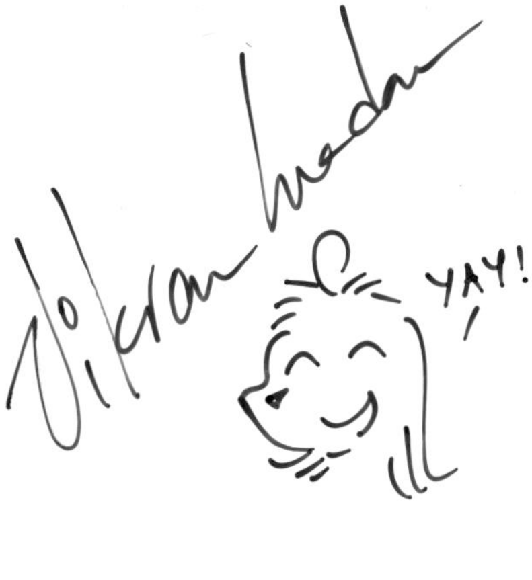
Vikram Madan
YAY!

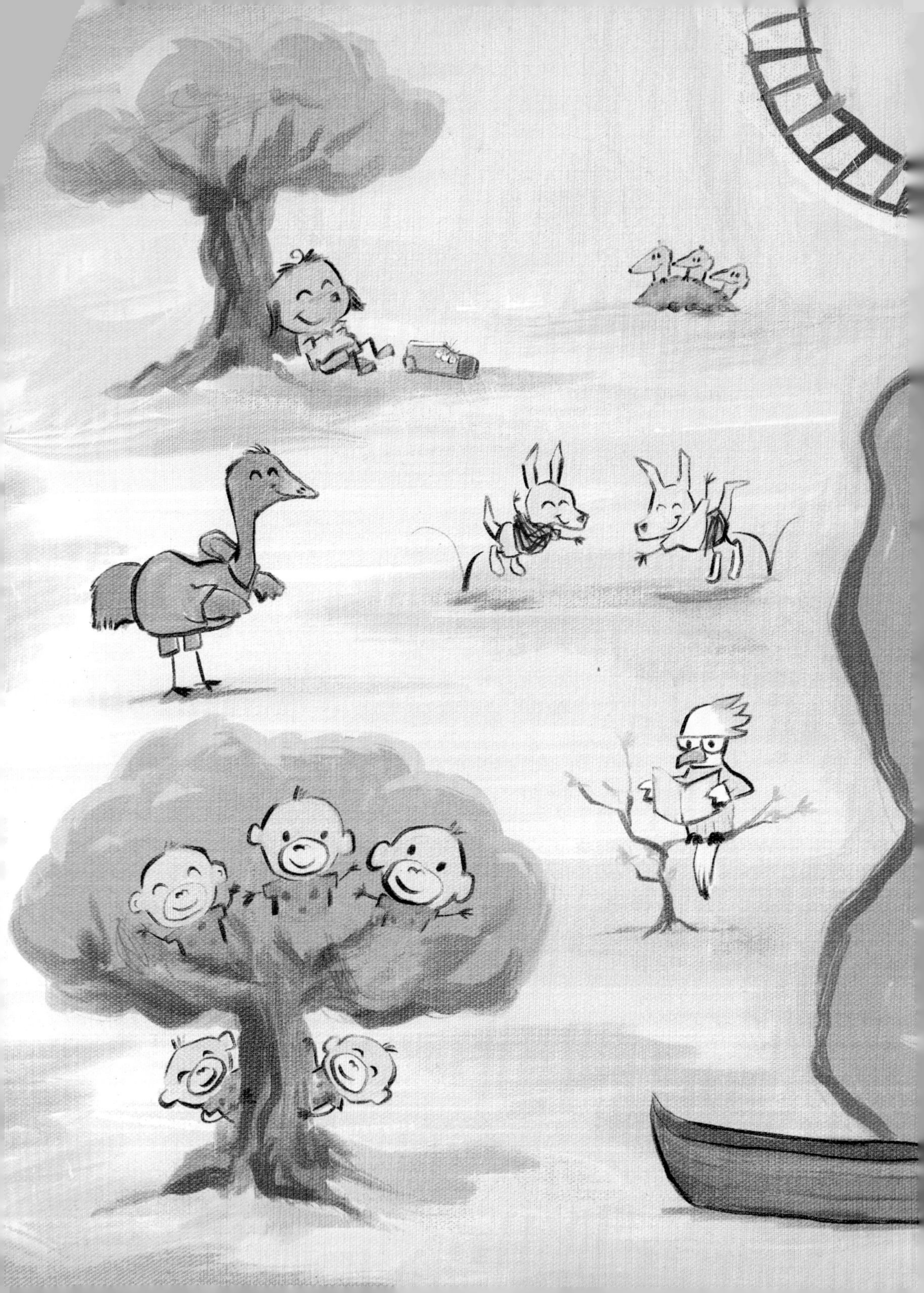

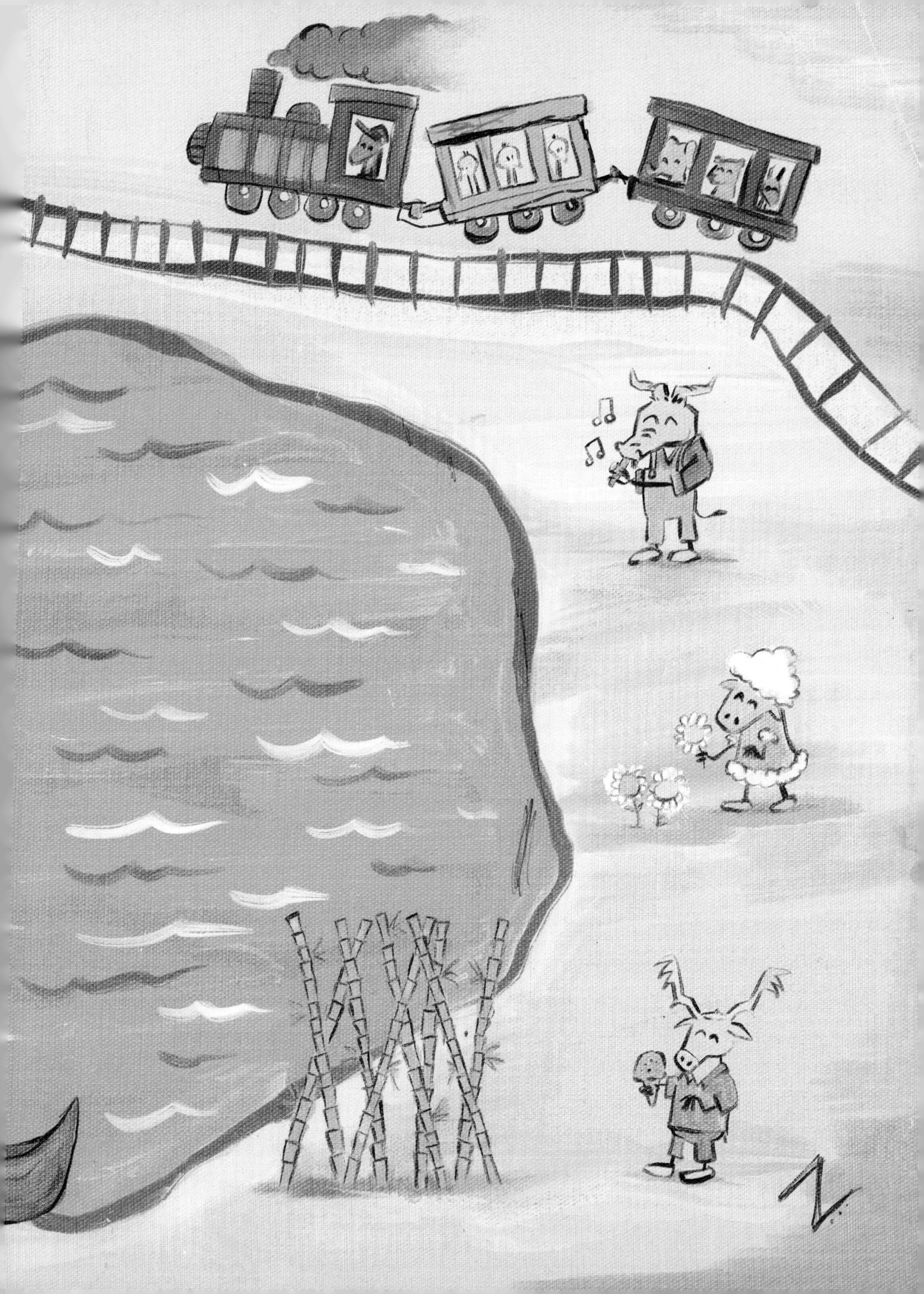

For Zooni, the sweetest dog
in the whole world.

Text and illustrations copyright © 2023 by Vikram Madan
All Rights Reserved
HOLIDAY HOUSE is registered in the U.S. Patent and Trademark Office.
Printed and bound in June 2023 at RRD, Dongguan, China.
The artwork was hand drawn on a tablet computer.
www.holidayhouse.com
First Edition
1 3 5 7 9 10 8 6 4 2
Library of Congress Cataloging-in-Publication Data is available.

ISBN: 978-0-8234-5357-3 (Hardcover)
ISBN: 978-0-8234-5616-1 (Paperback)

ZZZZZZ

ZOONI TALES

KEEP IT UP, PLUCKY PUP

BY VIKRAM MADAN

HOLIDAY HOUSE • NEW YORK

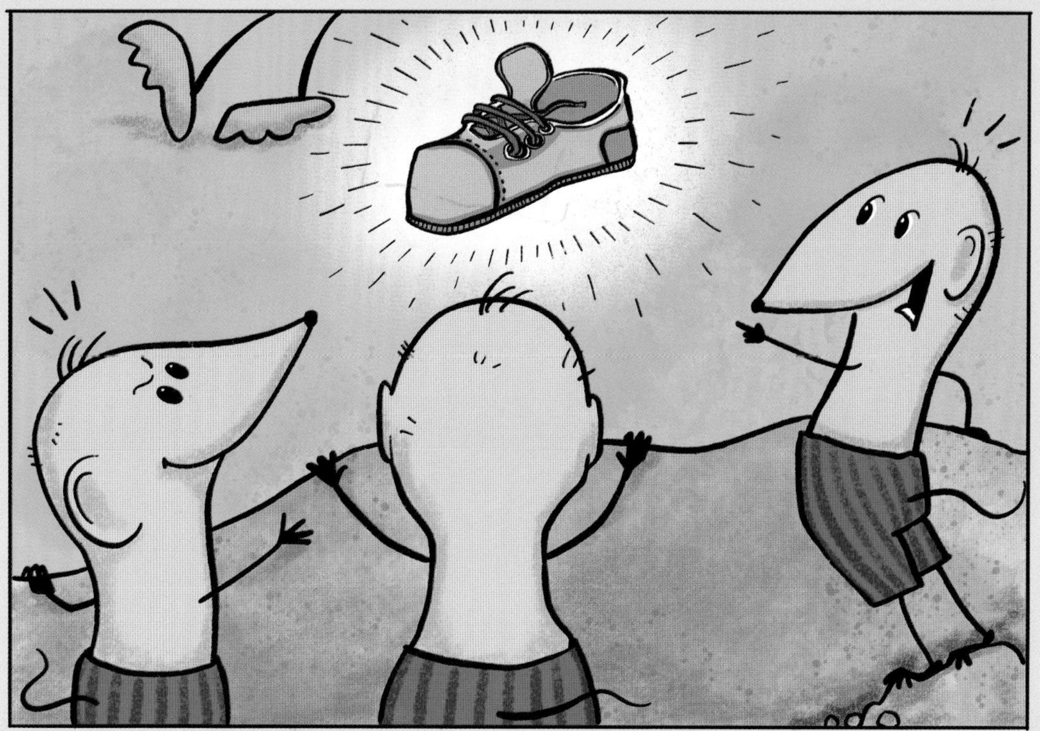

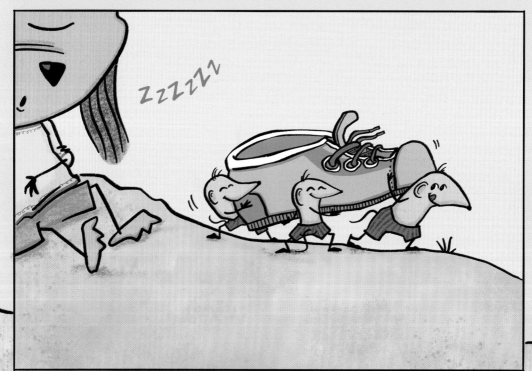

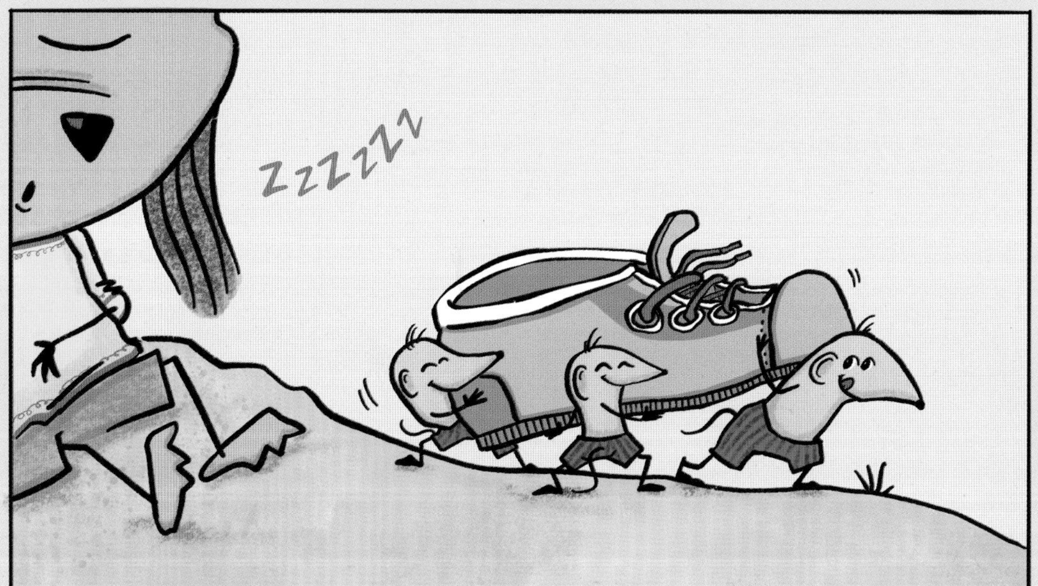
ZzZzZz

Contents

MISSING SHOE

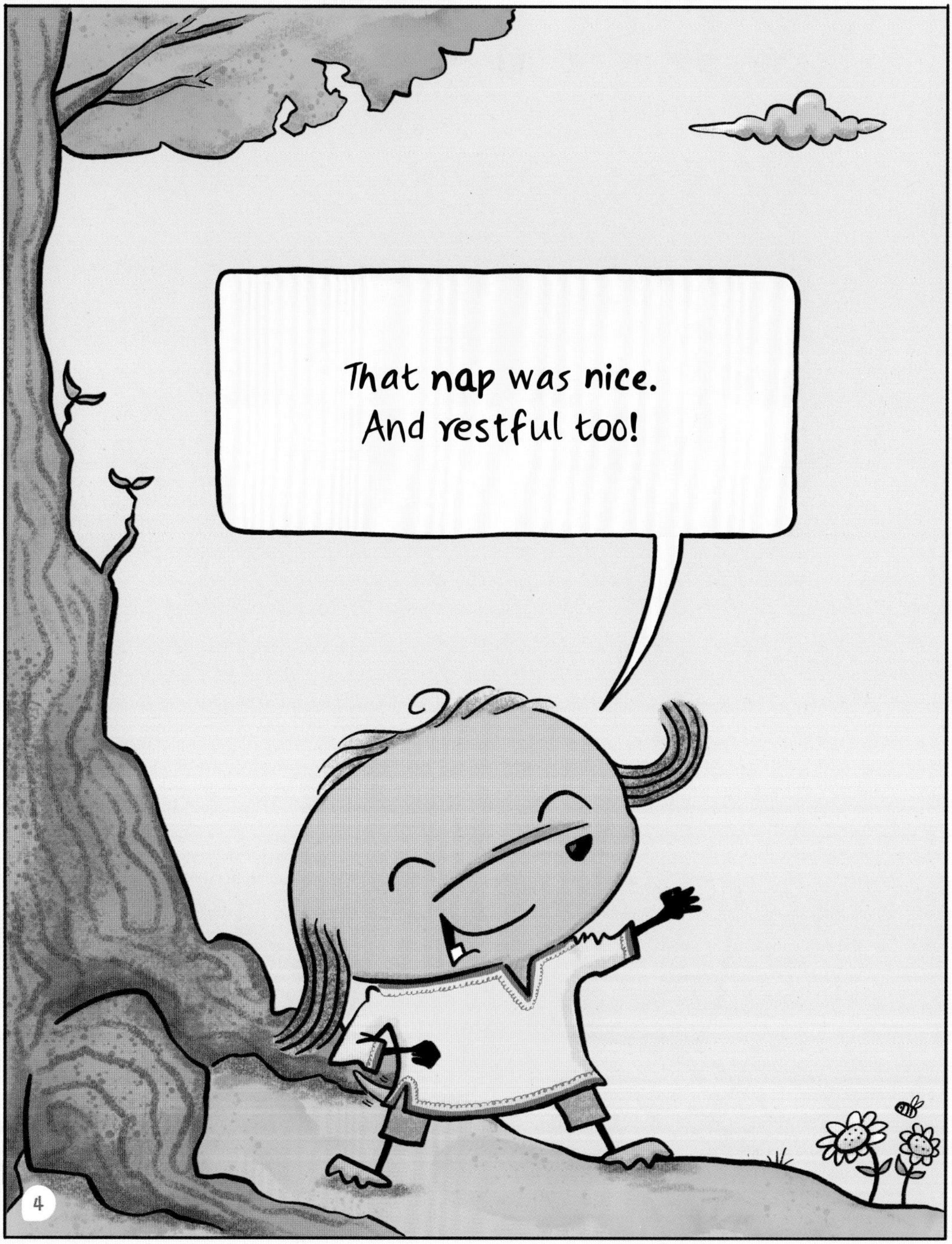
That nap was nice.
And restful too!

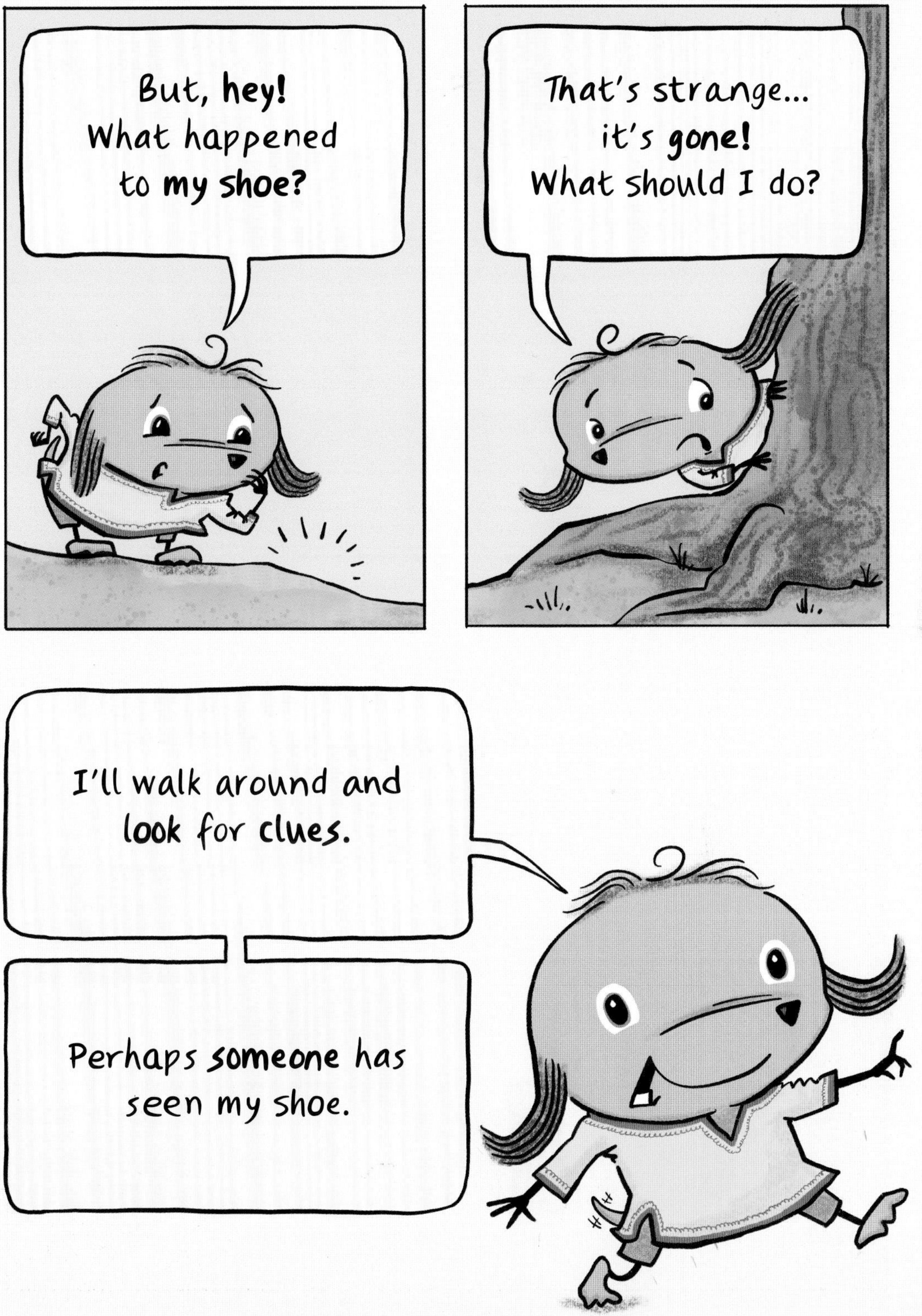
But, hey! What happened to my shoe?
That's strange... it's gone! What should I do?
I'll walk around and look for clues.
Perhaps someone has seen my shoe.

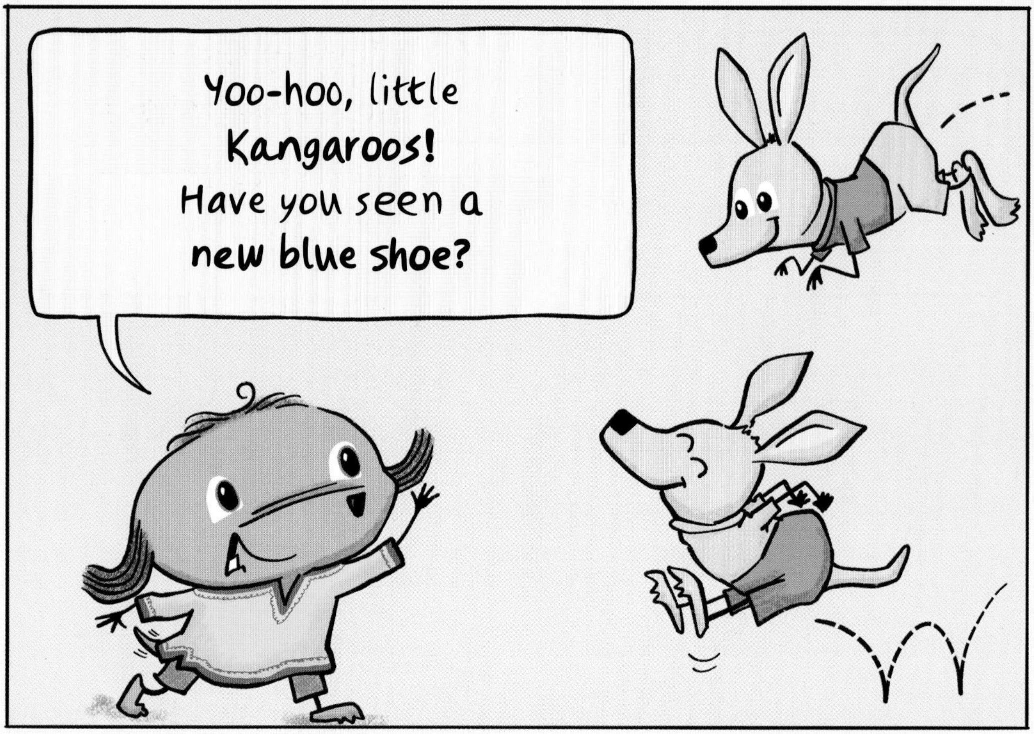
Yoo-hoo, little **Kangaroos!** Have you seen a **new blue shoe?**

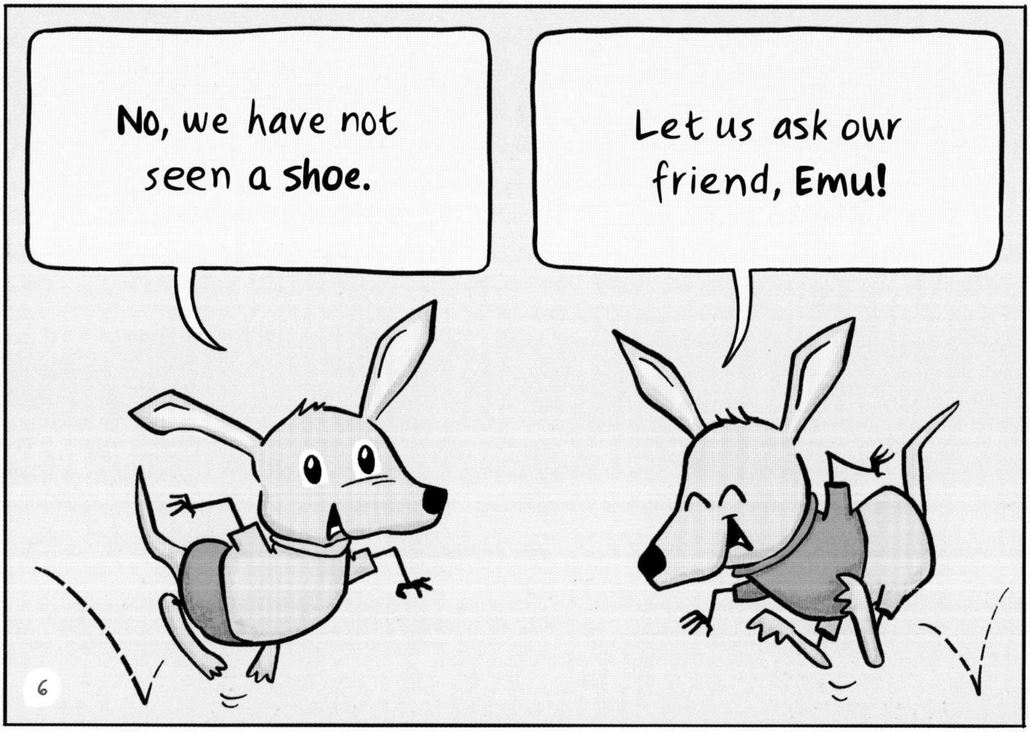
No, we have not seen a **shoe.**
Let us ask our friend, **Emu!**

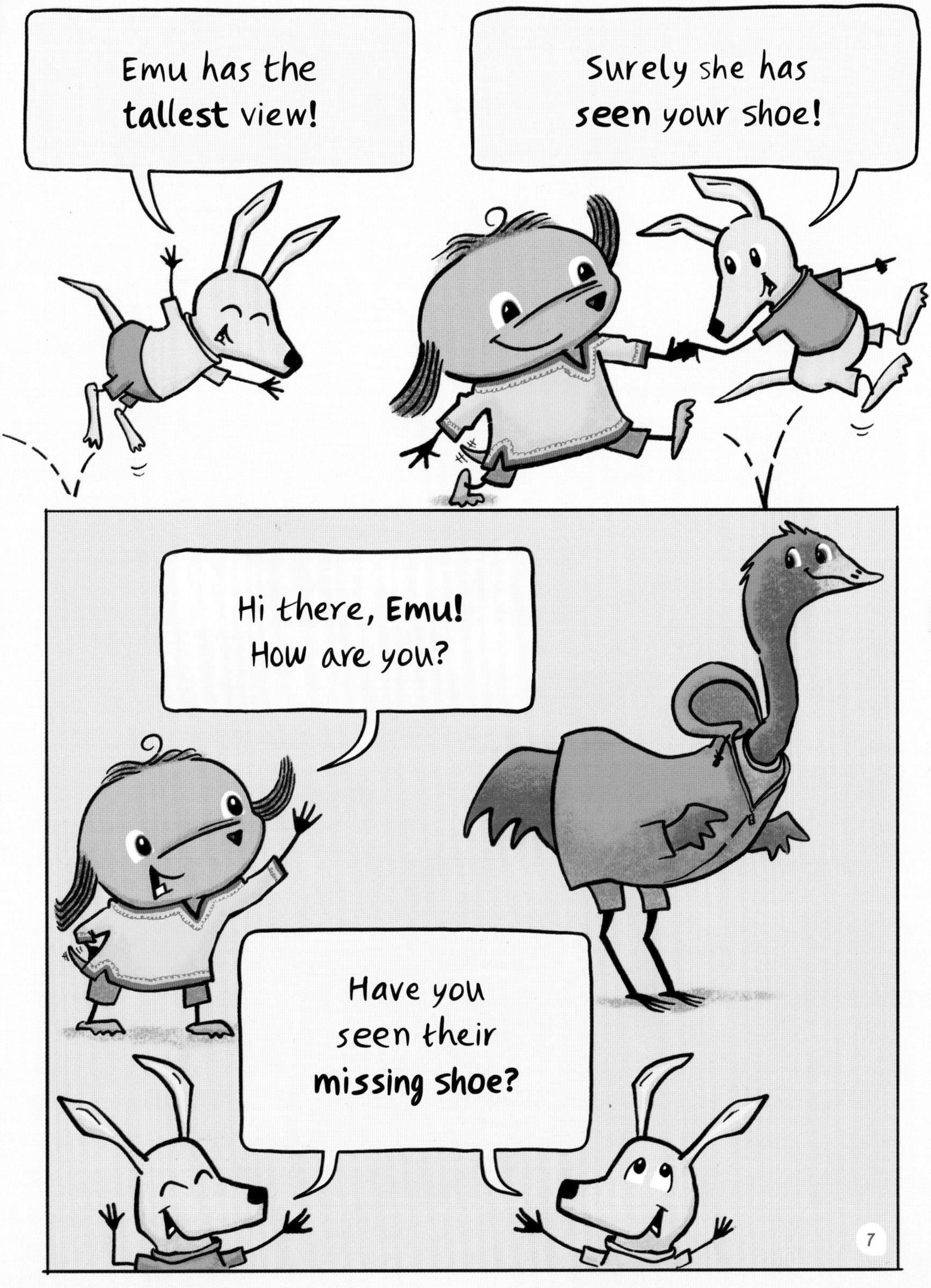
Emu has the **tallest** view!
Surely she has **seen** your shoe!
Hi there, **Emu!** How are you?
Have you seen their **missing shoe?**

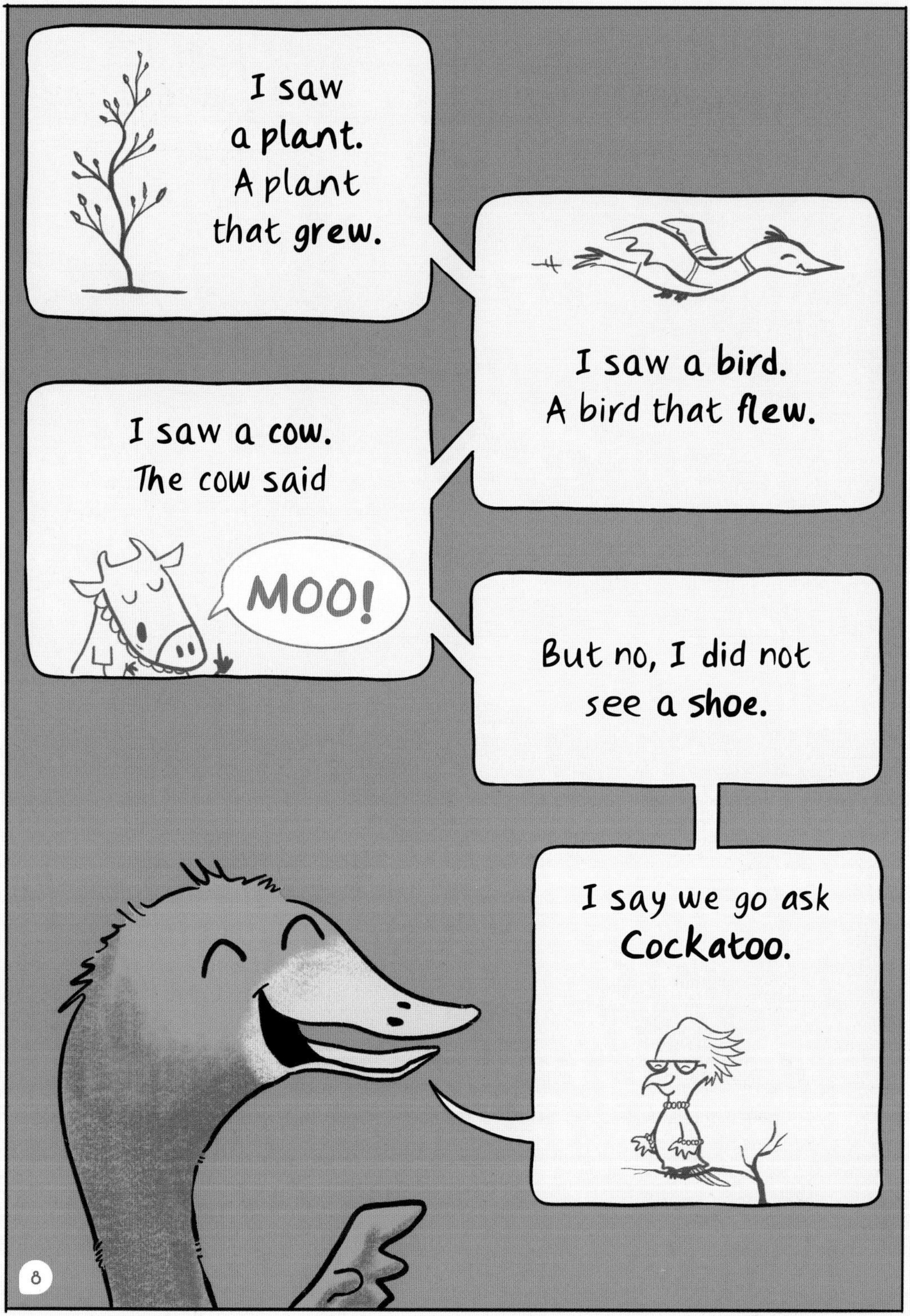
I saw a plant. A plant that grew.
I saw a bird. A bird that flew.
I saw a cow. The cow said
MOO!
But no, I did not see a shoe.
I say we go ask Cockatoo.

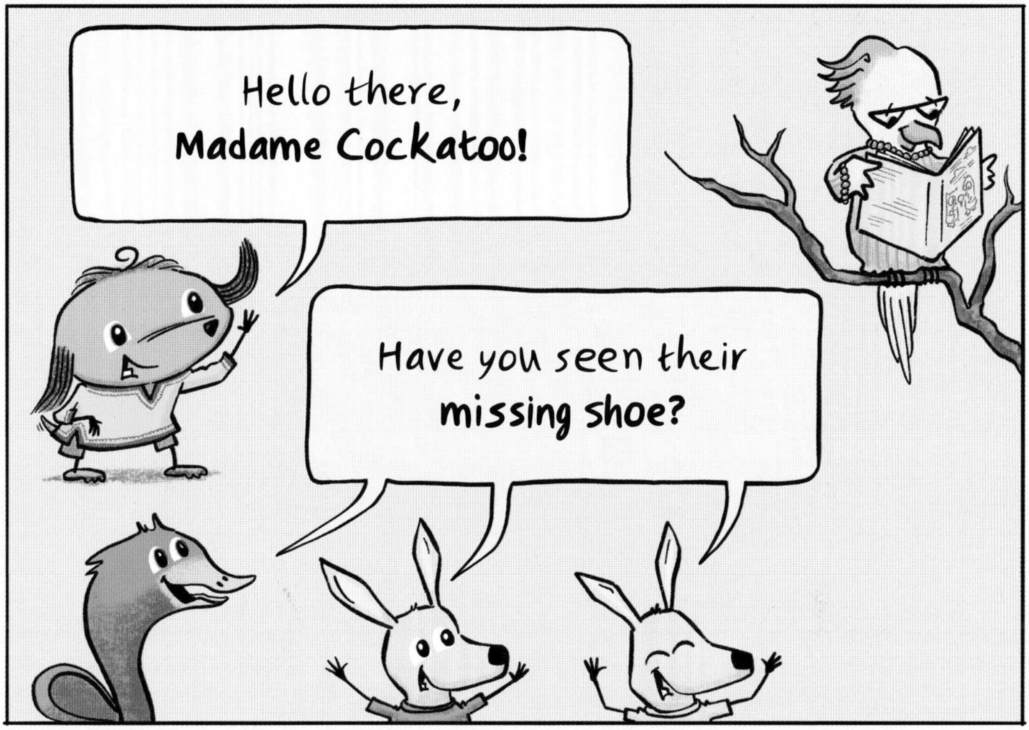
Hello there, Madame Cockatoo!
Have you seen their missing shoe?

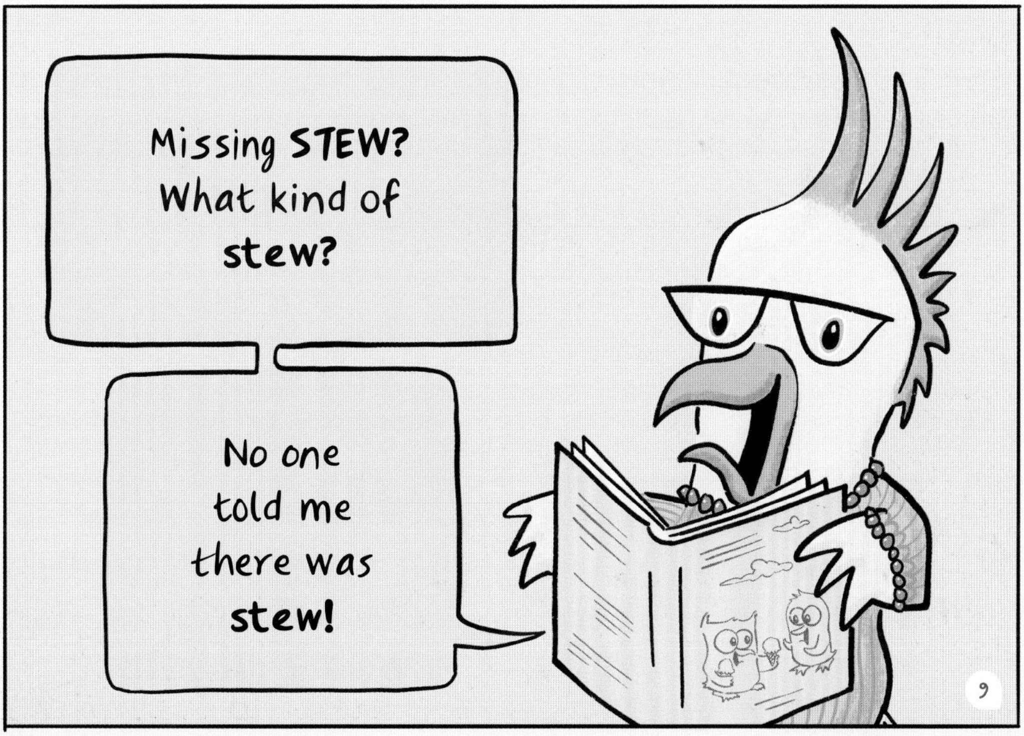
Missing STEW? What kind of stew?
No one told me there was stew!

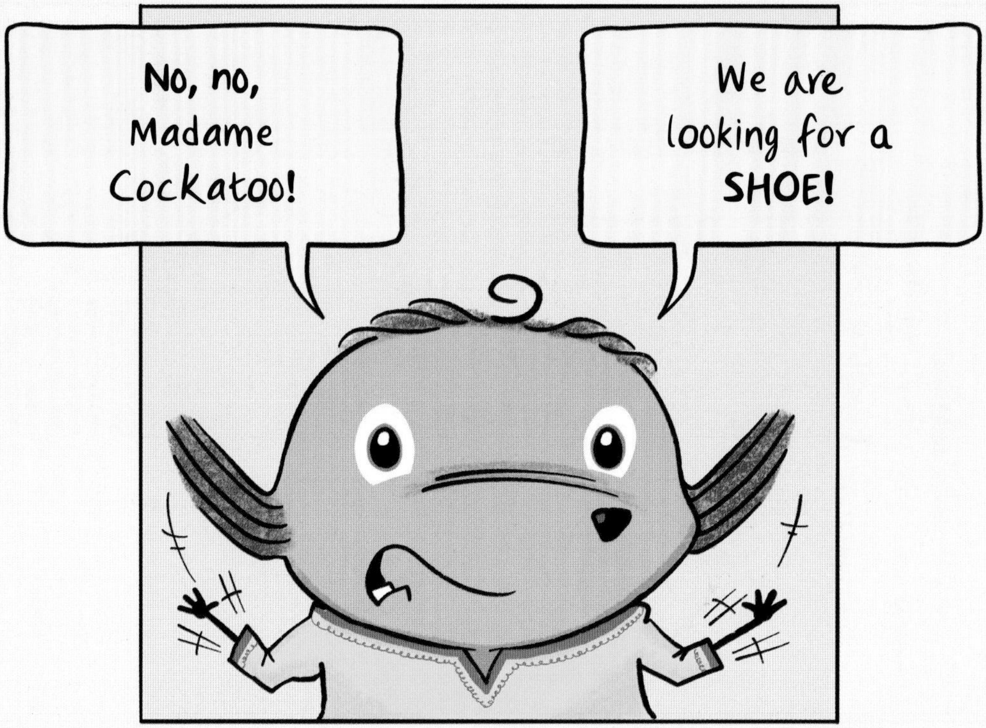

No, no, Madame Cockatoo!
We are looking for a **SHOE!**

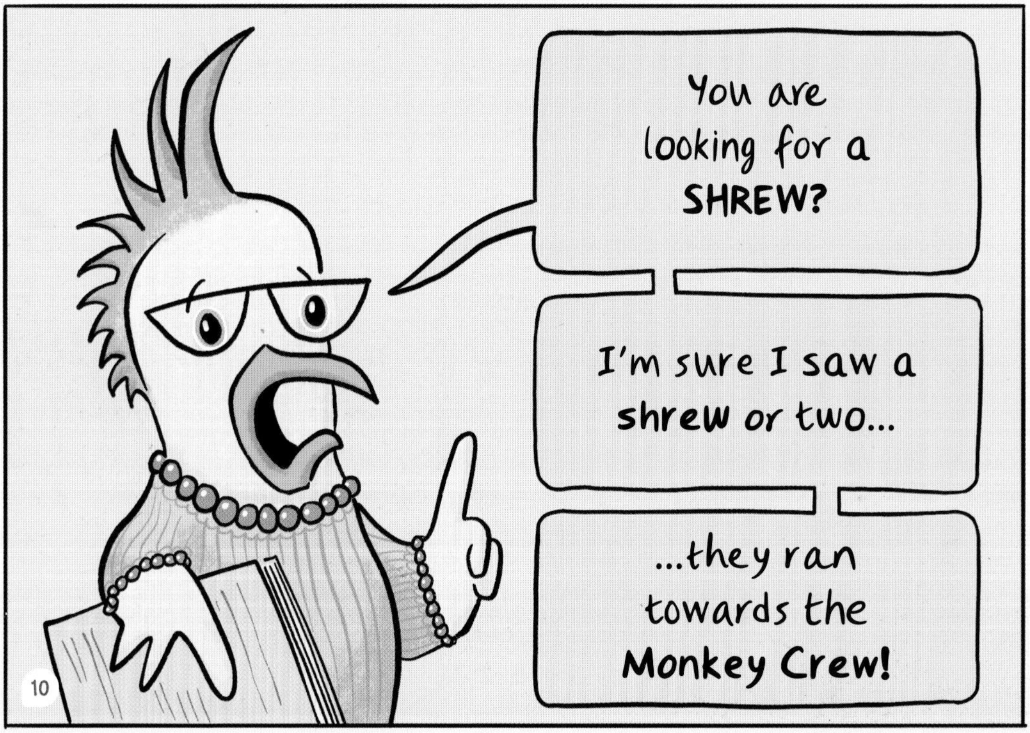

You are looking for a **SHREW?**
I'm sure I saw a **shrew** or two...
...they ran towards the **Monkey Crew!**

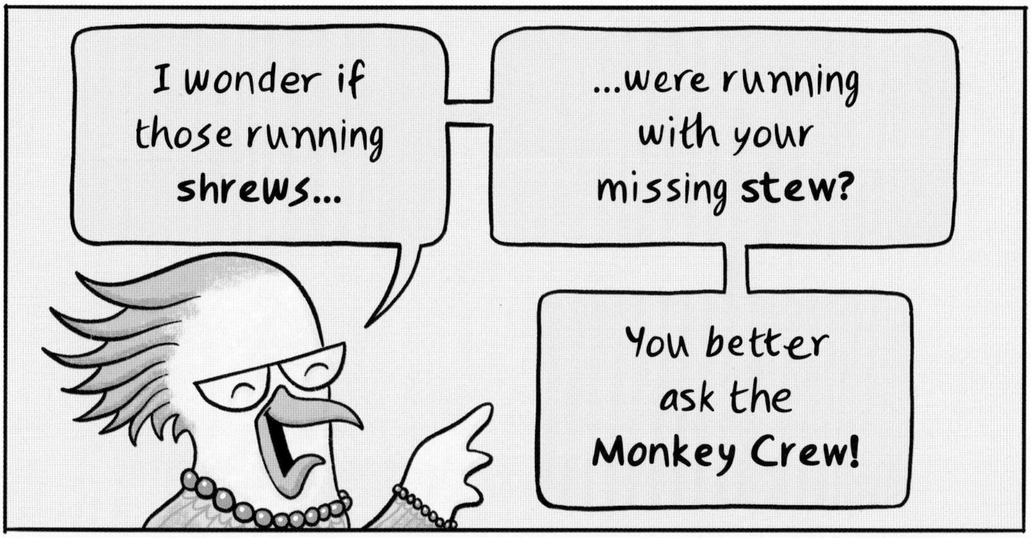
I wonder if those running shrews...
...were running with your missing stew?
You better ask the Monkey Crew!

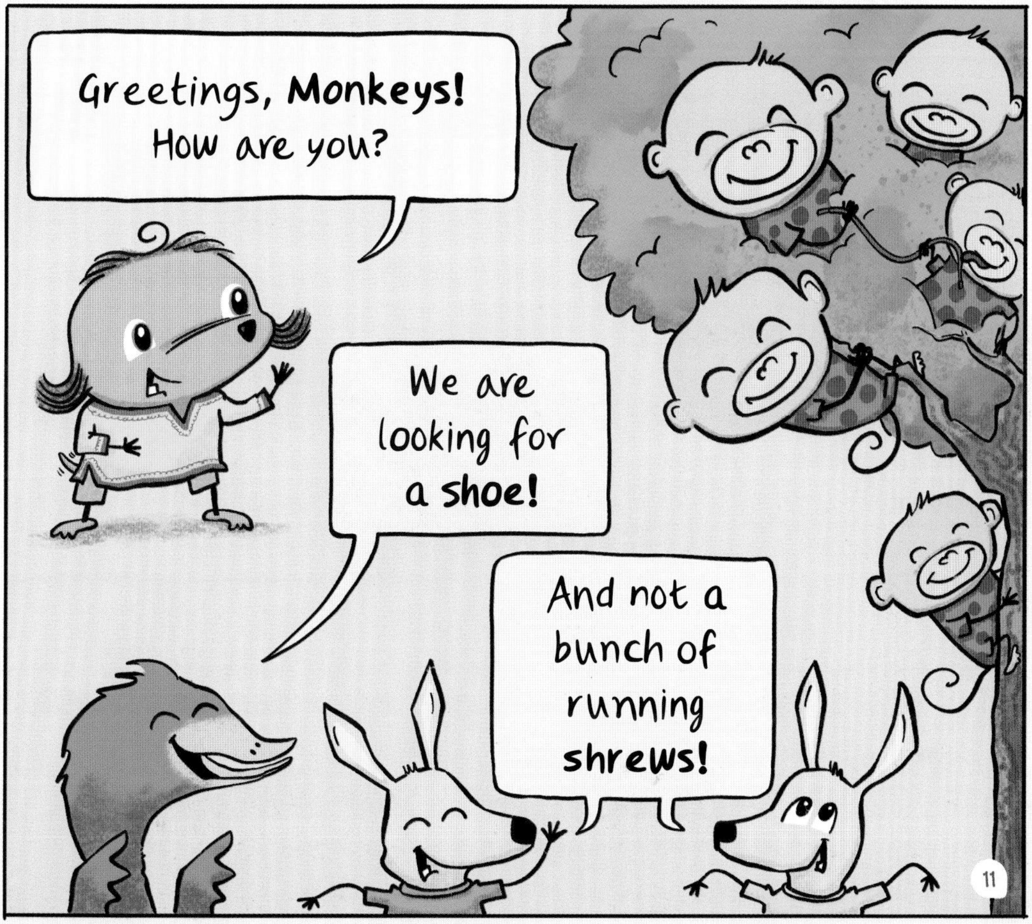
Greetings, Monkeys! How are you?
We are looking for a shoe!
And not a bunch of running shrews!

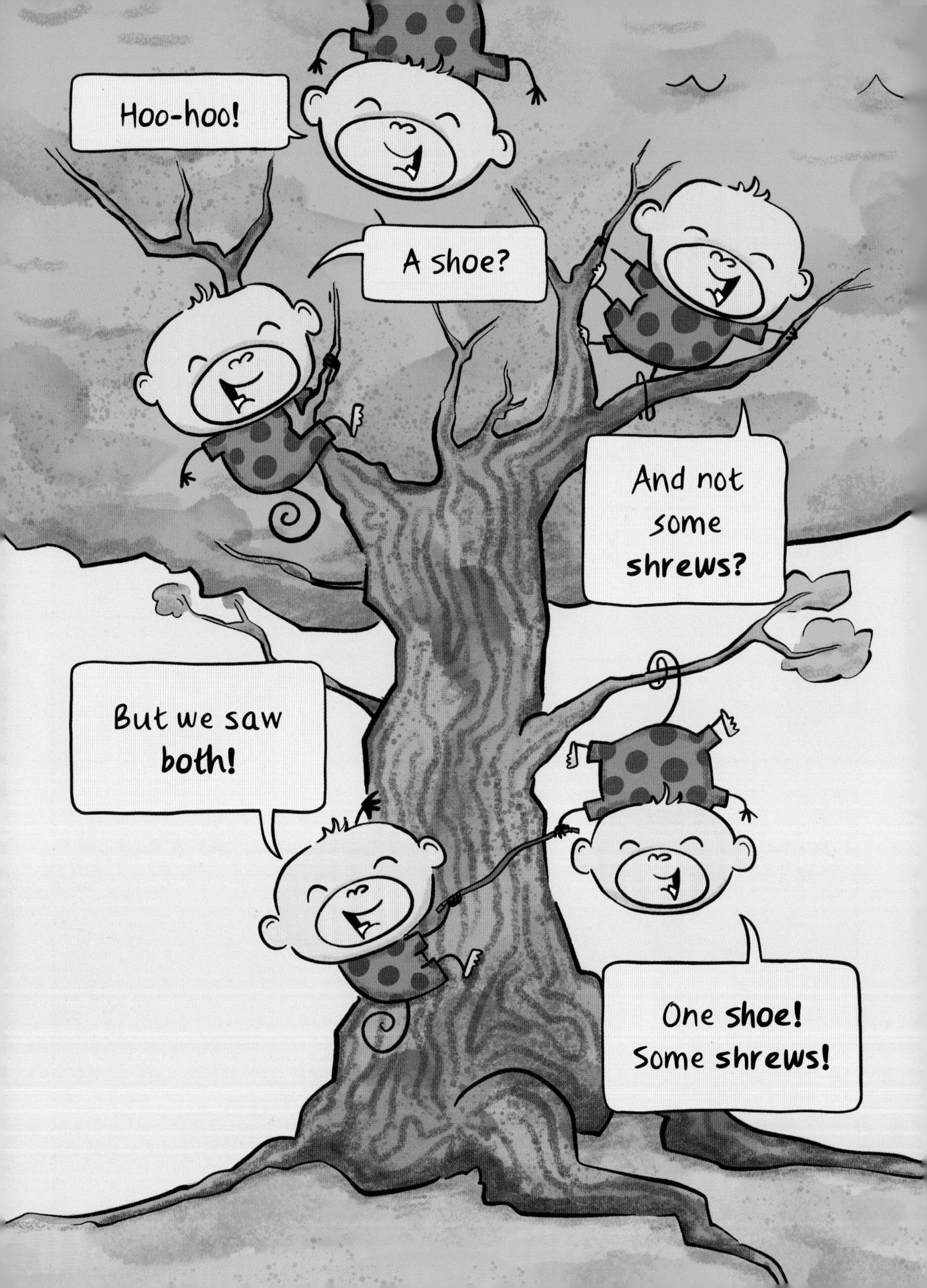
Hoo-hoo!
A shoe?
And not some **shrews?**
But we saw **both!**
One **shoe!** Some **shrews!**

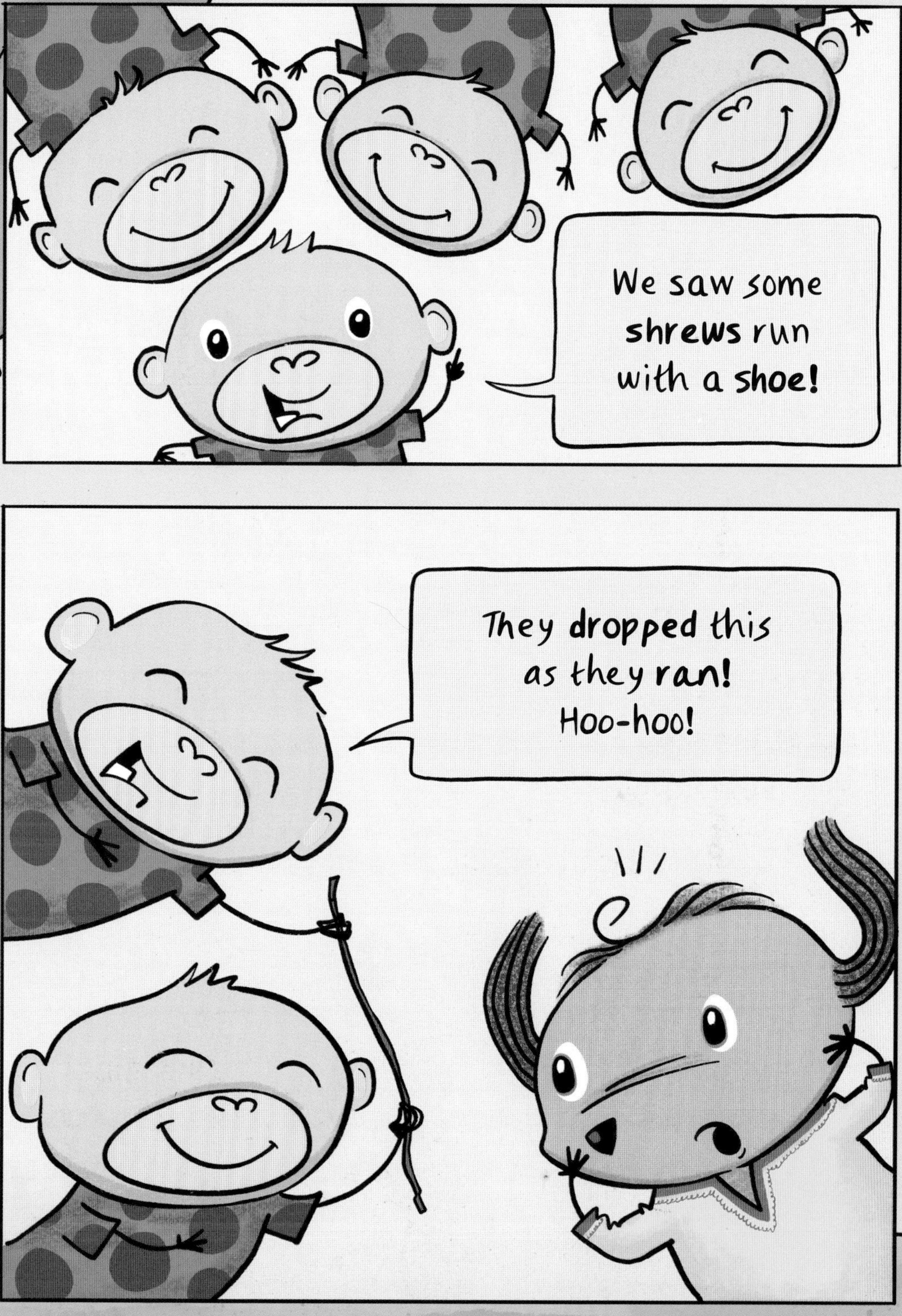
We saw some **shrews** run with a **shoe**!
They **dropped** this as they **ran**! Hoo-hoo!

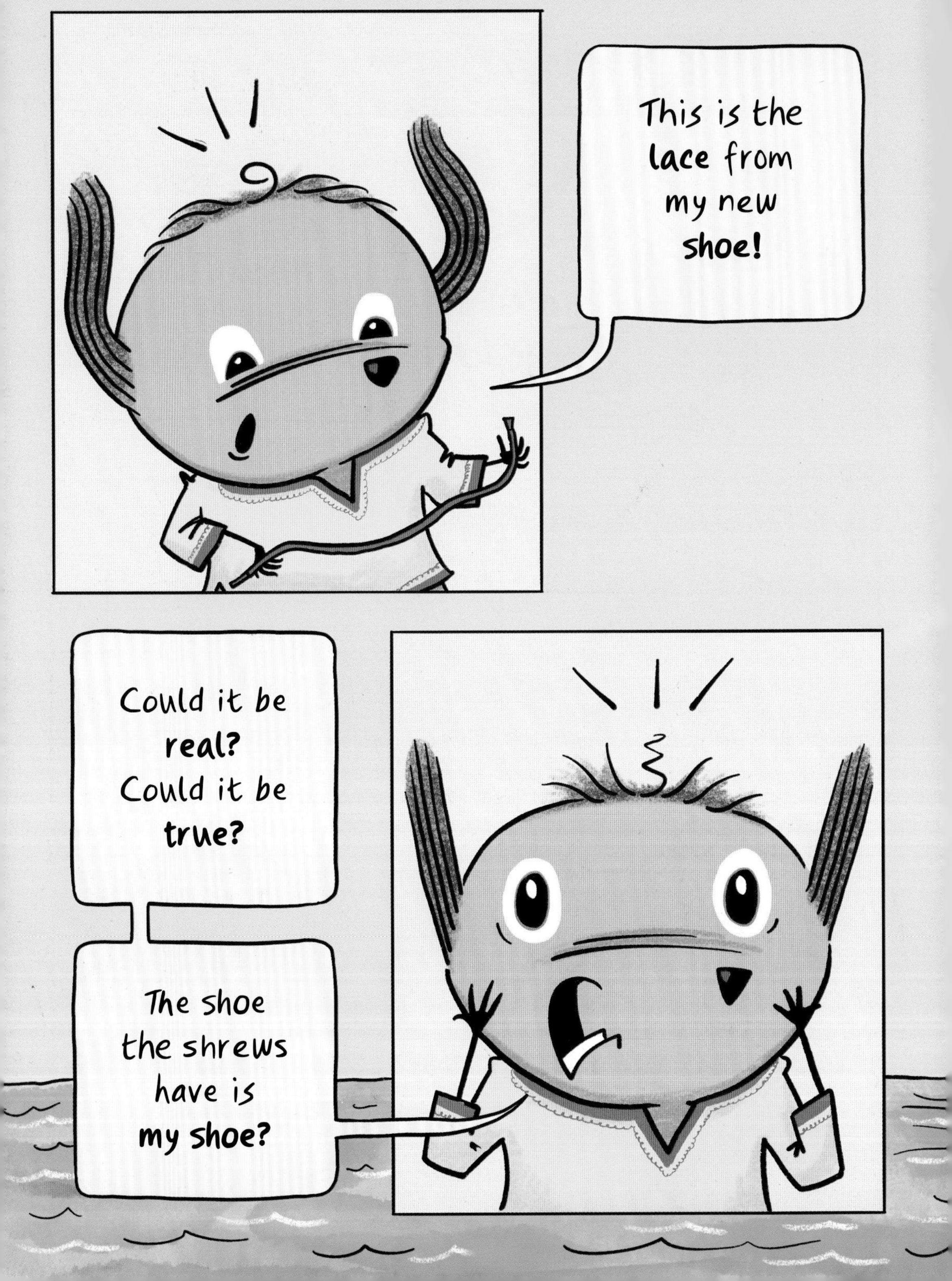
This is the **lace** from my new **shoe!**
Could it be **real?** Could it be **true?**
The shoe the shrews have is **my shoe?**

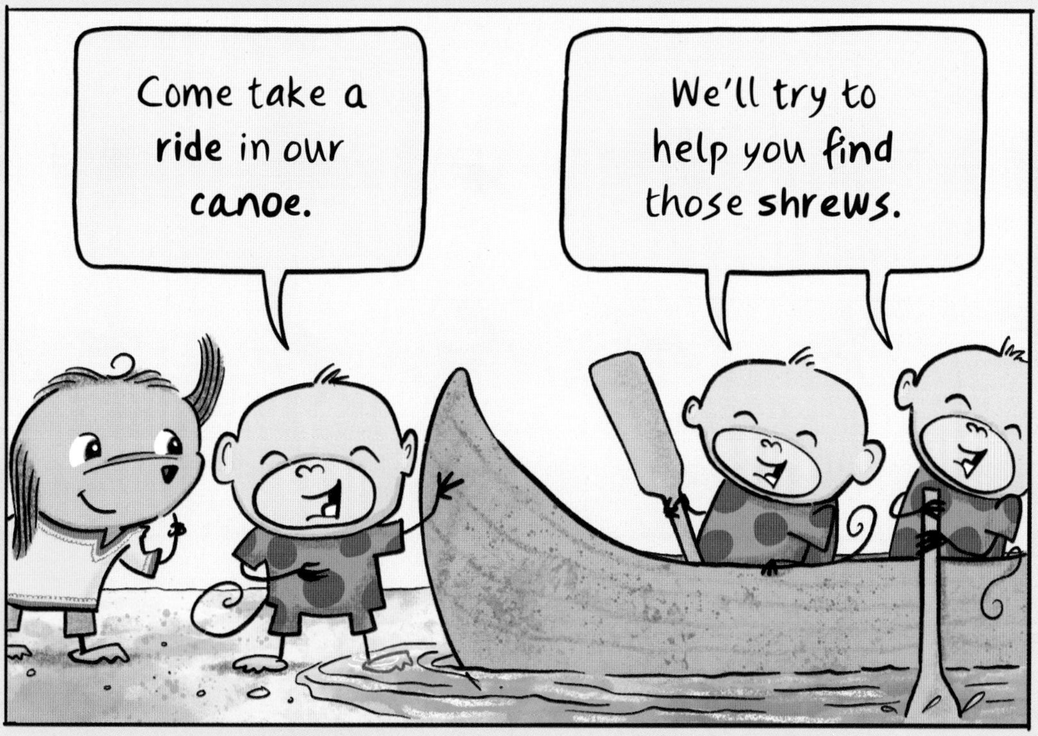
Come take a ride in our canoe.
We'll try to help you find those shrews.

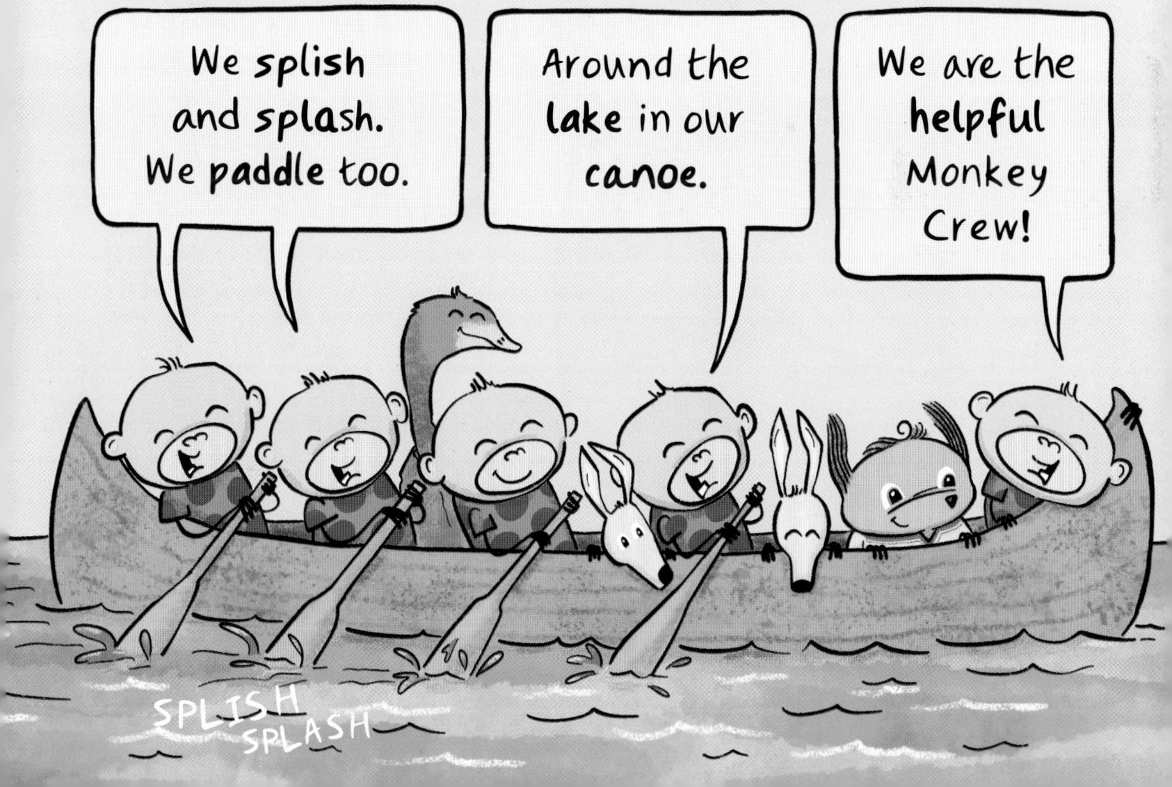
We splish and splash. We paddle too.
Around the lake in our canoe.
We are the helpful Monkey Crew!
SPLISH SPLASH

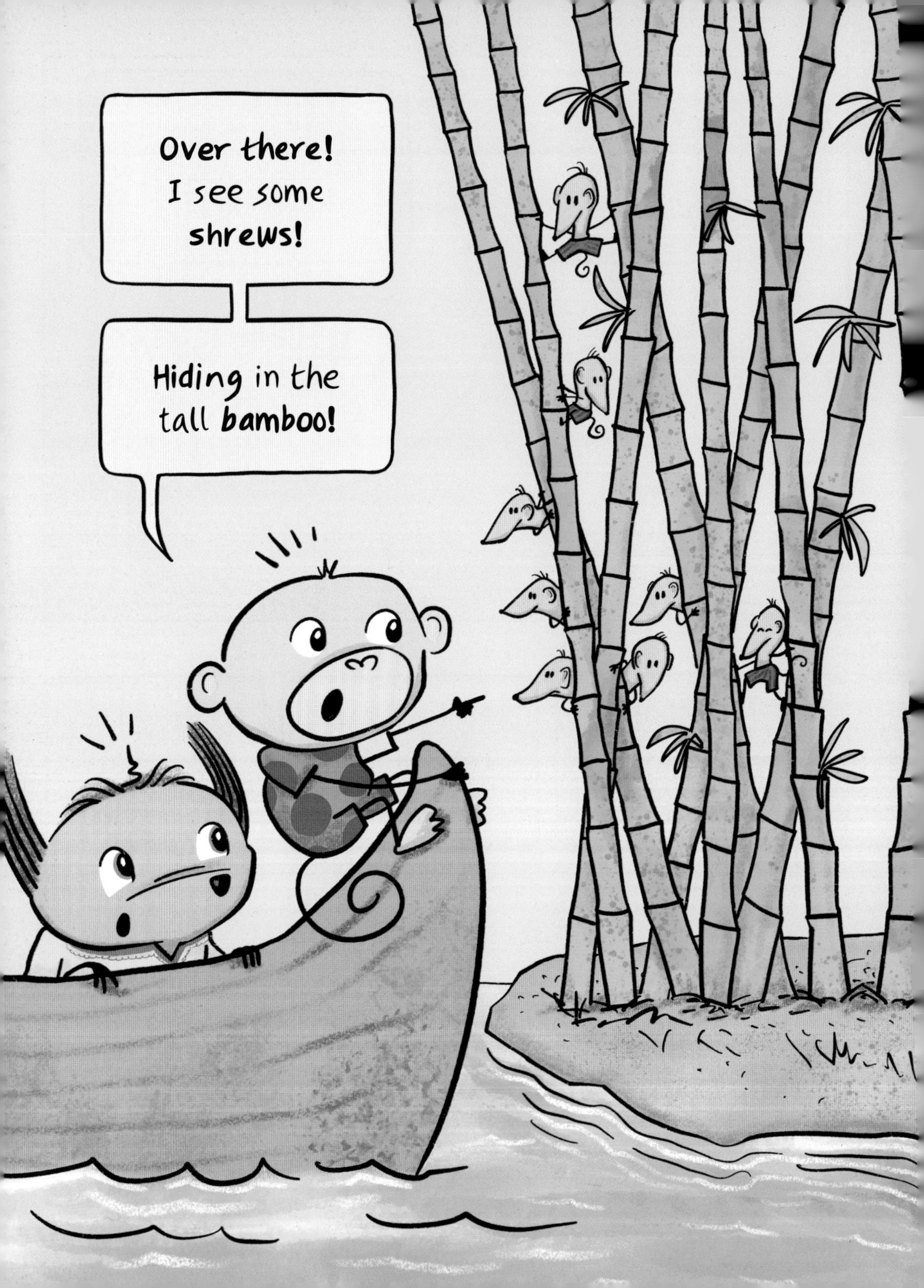
Over there! I see some shrews!
Hiding in the tall bamboo!

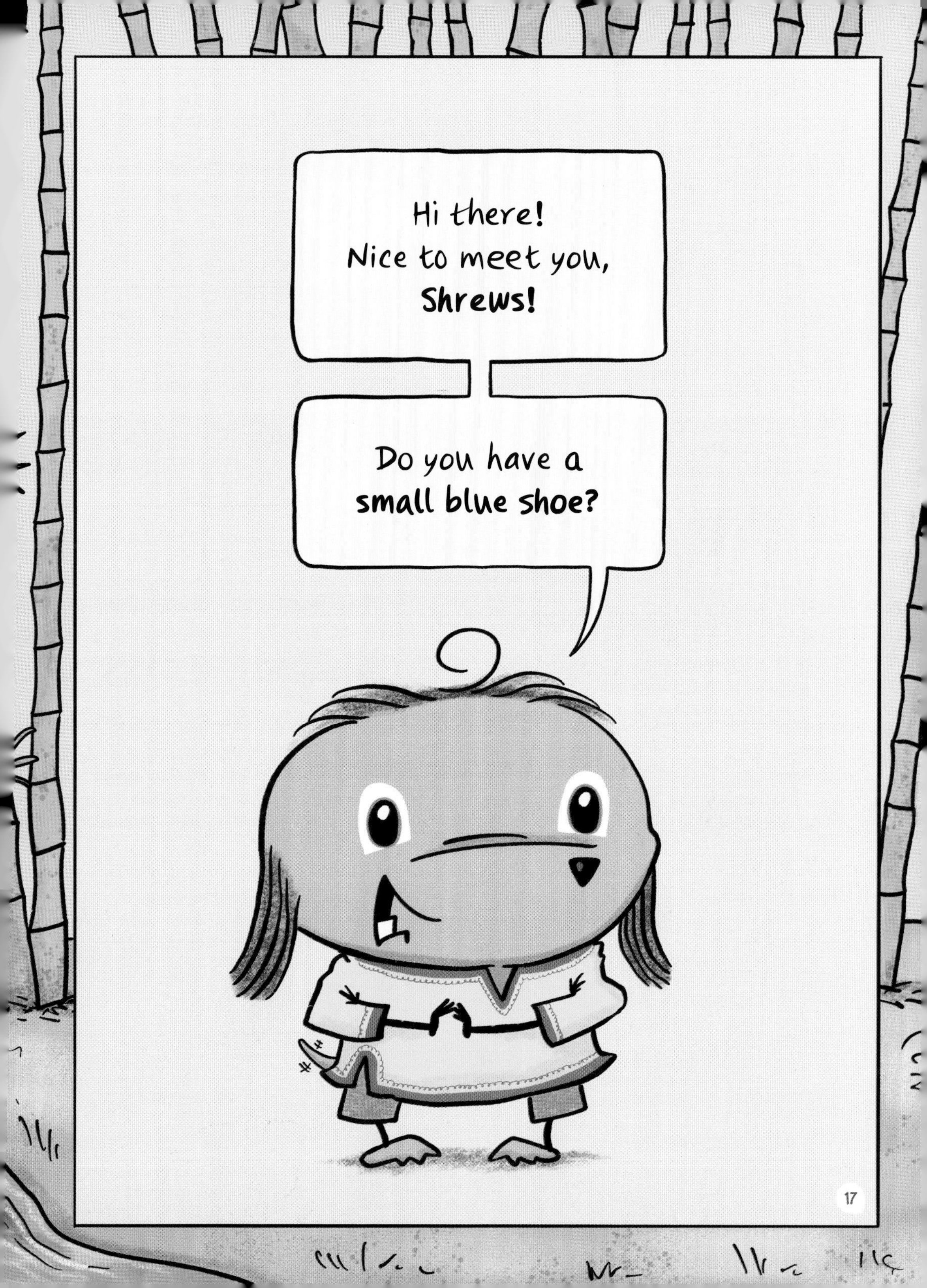
Hi there!
Nice to meet you,
Shrews!
Do you have a
small blue shoe?

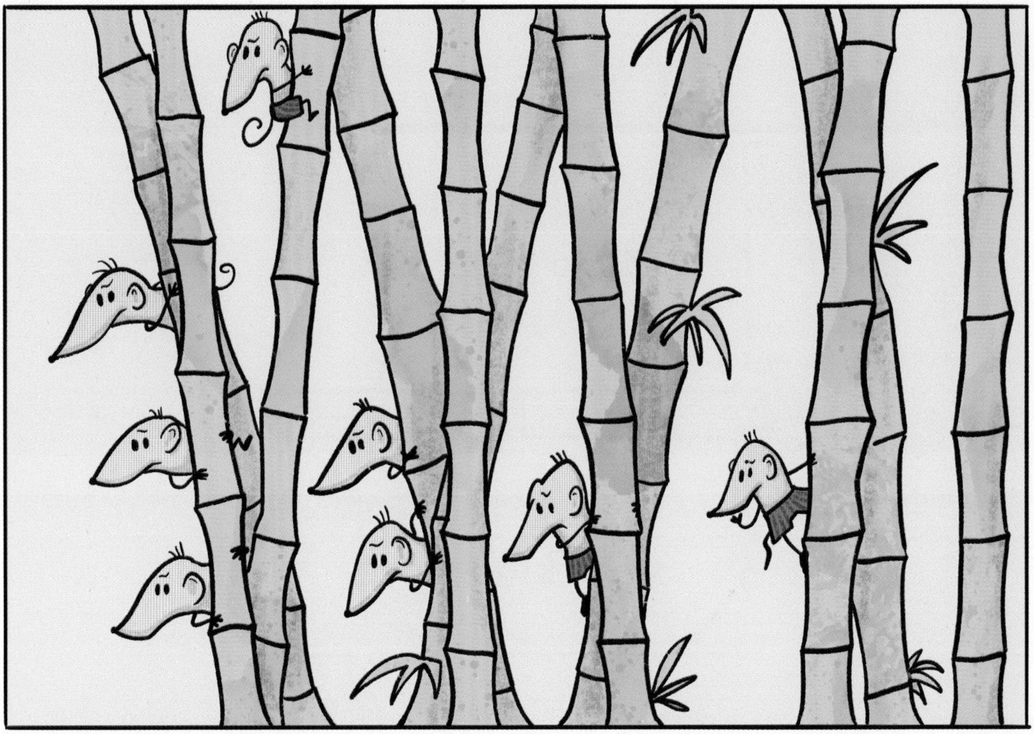

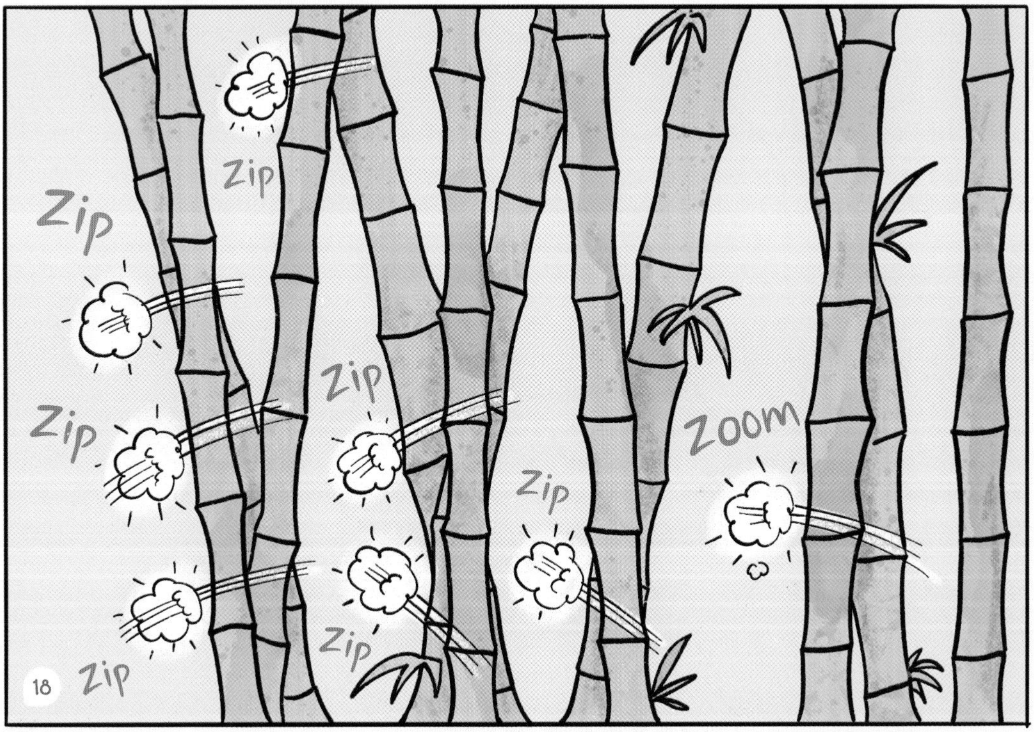
Zip
Zip
Zip
Zip
Zip
Zoom
Zip
Zip

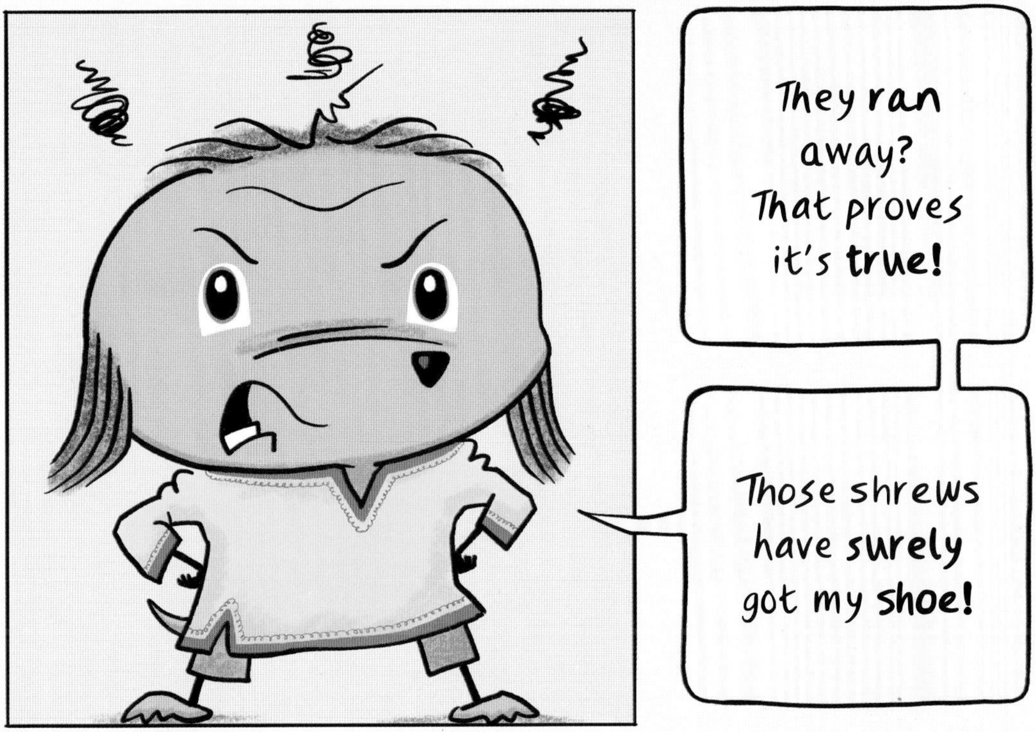
They ran away? That proves it's **true!**
Those shrews have **surely** got my **shoe!**

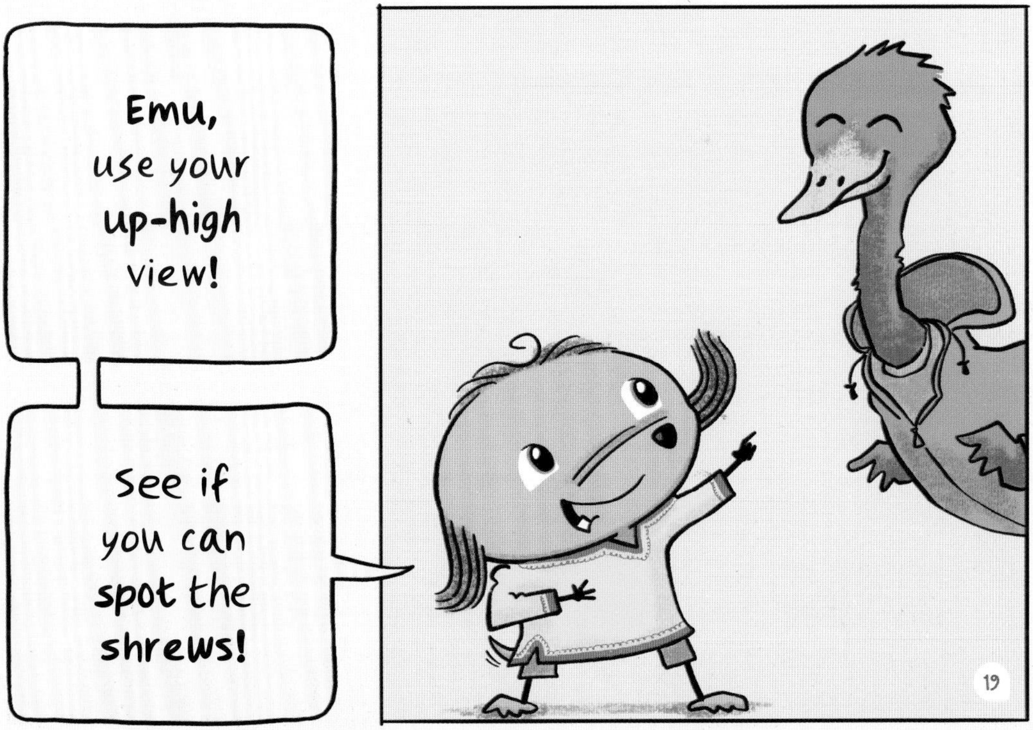
Emu, use your **up-high** view!
See if you can **spot** the **shrews!**

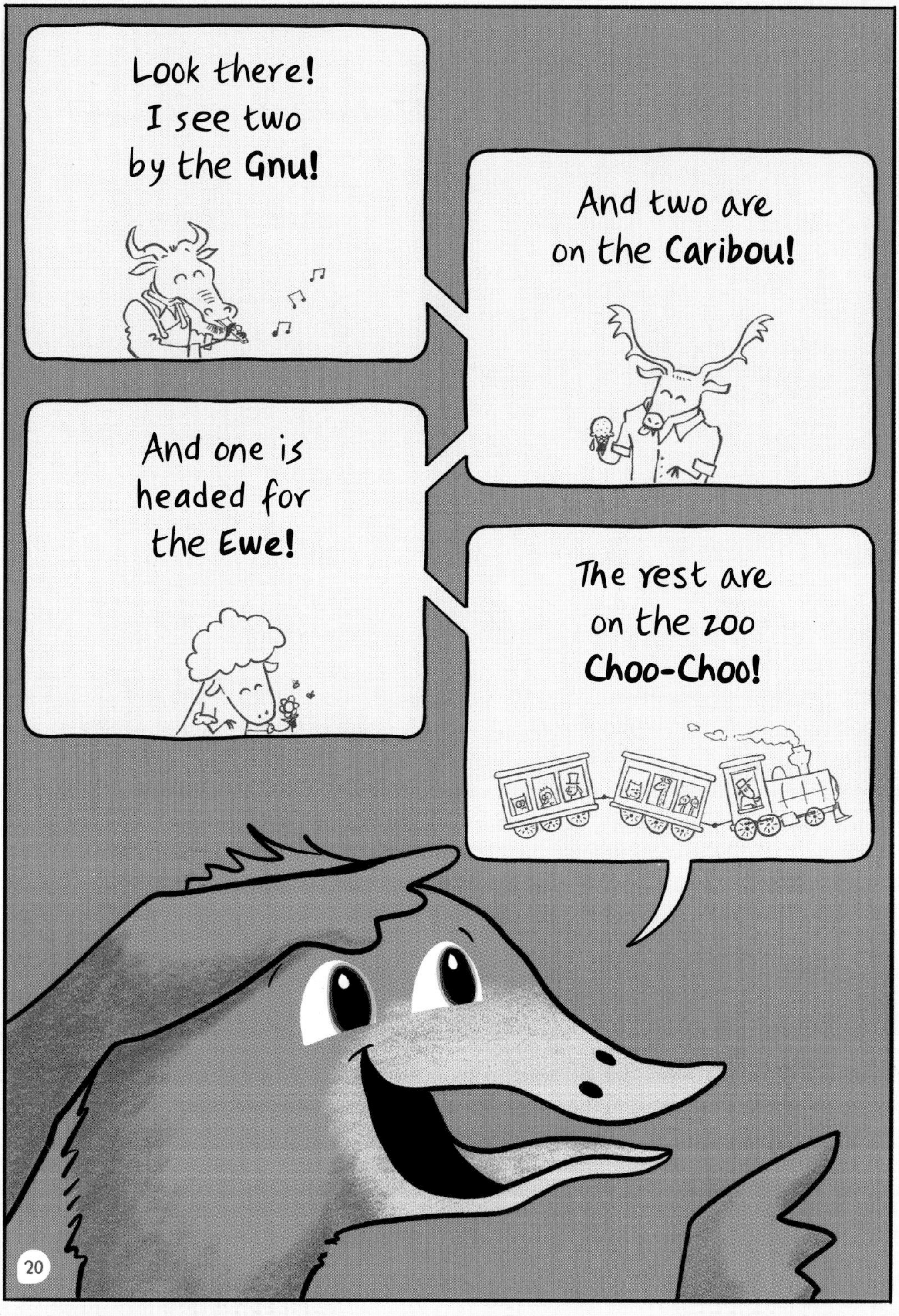
Look there! I see two by the Gnu!
And two are on the Caribou!
And one is headed for the Ewe!
The rest are on the zoo Choo-Choo!

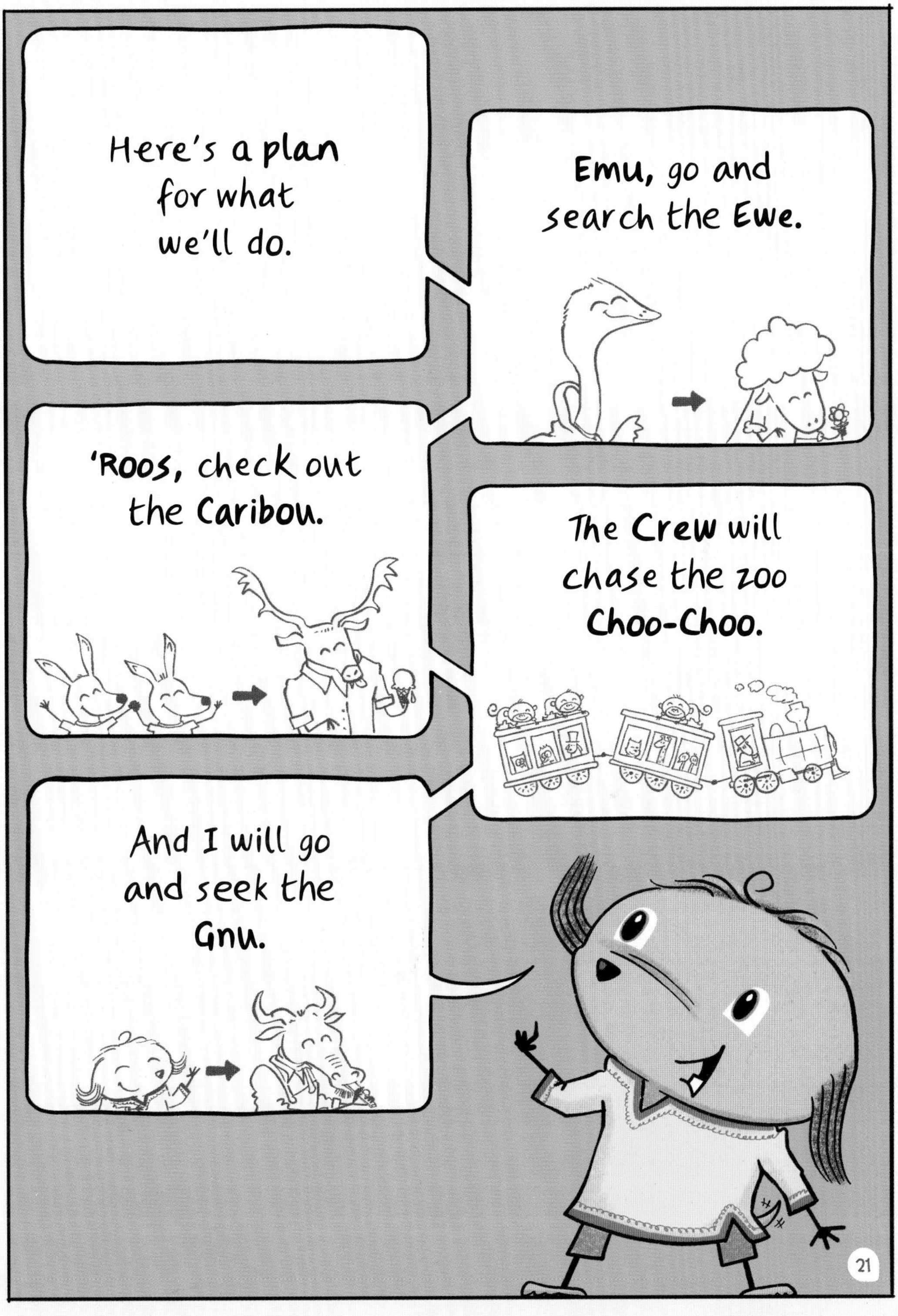

Here's a plan for what we'll do.
Emu, go and search the Ewe.
'Roos, check out the Caribou.
The Crew will chase the zoo Choo-Choo.
And I will go and seek the Gnu.

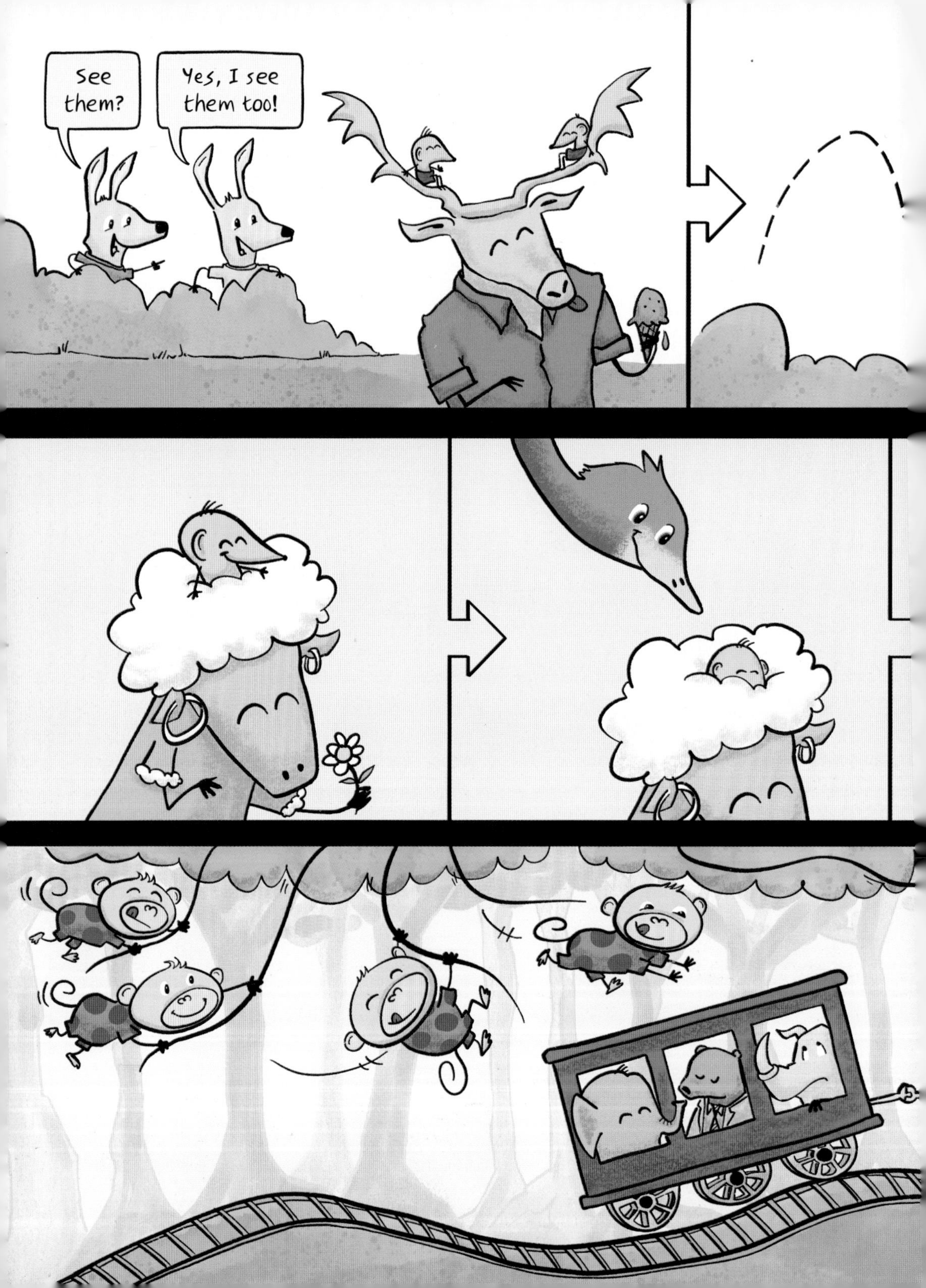
See them?
Yes, I see them too!

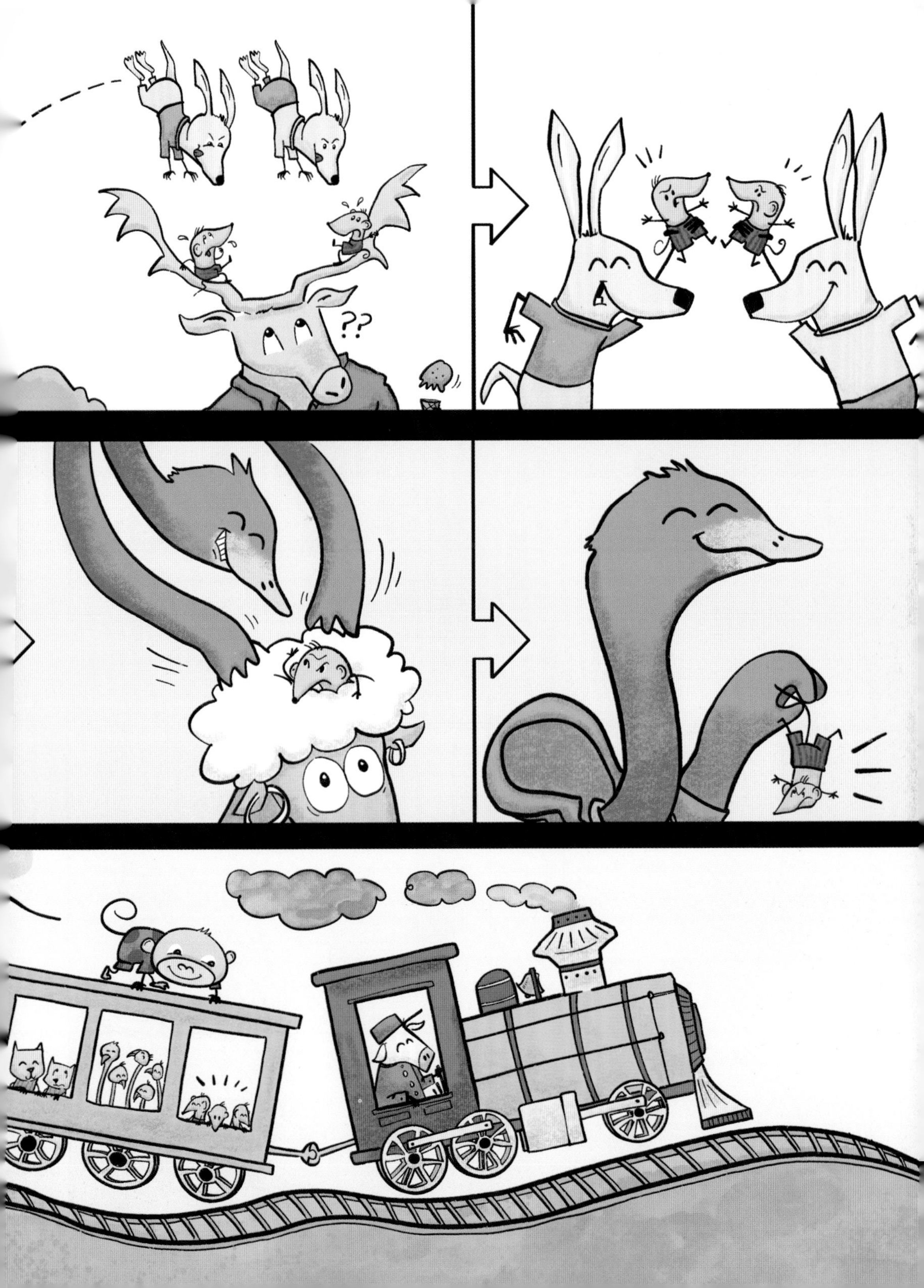
??

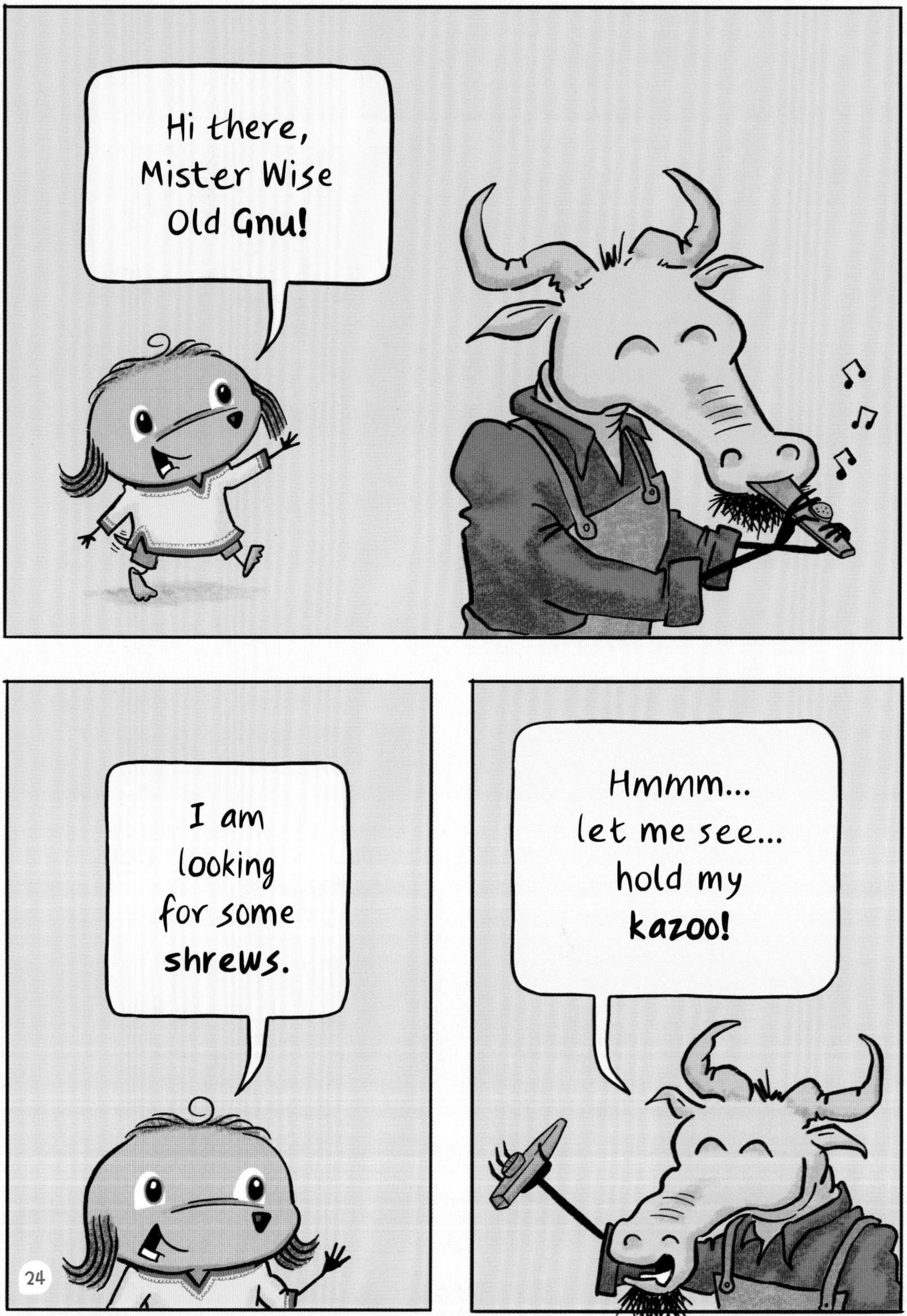
Hi there, Mister Wise Old Gnu!
I am looking for some **shrews**.
Hmmm... let me see... hold my **kazoo**!

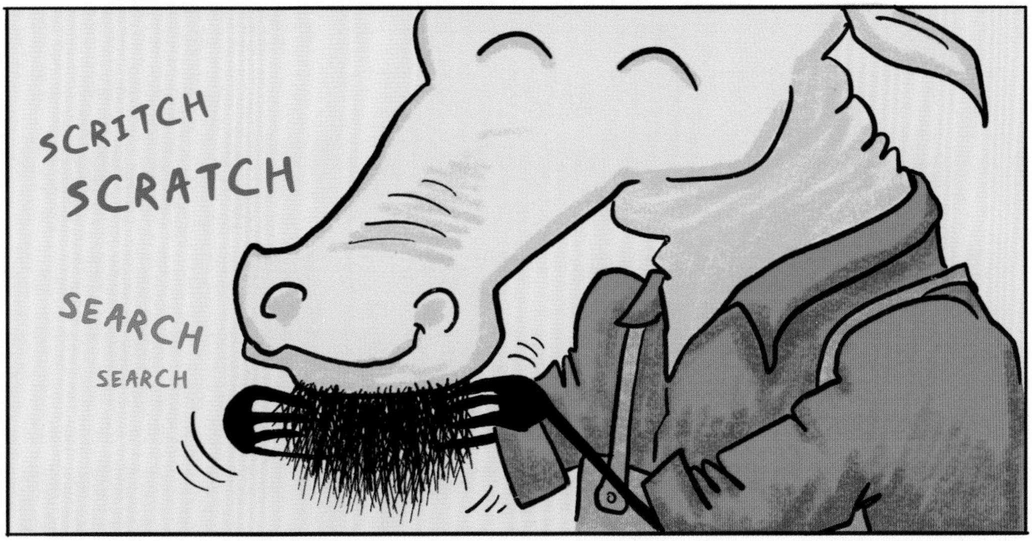
SCRITCH
SCRATCH
SEARCH
SEARCH

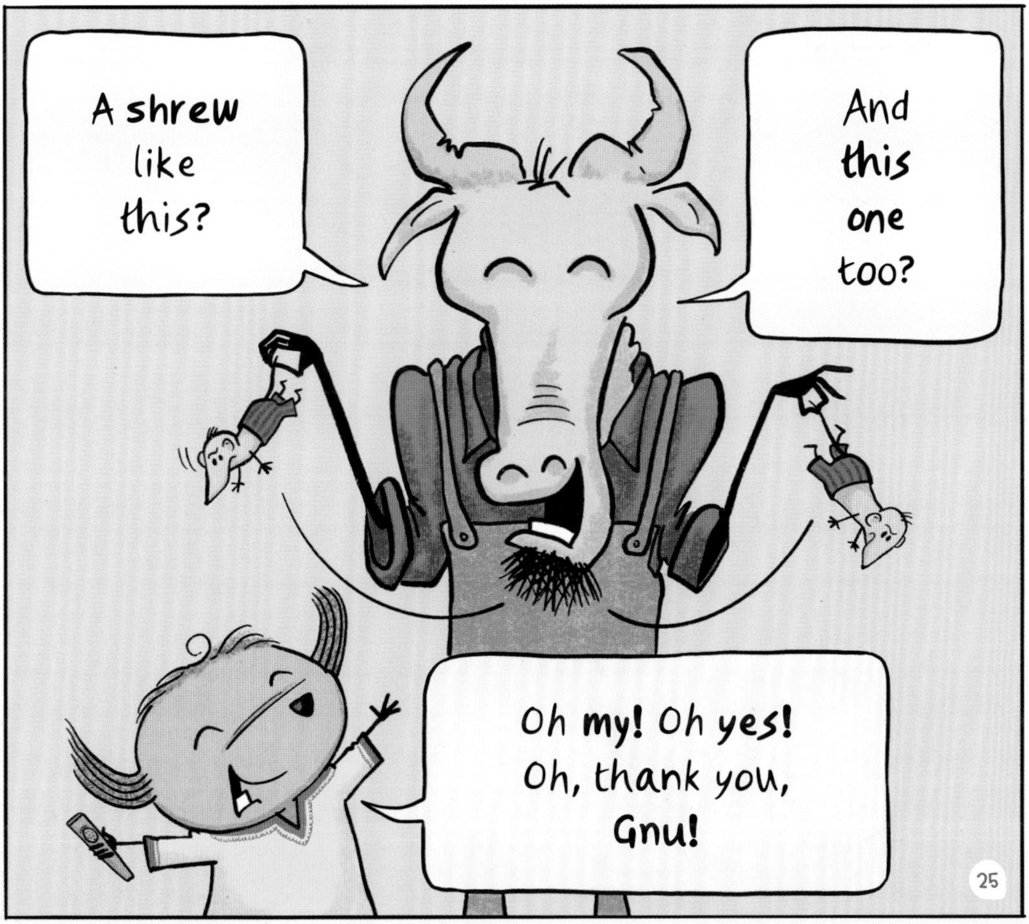
A shrew like this?
And this one too?
Oh my! Oh yes! Oh, thank you, Gnu!

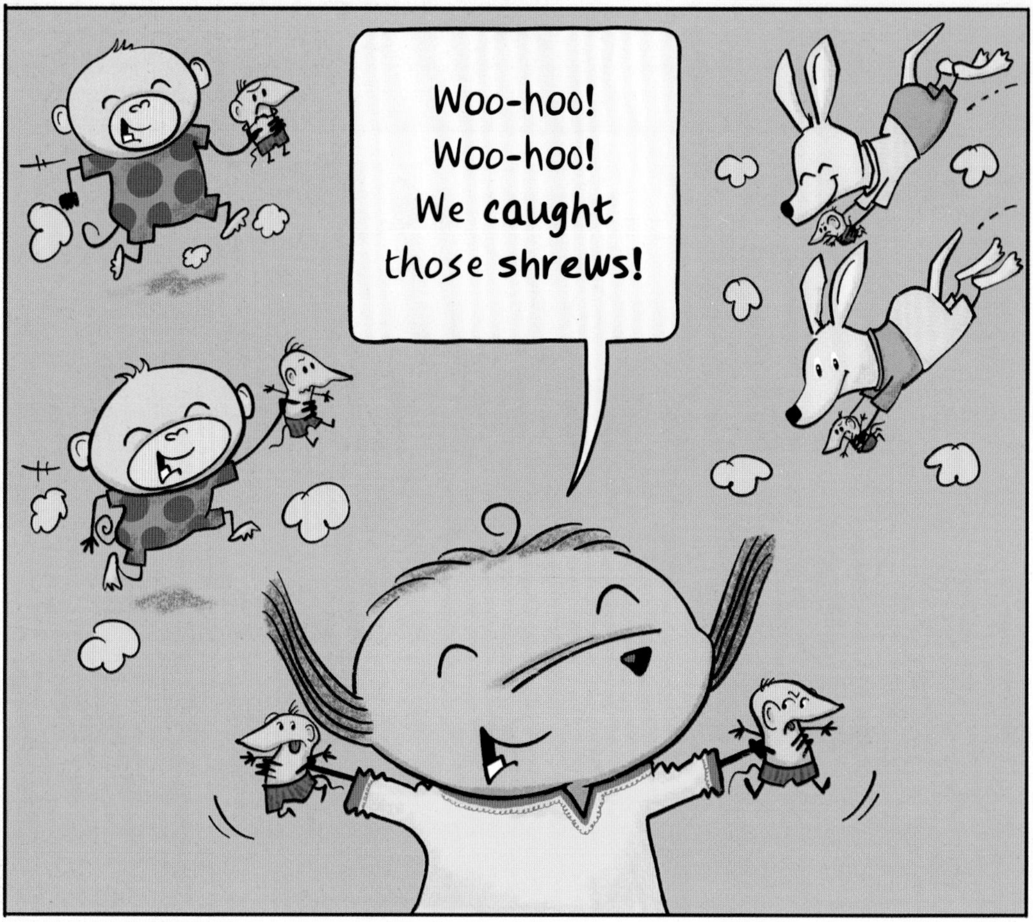
Woo-hoo!
Woo-hoo!
We caught those shrews!

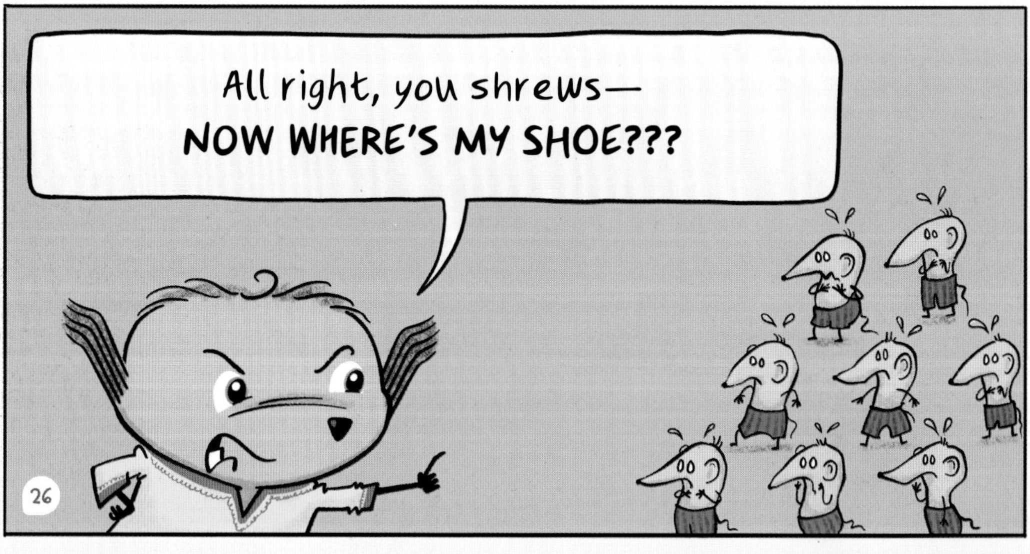
All right, you shrews—
NOW WHERE'S MY SHOE???

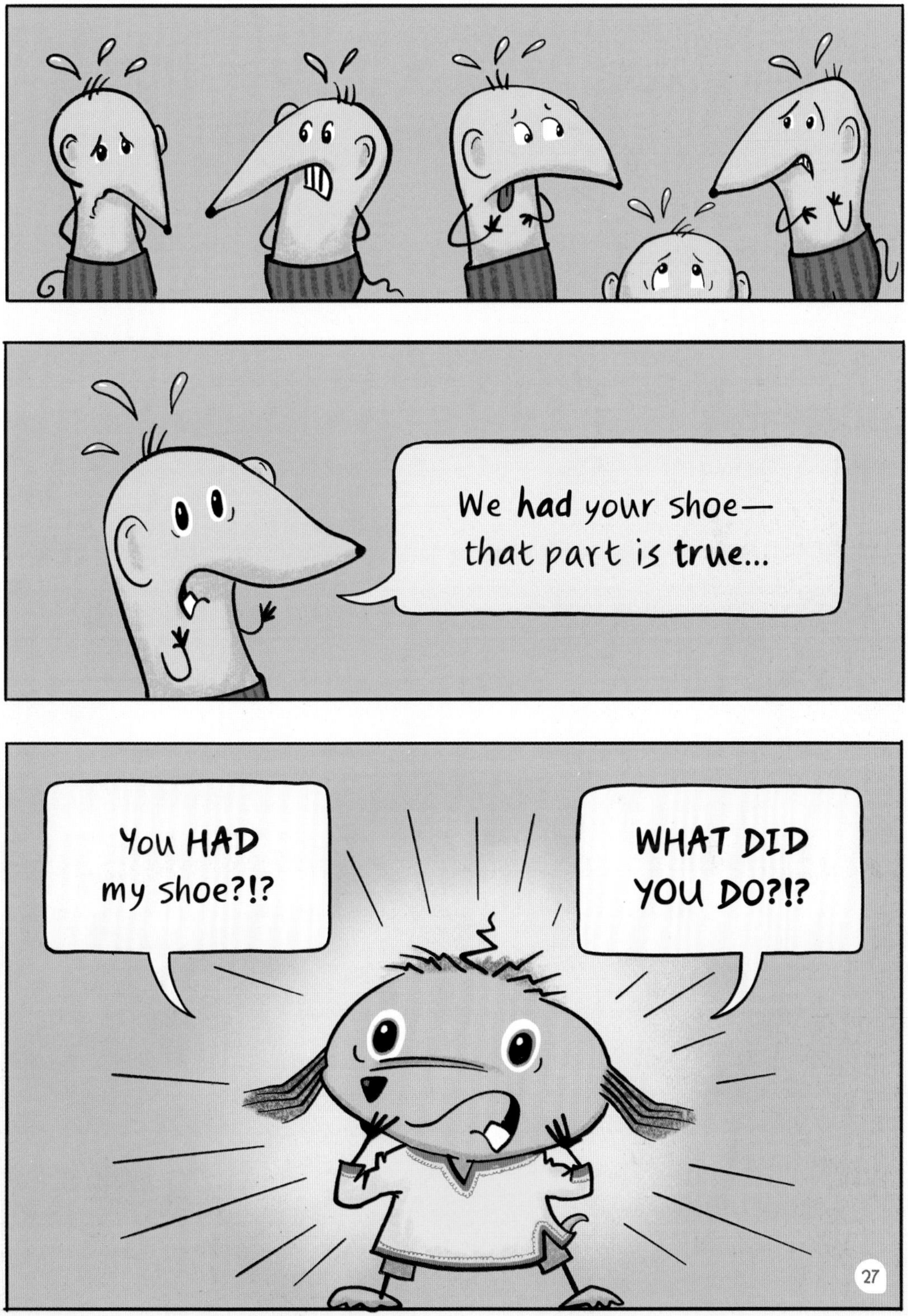
We had your shoe—
that part is true...
You HAD my shoe?!?
WHAT DID YOU DO?!?

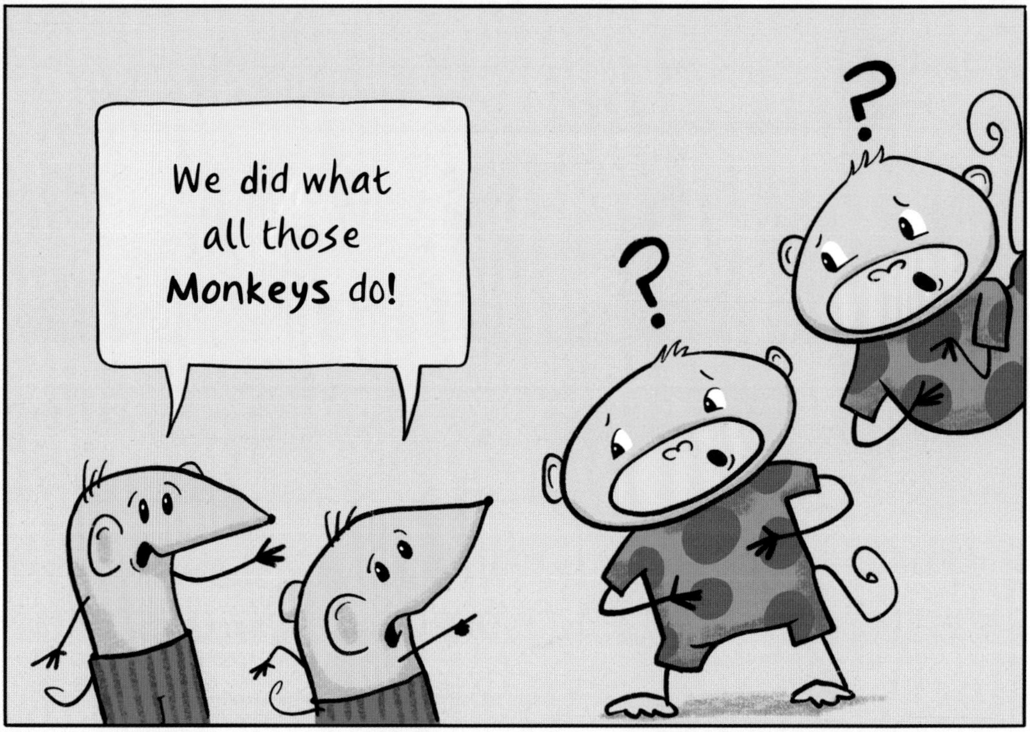
We did what all those Monkeys do!

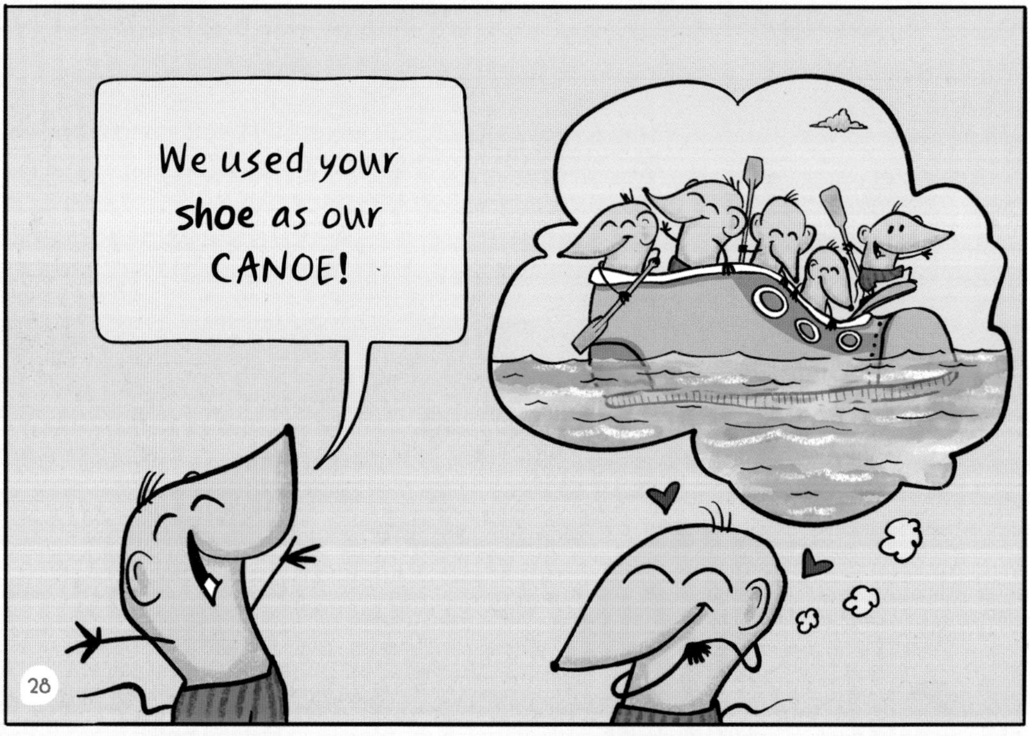
We used your shoe as our CANOE!

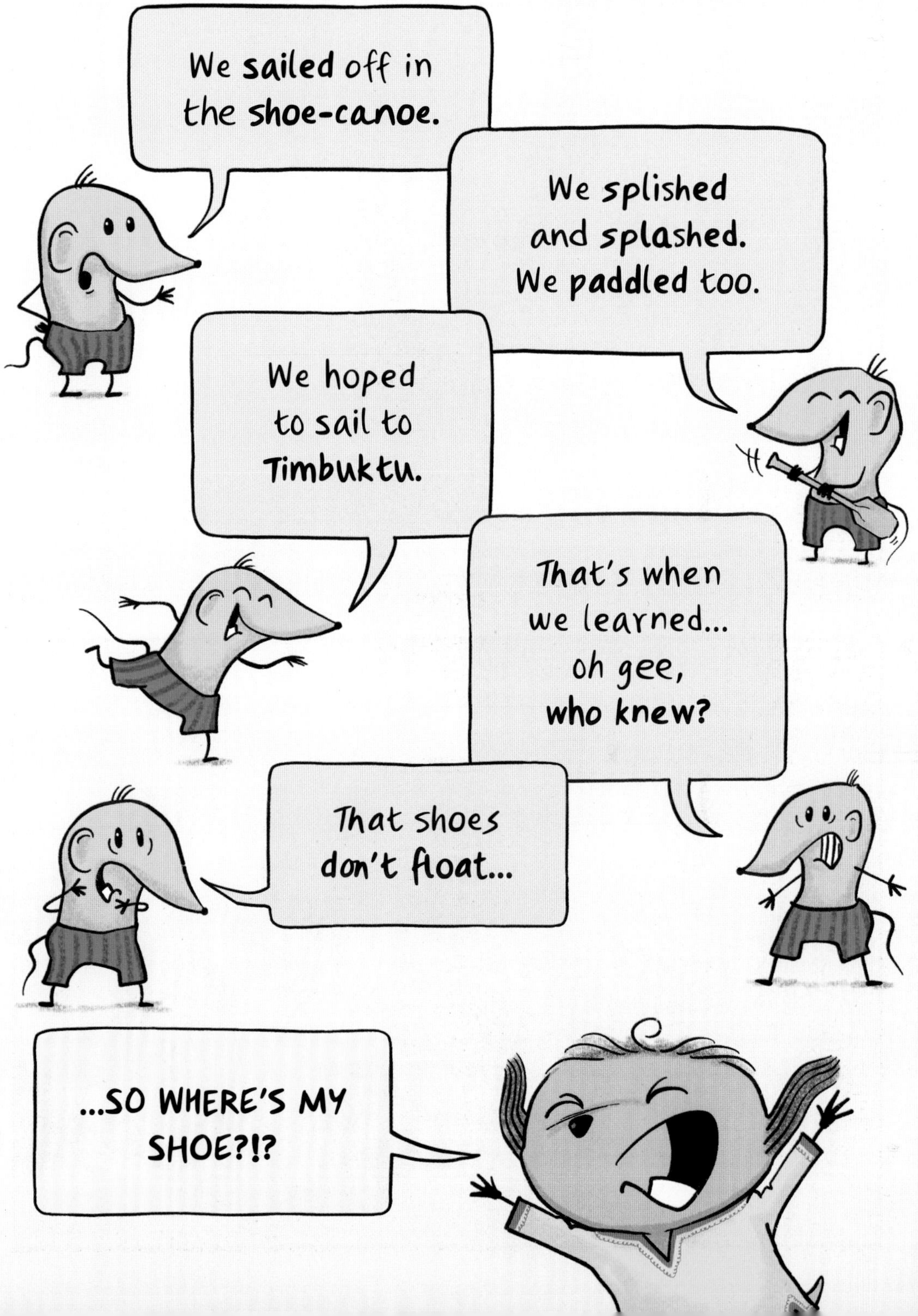
We sailed off in the shoe-canoe.
We splished and splashed. We paddled too.
We hoped to sail to Timbuktu.
That's when we learned... oh gee, who knew?
That shoes don't float...
...SO WHERE'S MY SHOE?!?

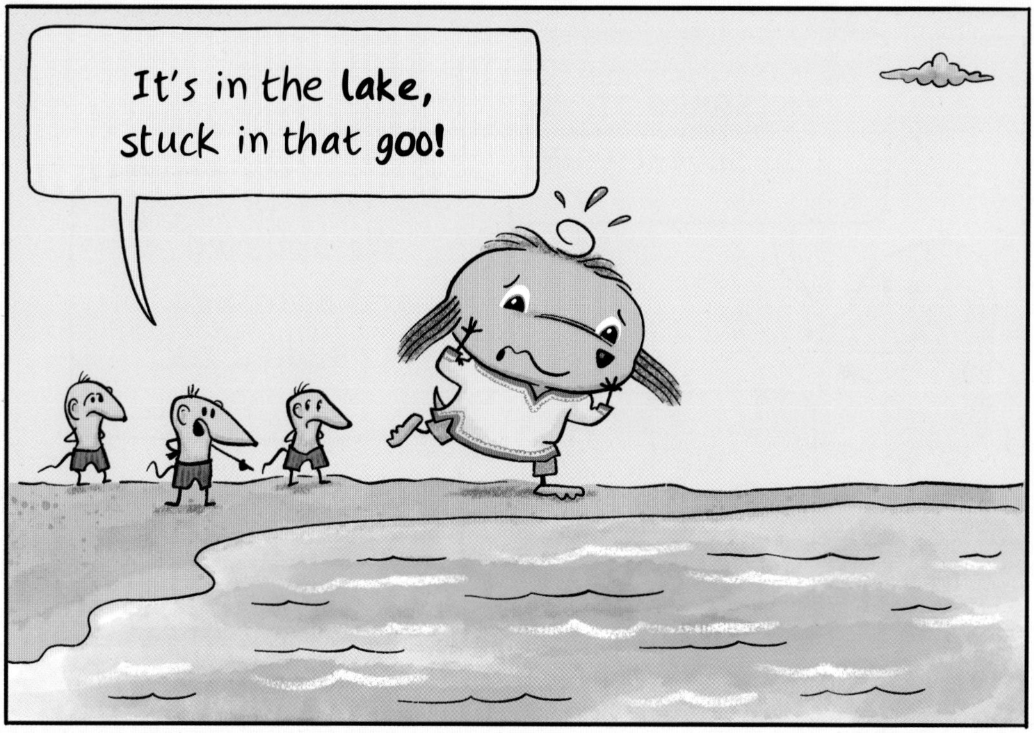
It's in the lake, stuck in that goo!

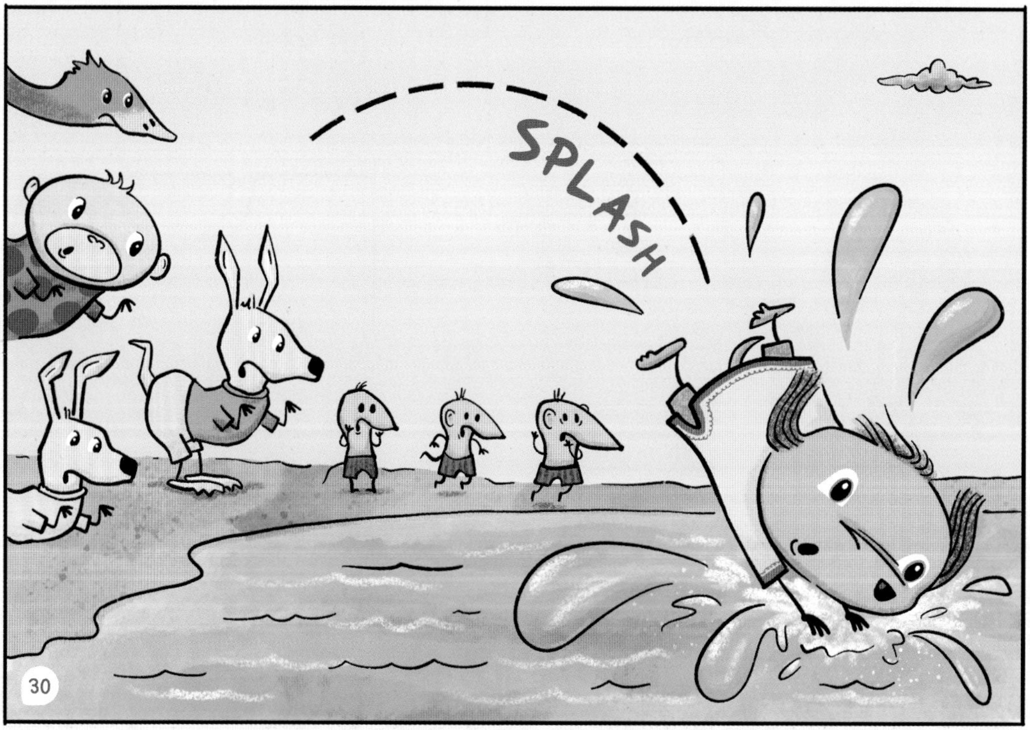
SPLASH

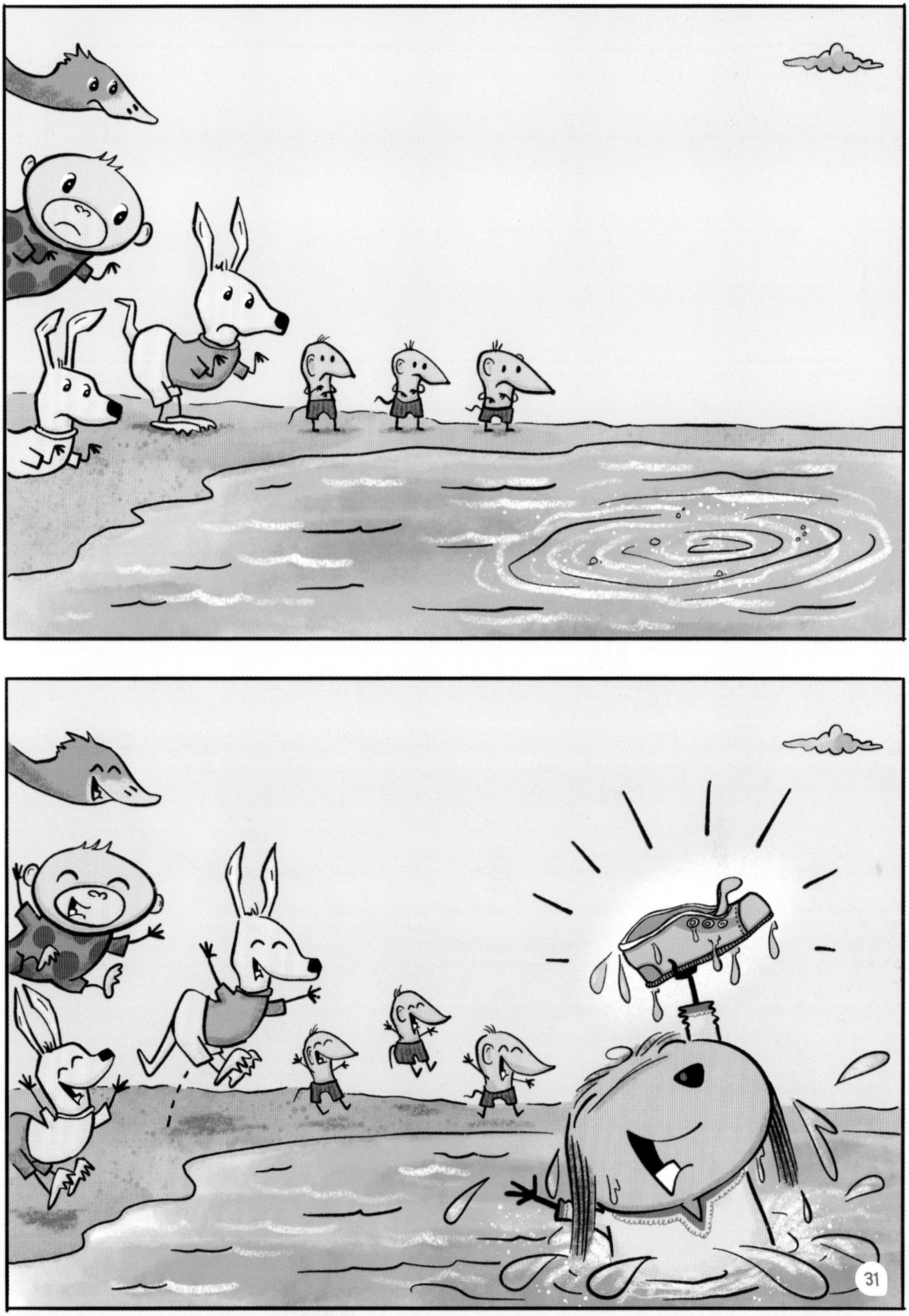

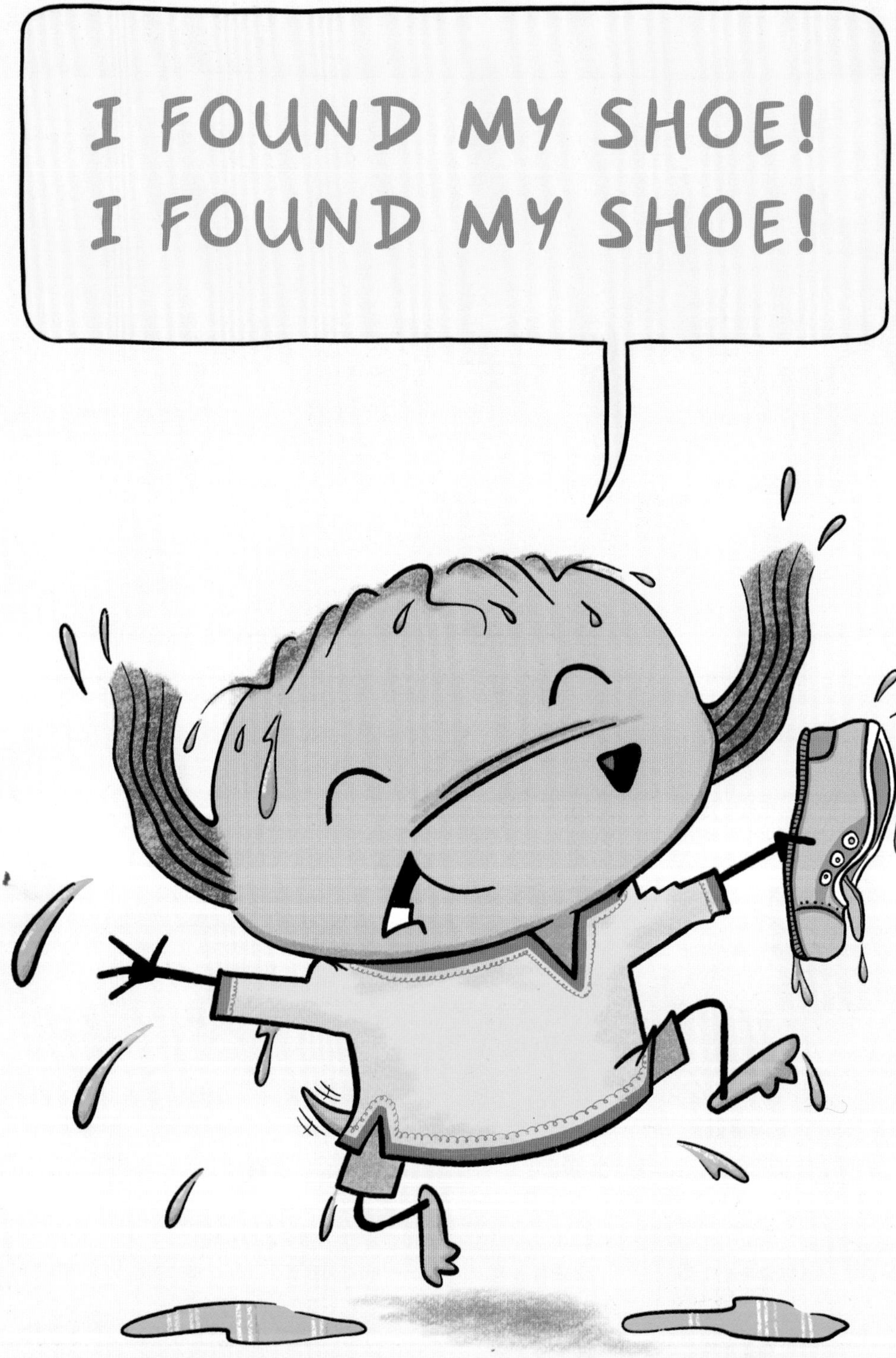
I FOUND MY SHOE! I FOUND MY SHOE!

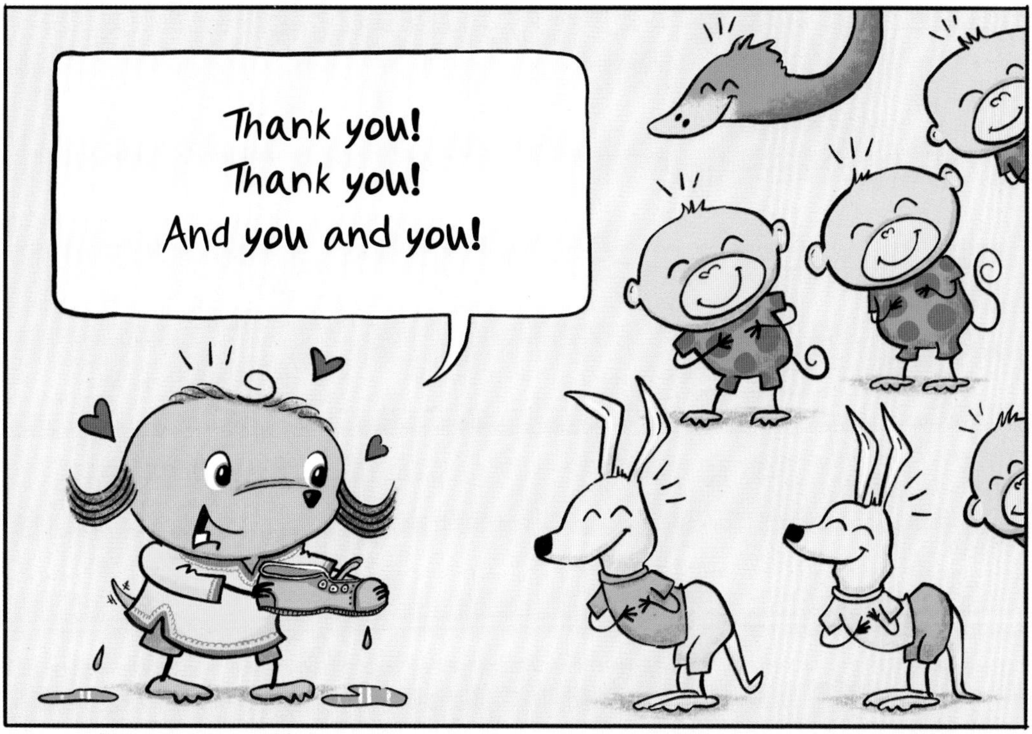
Thank you!
Thank you!
And you and you!

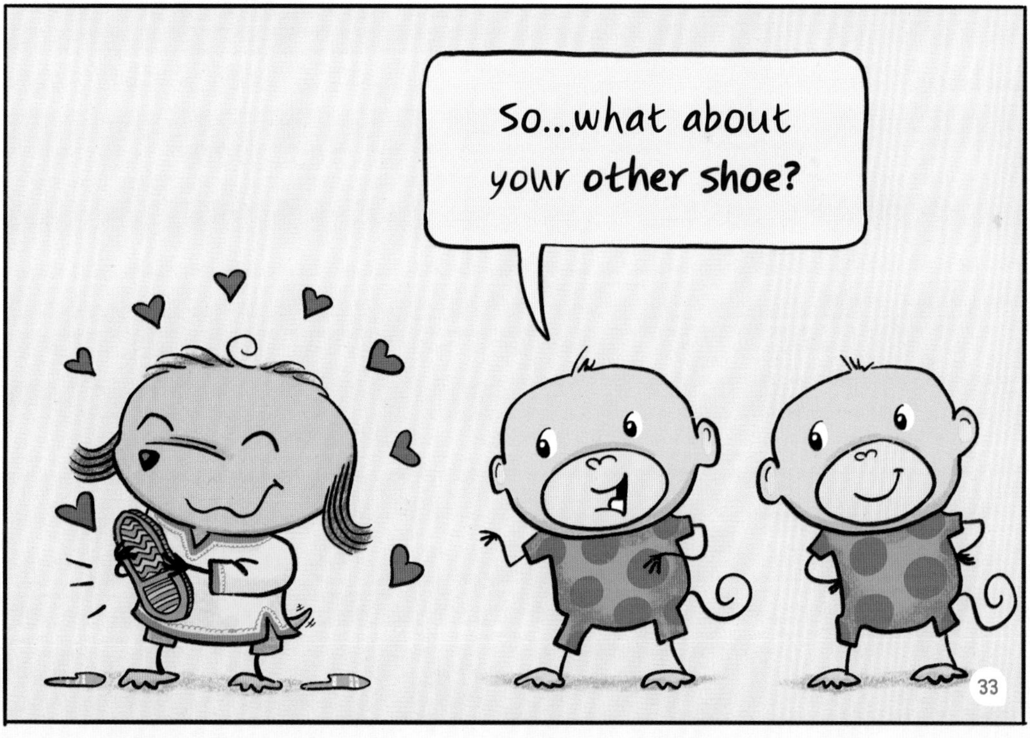
So...what about your other shoe?

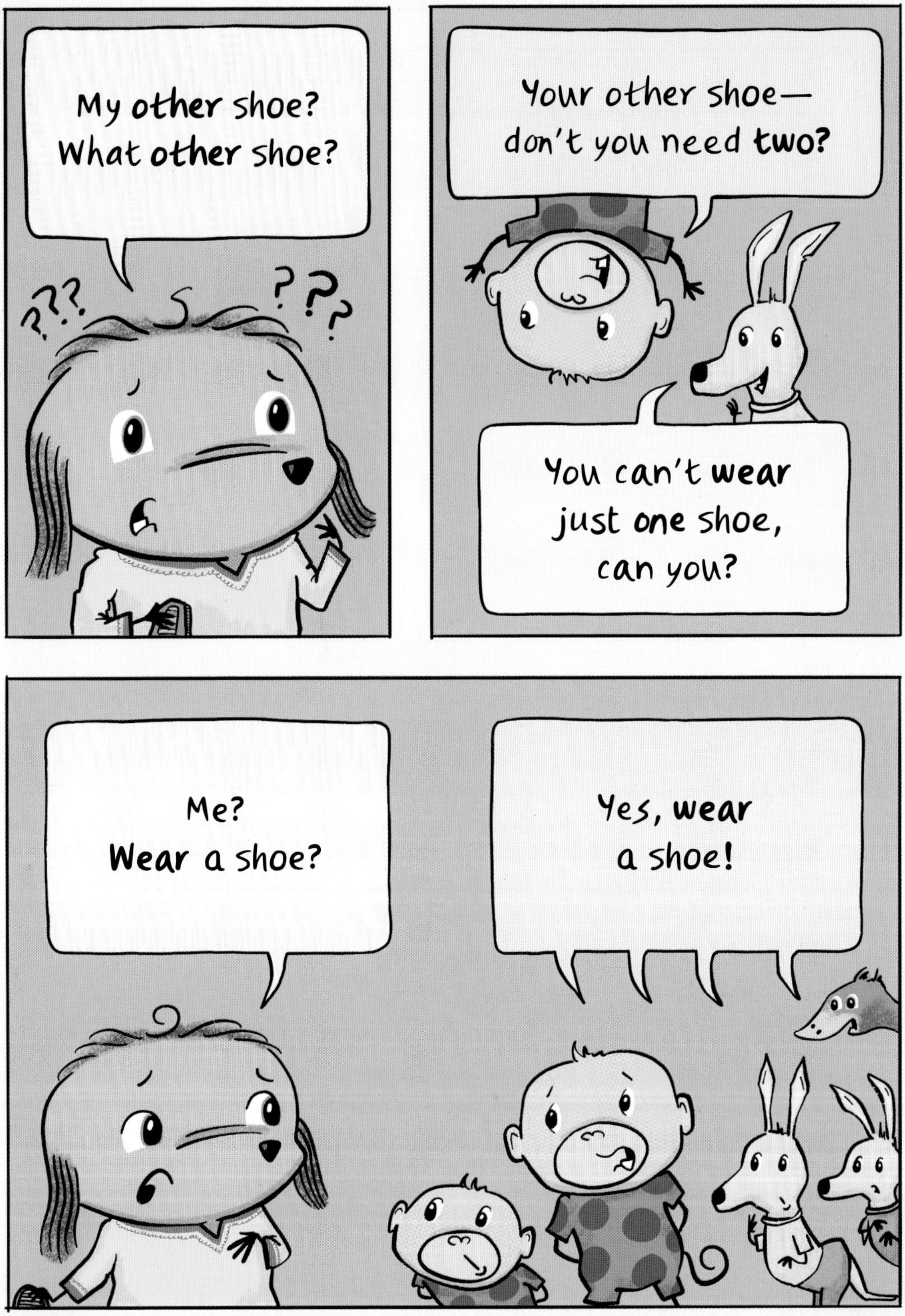
My other shoe? What other shoe?
???
???
Your other shoe— don't you need two?
You can't wear just one shoe, can you?
Me? Wear a shoe?
Yes, wear a shoe!

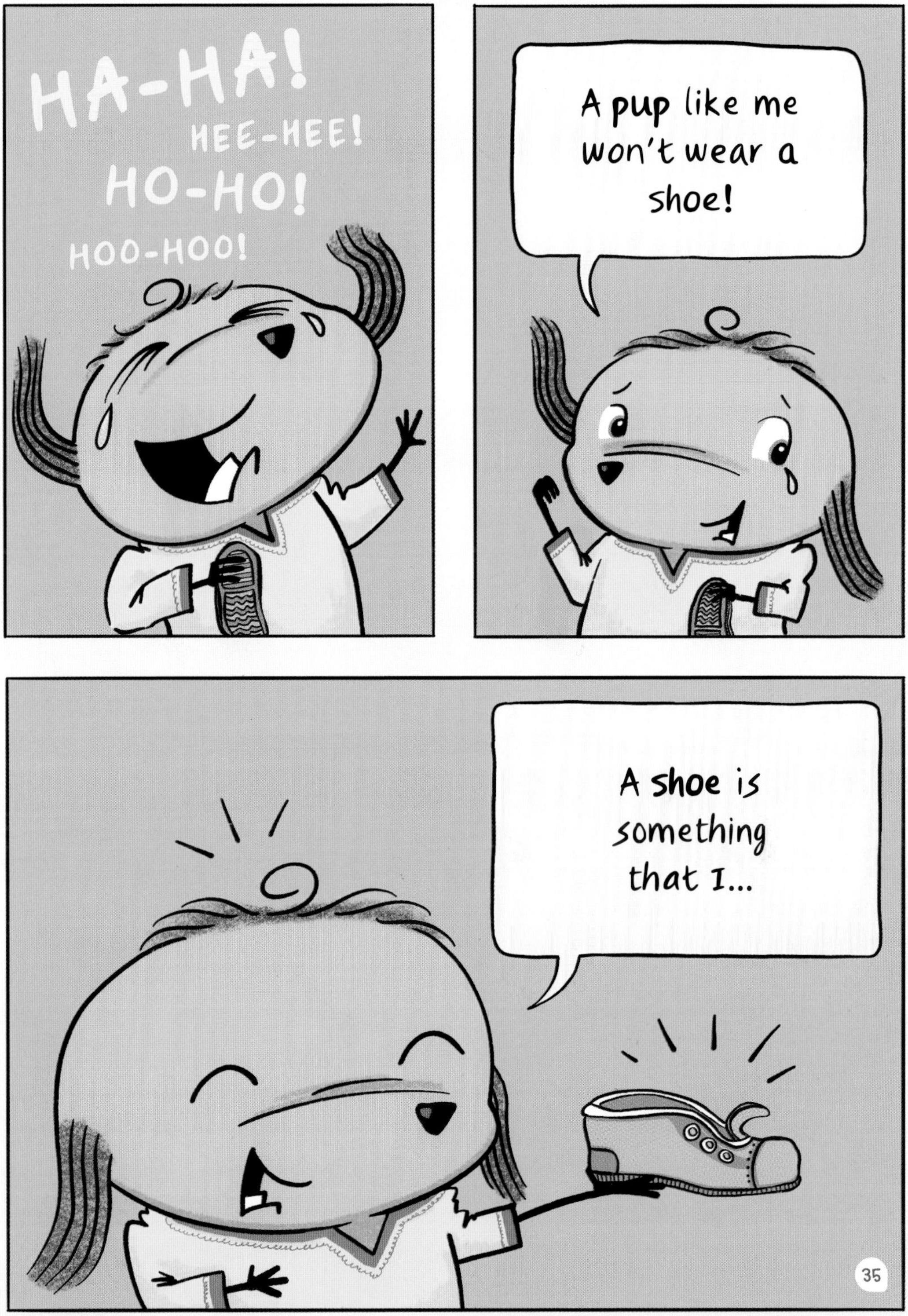
HA-HA!
HEE-HEE!
HO-HO!
HOO-HOO!
A pup like me won't wear a shoe!
A shoe is something that I...

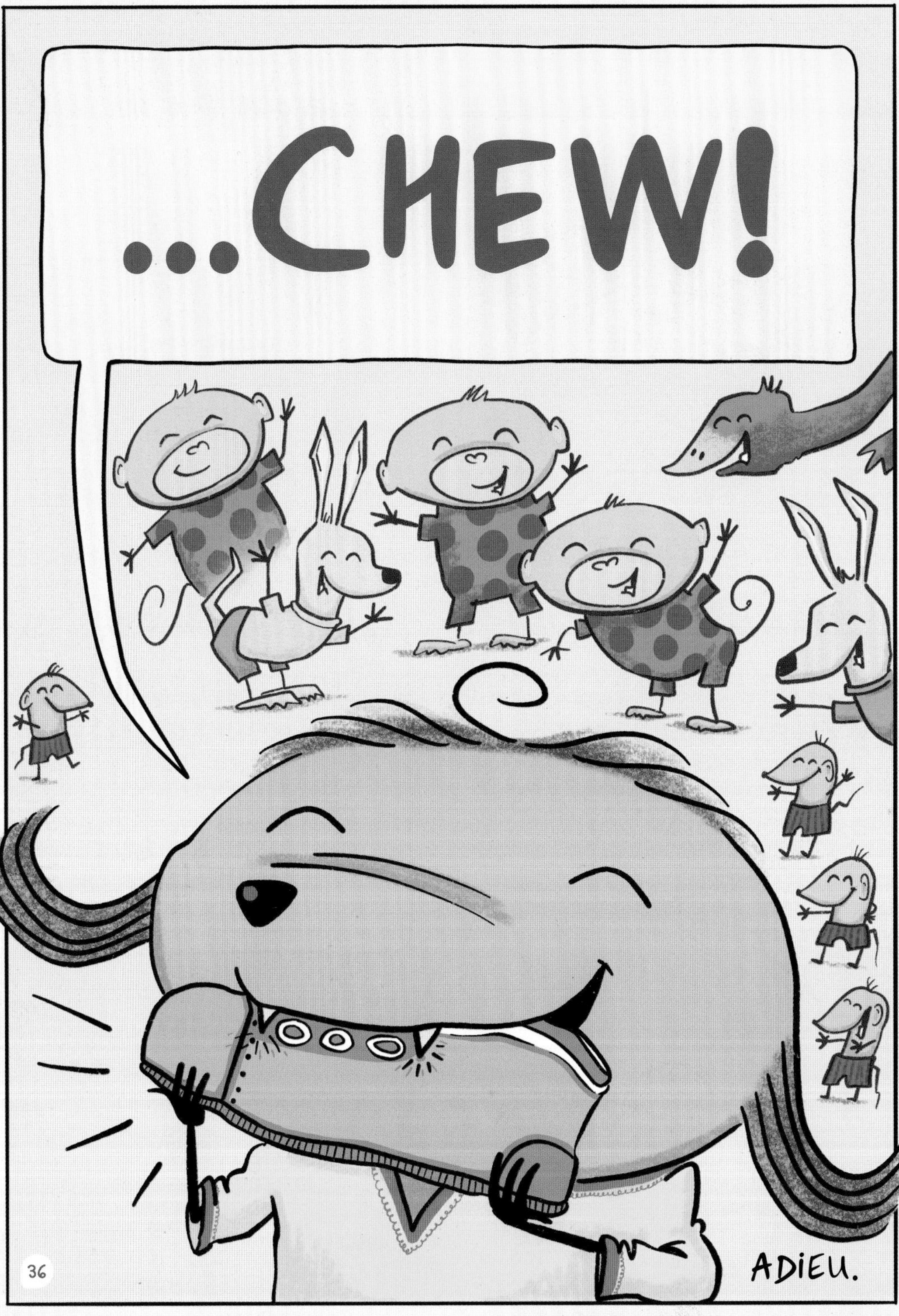
...CHEW!
ADIEU.

ZOONI LOVES... RACING

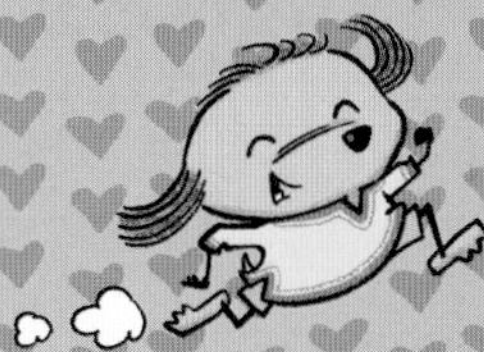

Race a **Donkey**, race a **Sheep**.

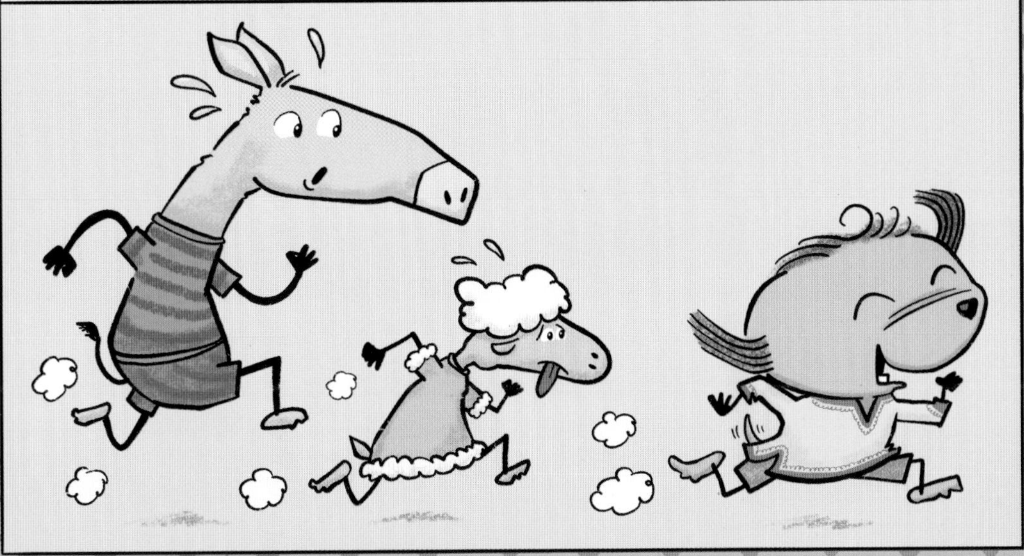

Race a **Panda** in a **jeep**.

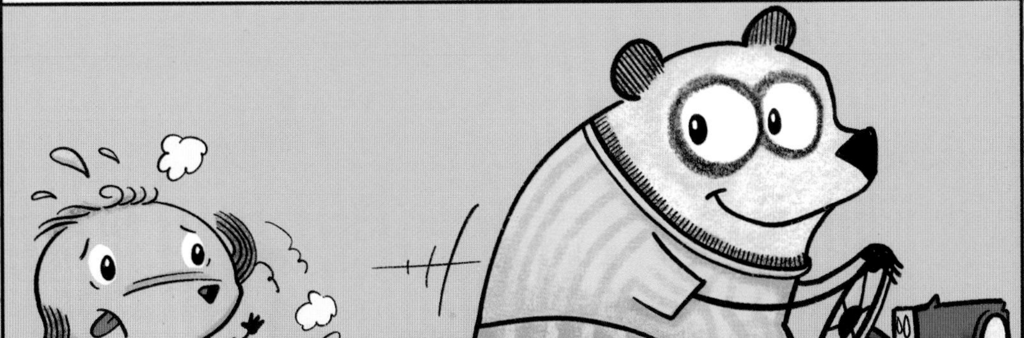

Race a **Dolphin** in the deep.

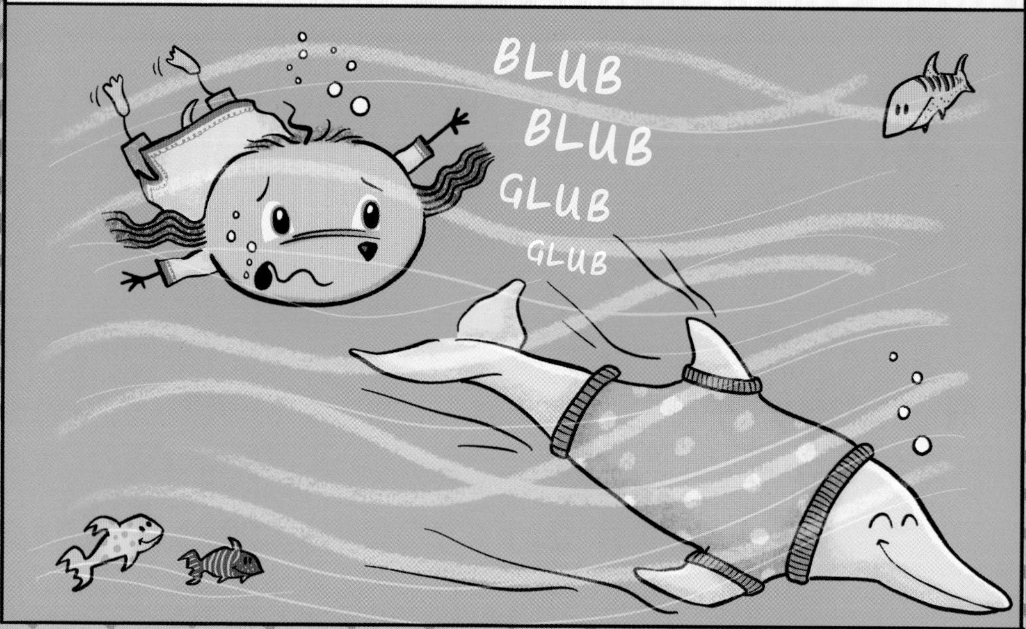
BLUB
BLUB
GLUB
GLUB

Race a **Bird** that goes...

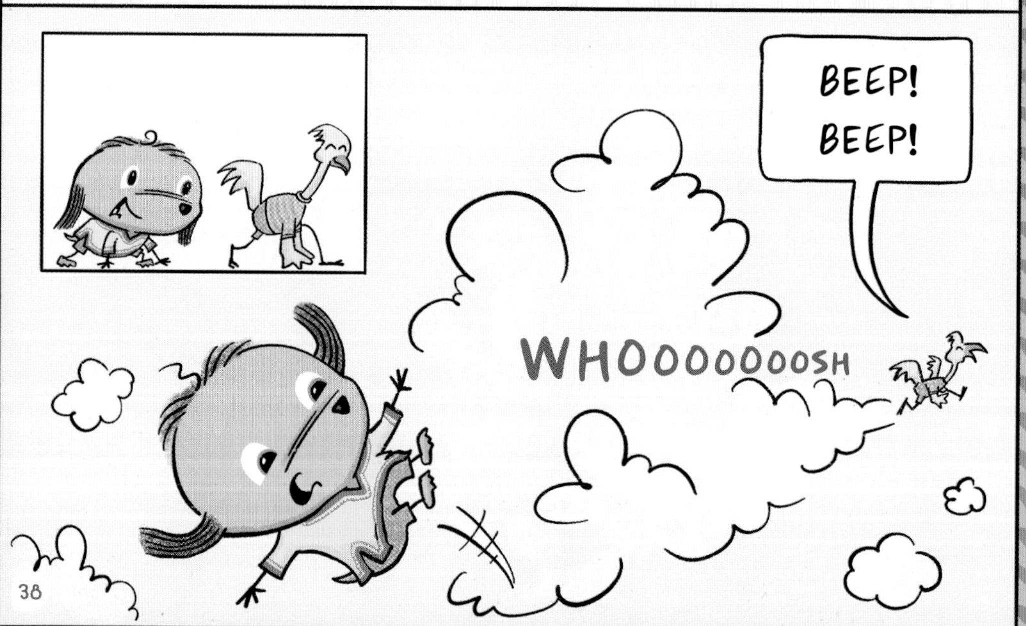
BEEP!
BEEP!
WHOOOOOOOOSH

Race a **Rabbit,** hop and leap.

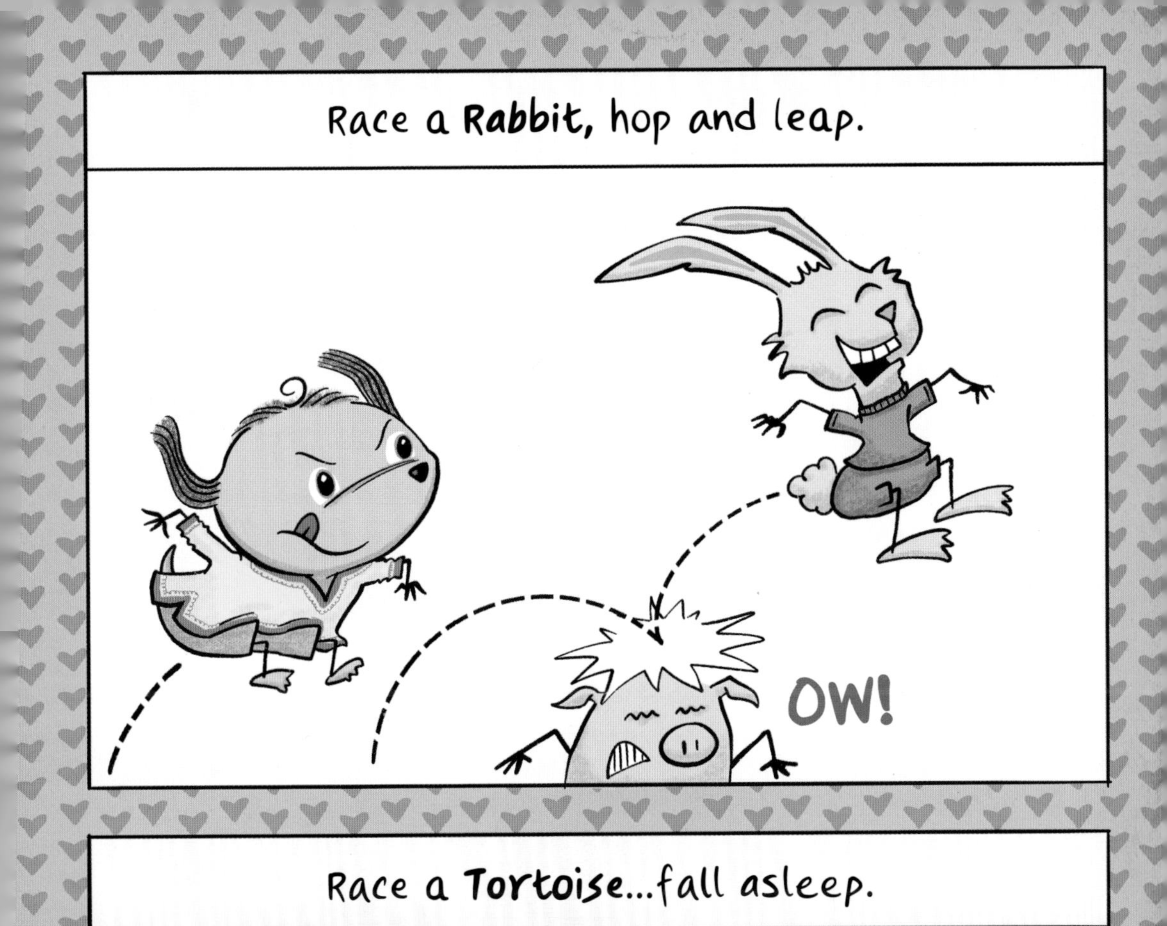
OW!

Race a **Tortoise**...fall asleep.

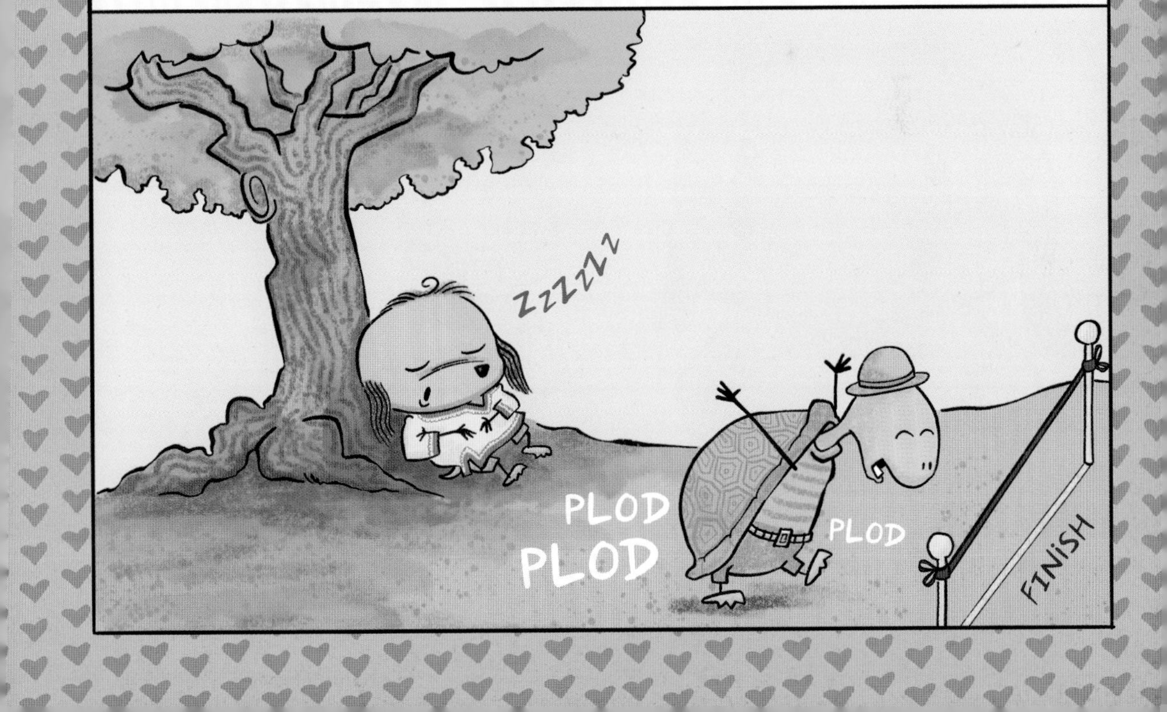
ZzZzzz
PLOD
PLOD
PLOD
FINISH

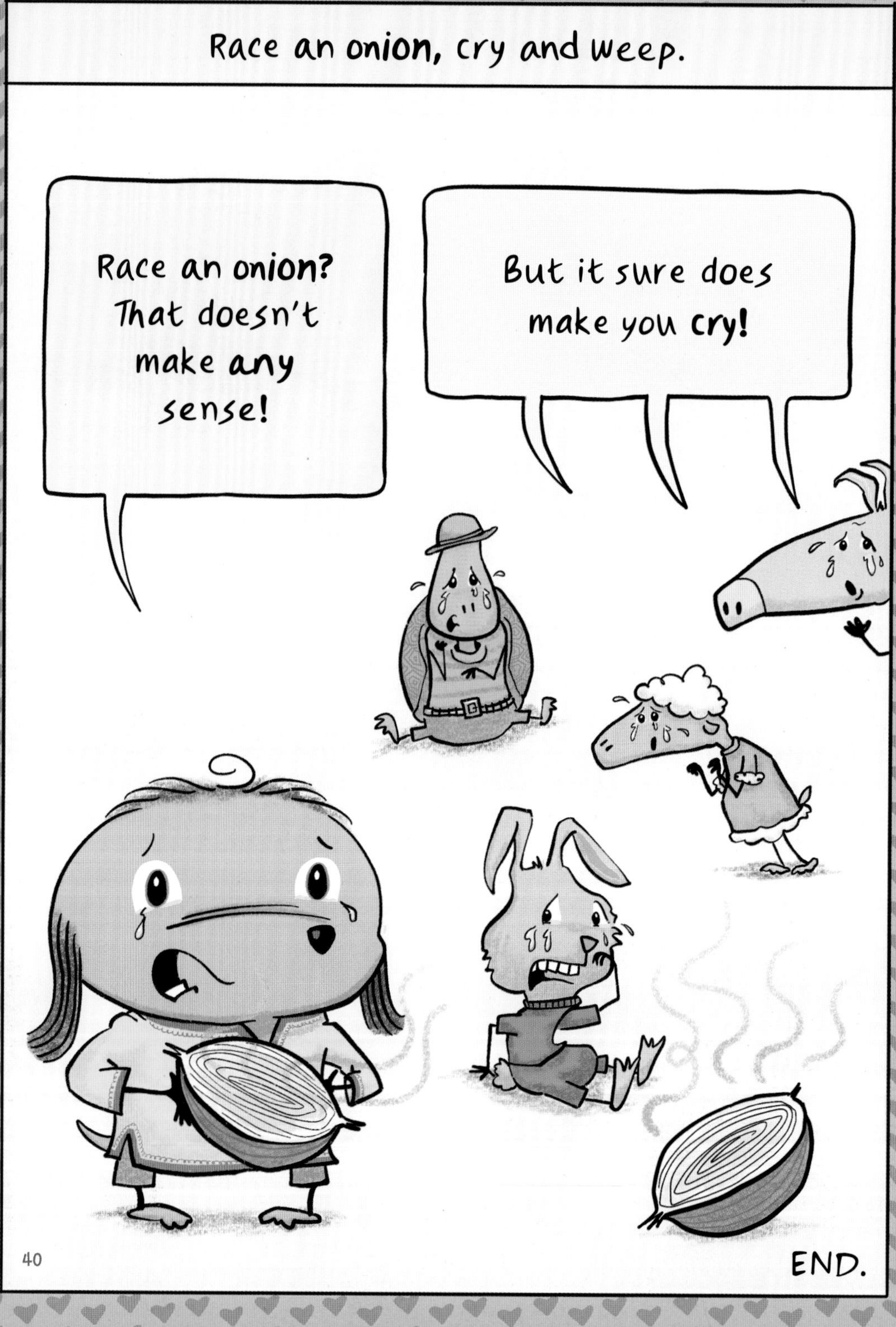
Race an onion, cry and weep.
Race an onion? That doesn't make any sense!
But it sure does make you cry!
END.

RESCUE

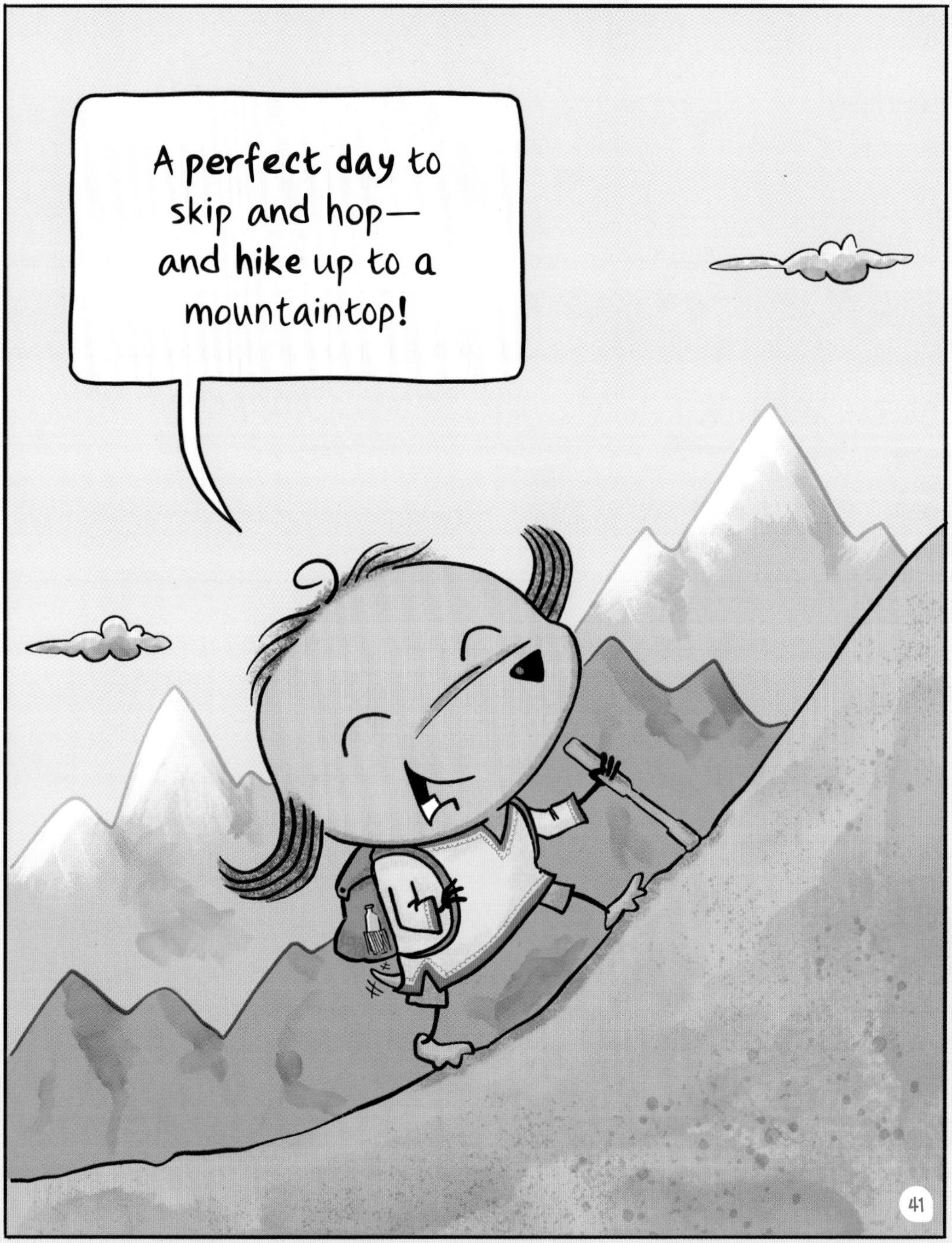
A perfect day to skip and hop— and hike up to a mountaintop!

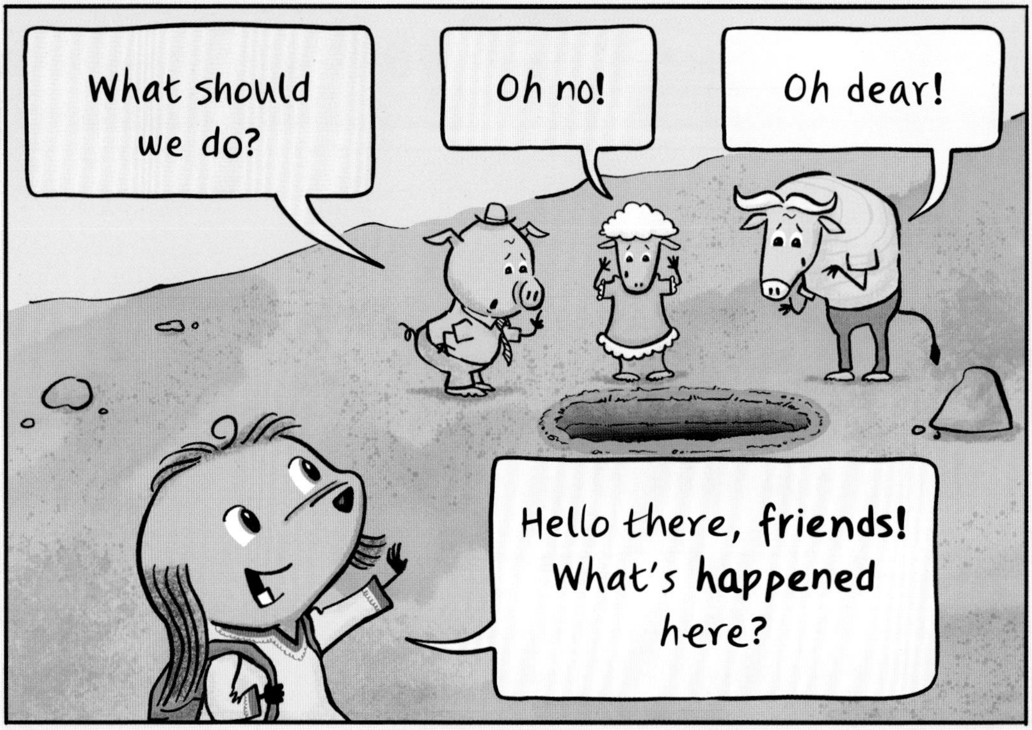
What should we do?
Oh no!
Oh dear!
Hello there, friends! What's happened here?

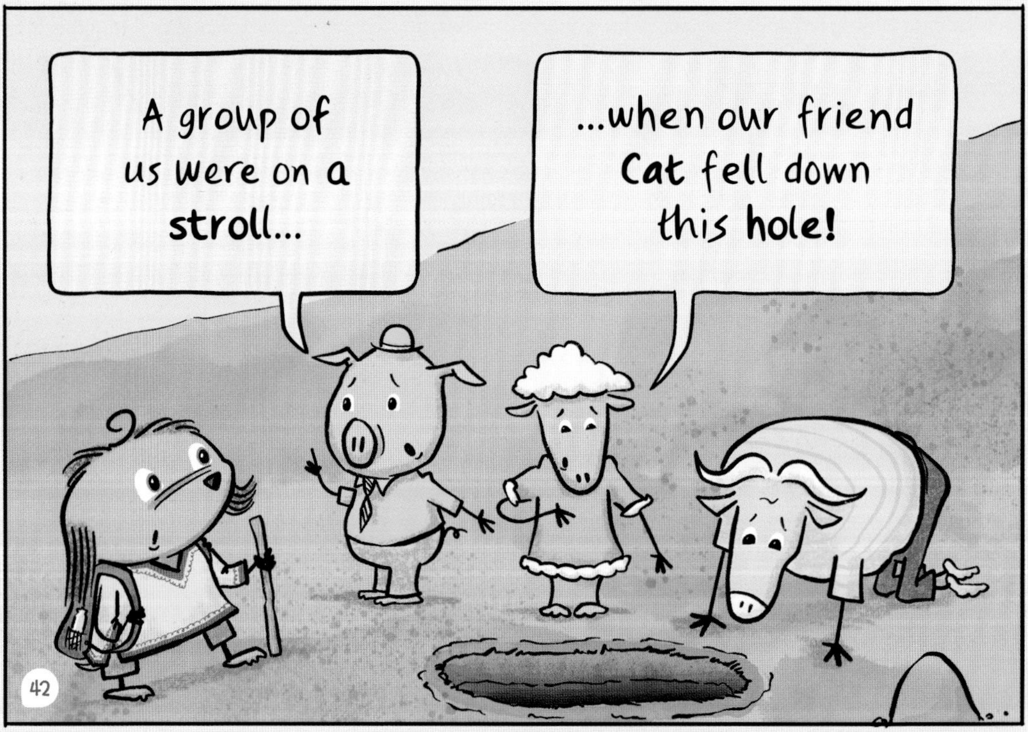
A group of us were on a stroll...
...when our friend Cat fell down this hole!

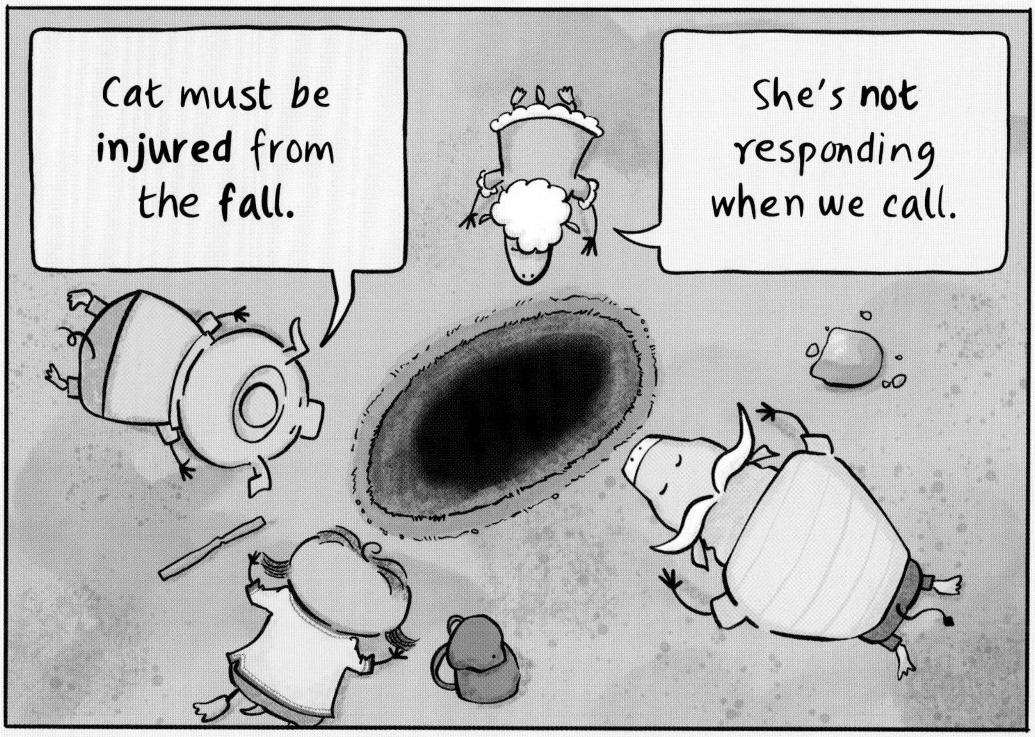
Cat must be injured from the fall.
She's not responding when we call.

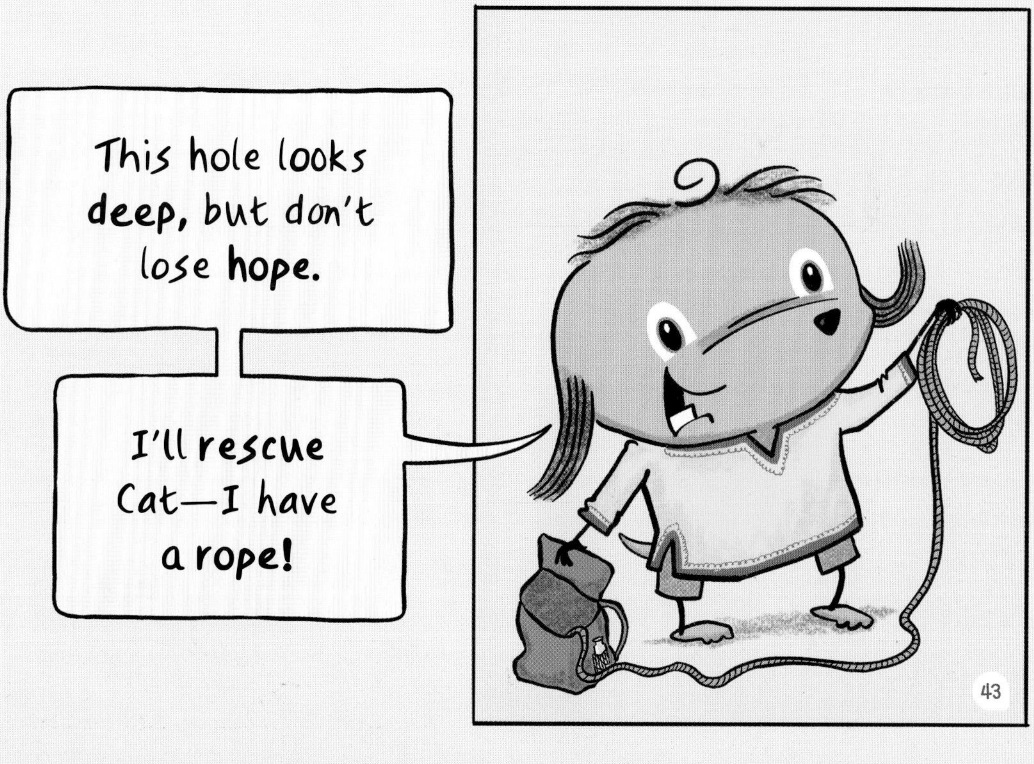
This hole looks deep, but don't lose hope.
I'll rescue Cat—I have a rope!

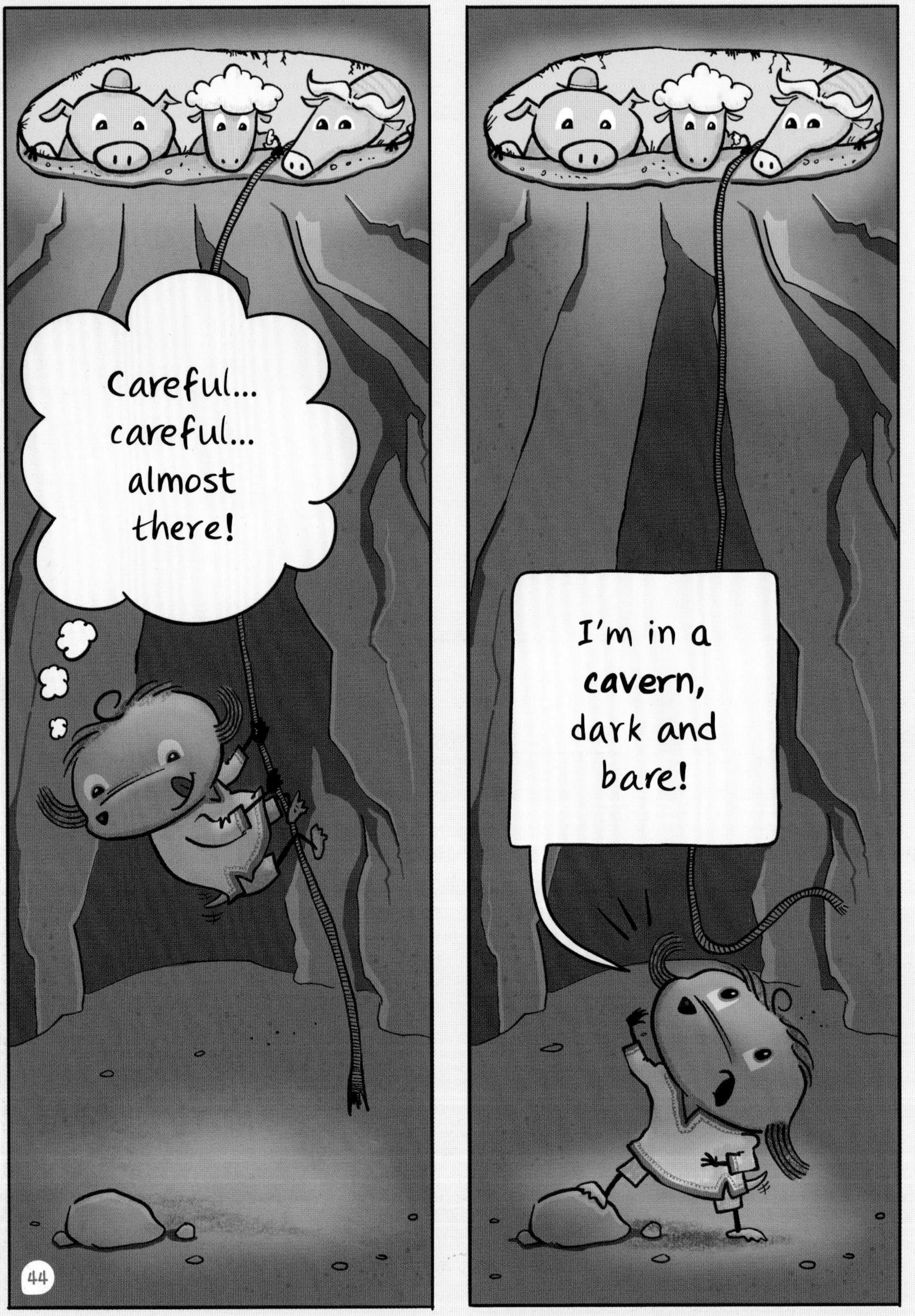
Careful... careful... almost there!
I'm in a **cavern**, dark and bare!

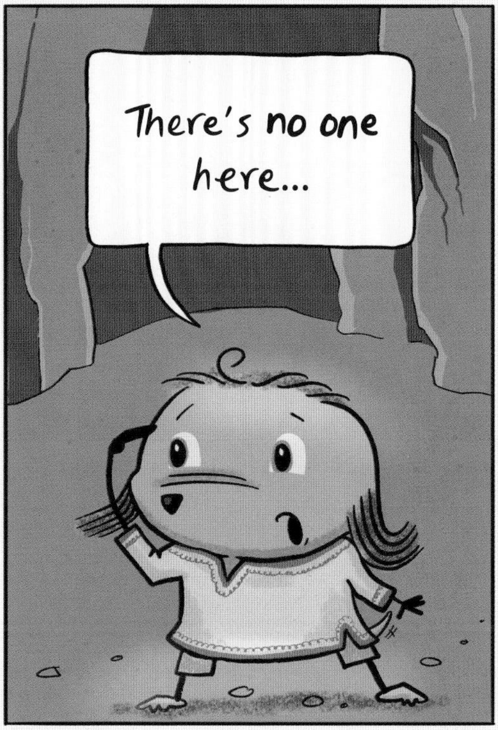
There's no one here...

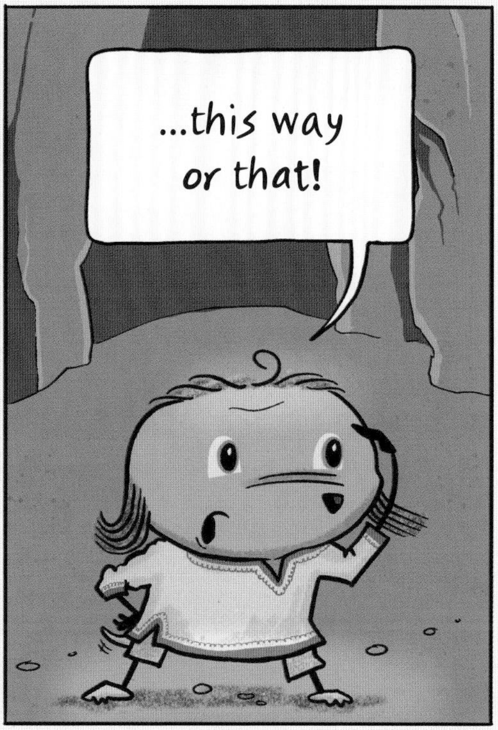
...this way or that!

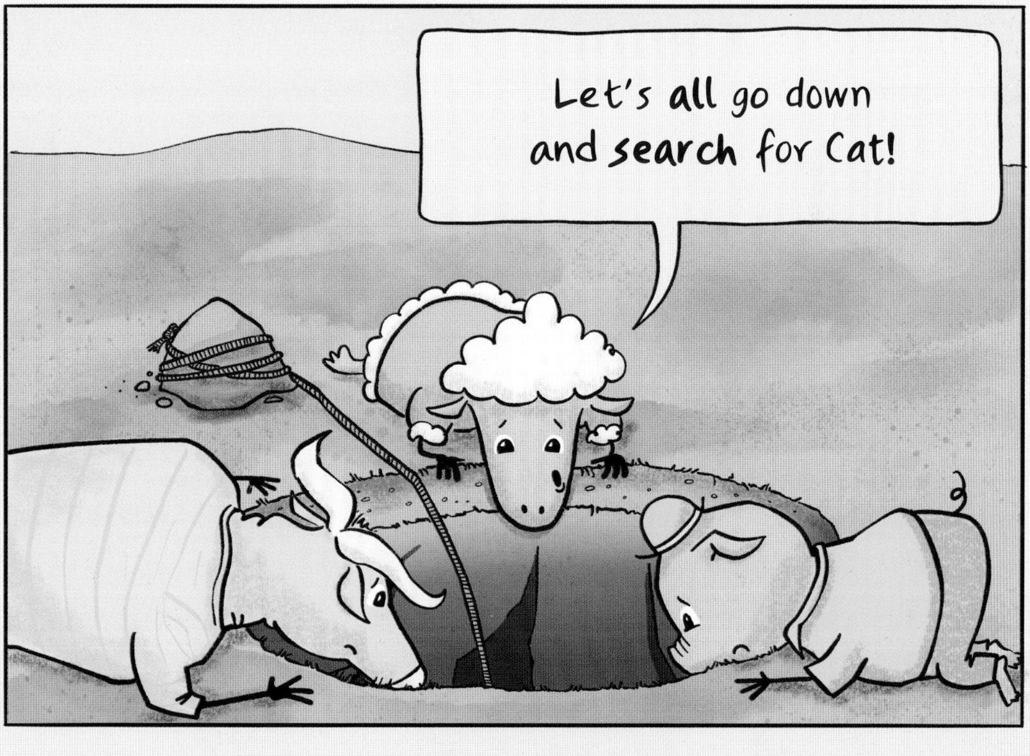
Let's all go down and search for Cat!

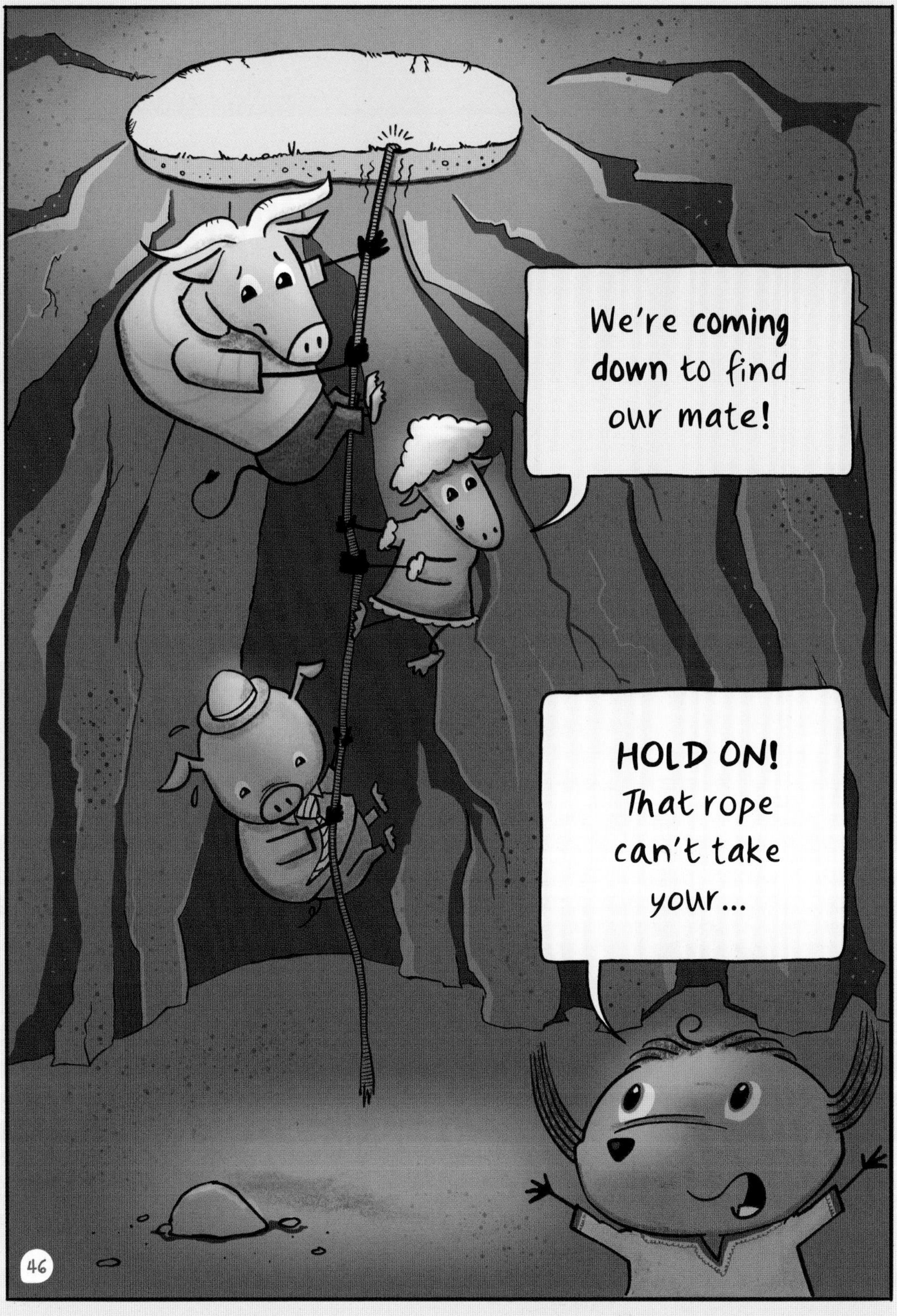
We're coming down to find our mate!
HOLD ON! That rope can't take your...

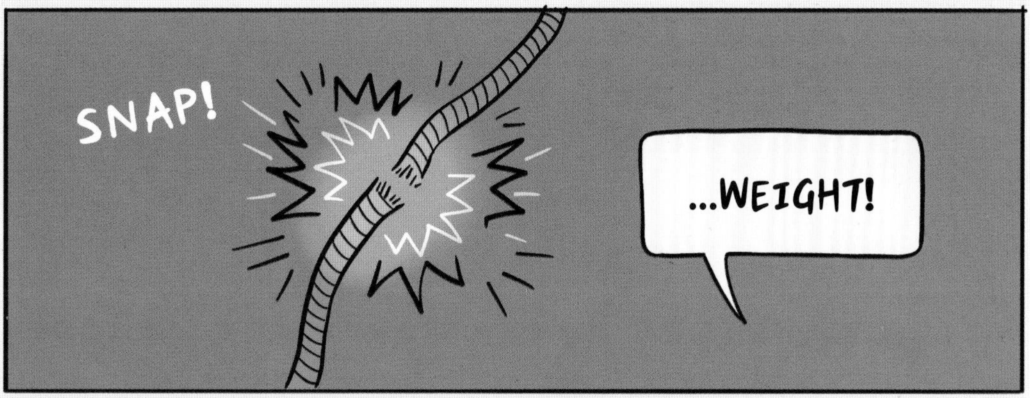
SNAP!
...WEIGHT!

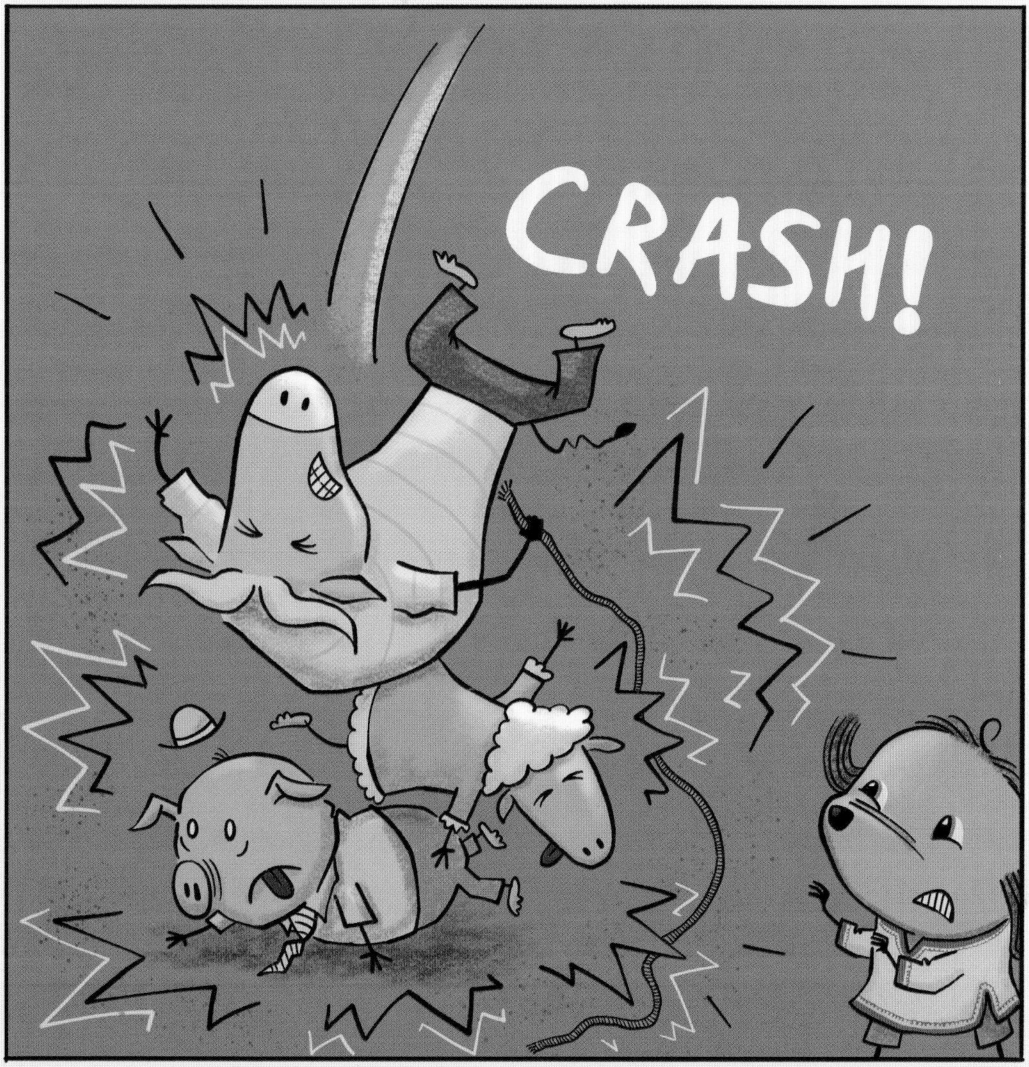
CRASH!

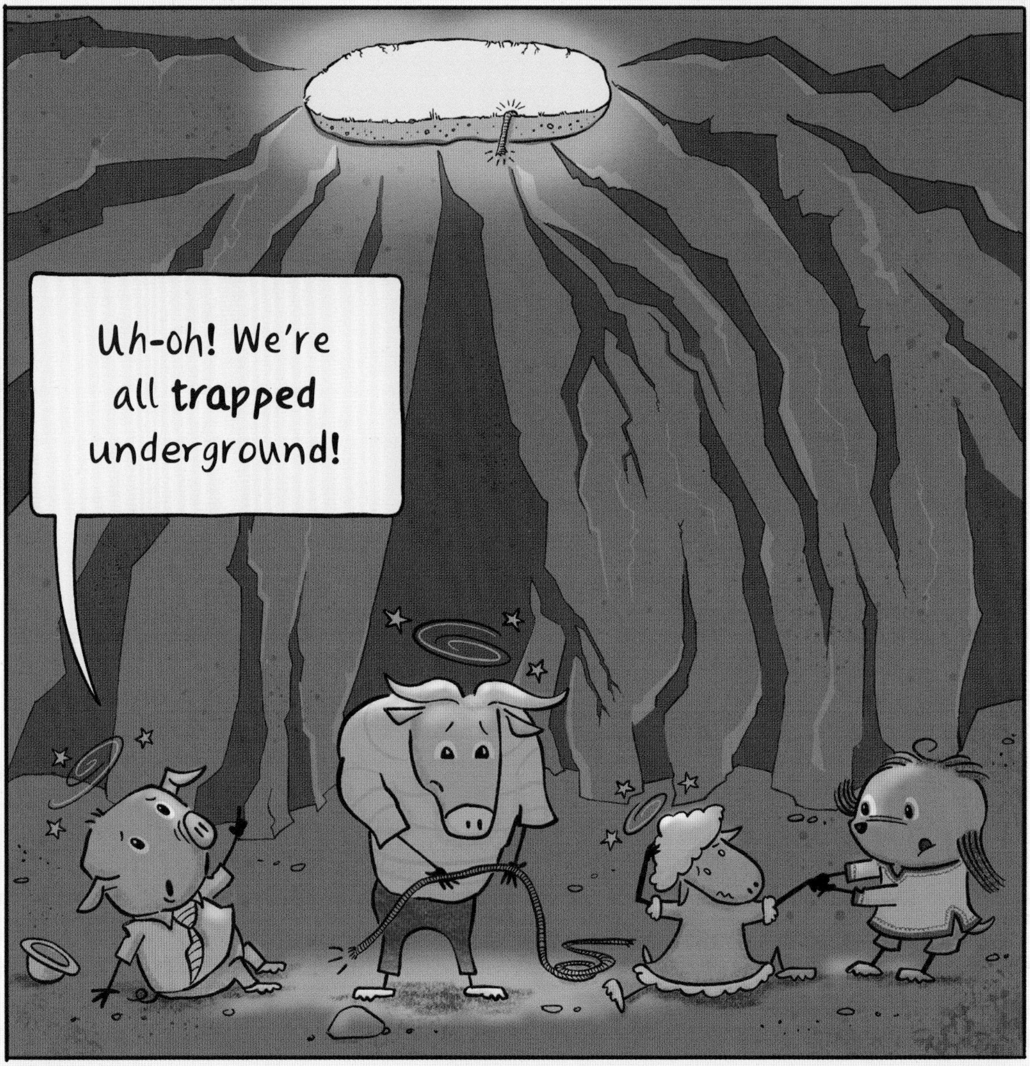
Uh-oh! We're all **trapped** underground!

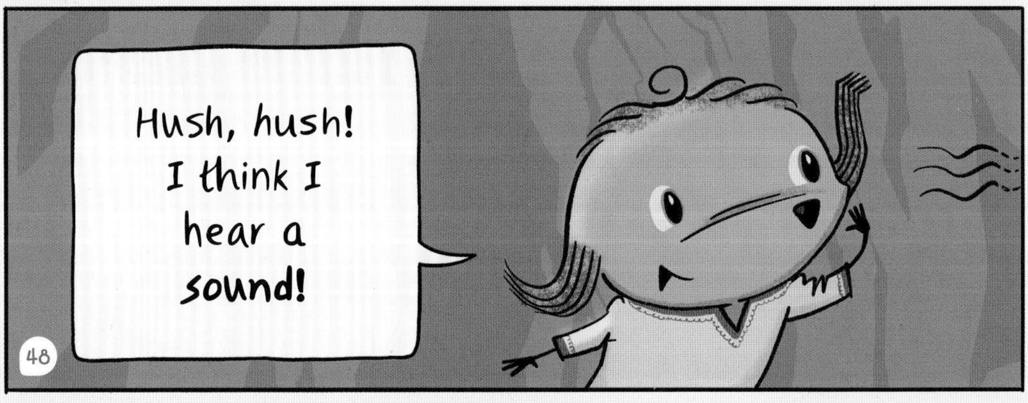
Hush, hush! I think I hear a **sound**!

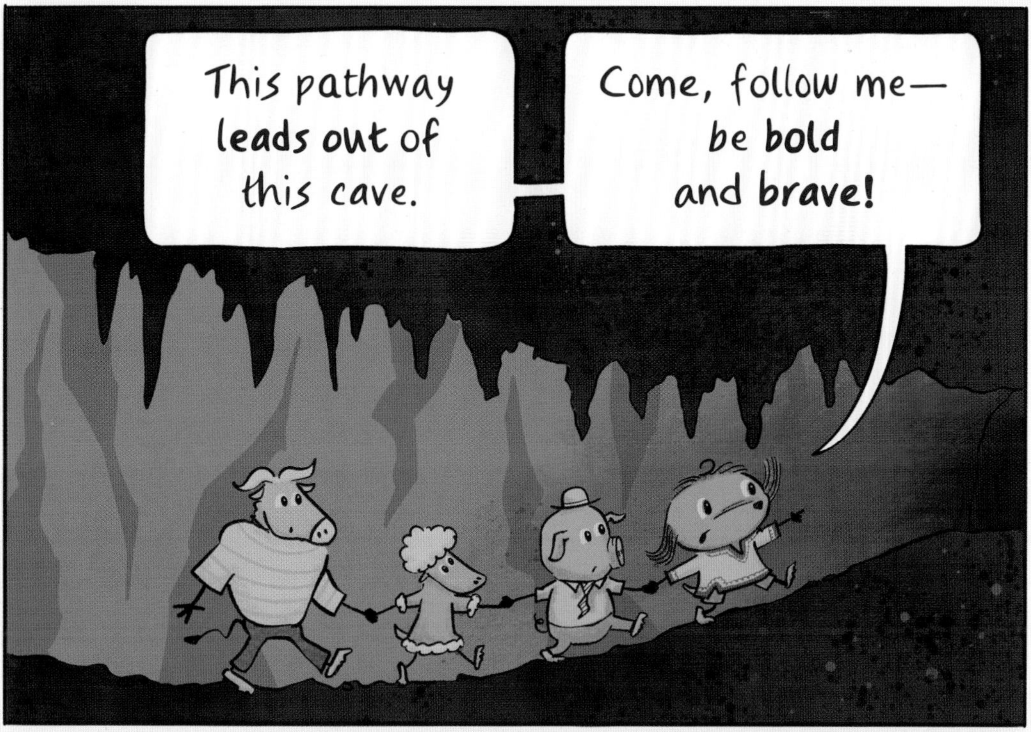
This pathway leads out of this cave.
Come, follow me—be bold and brave!

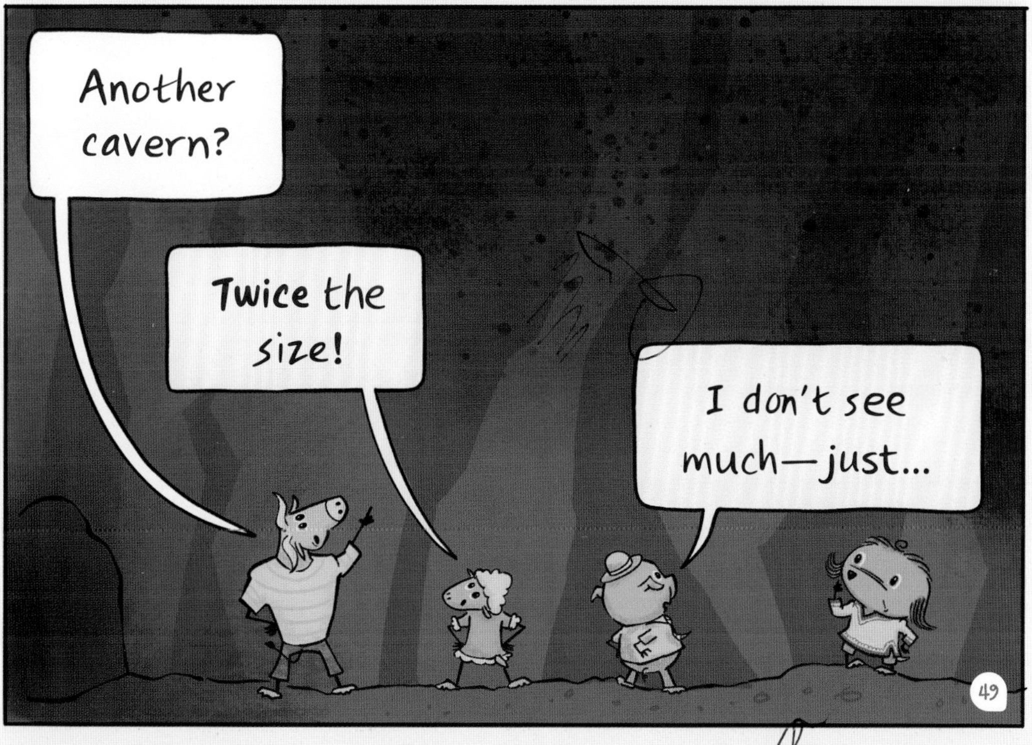
Another cavern?
Twice the size!
I don't see much—just...

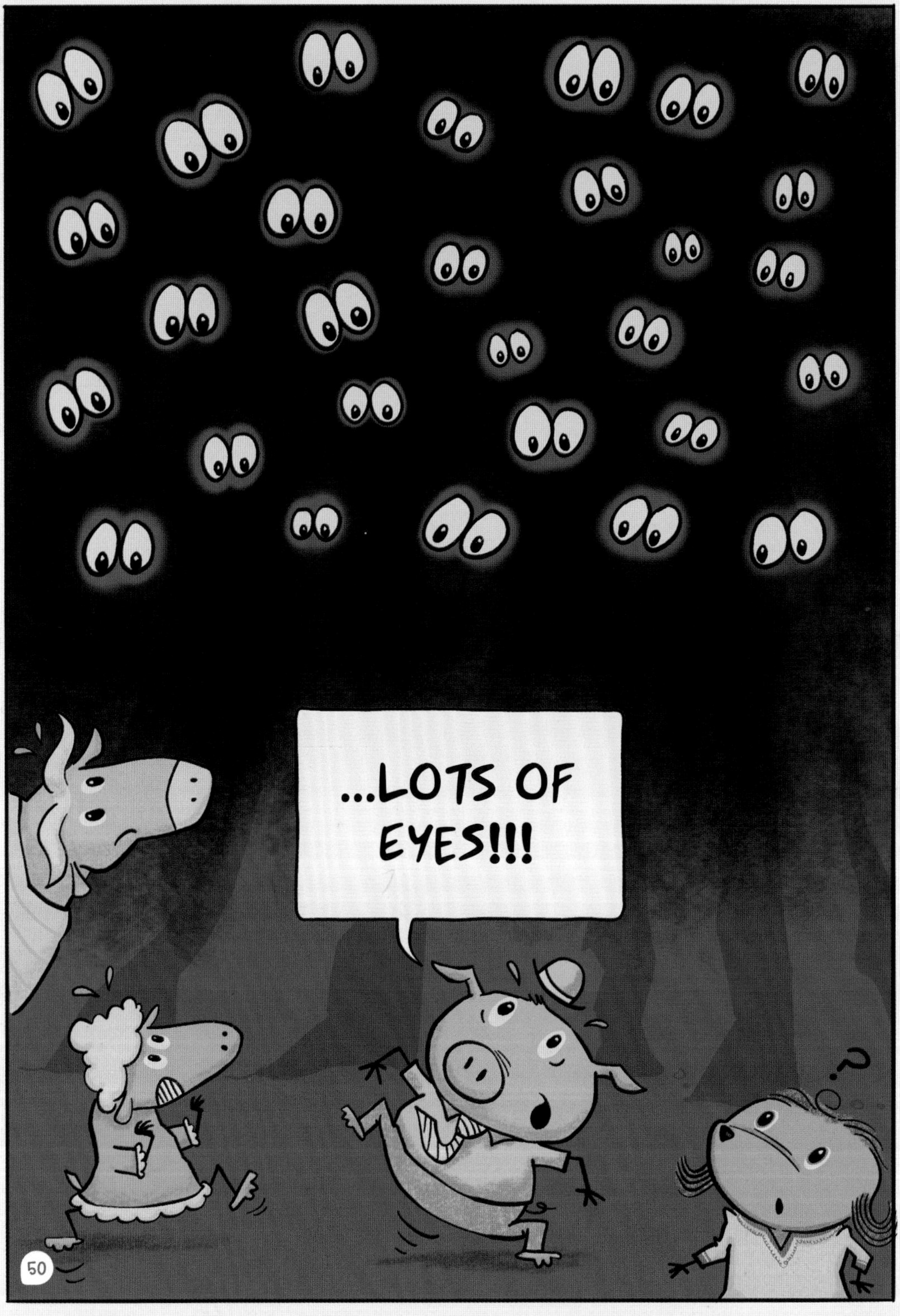
...LOTS OF
EYES!!!
?

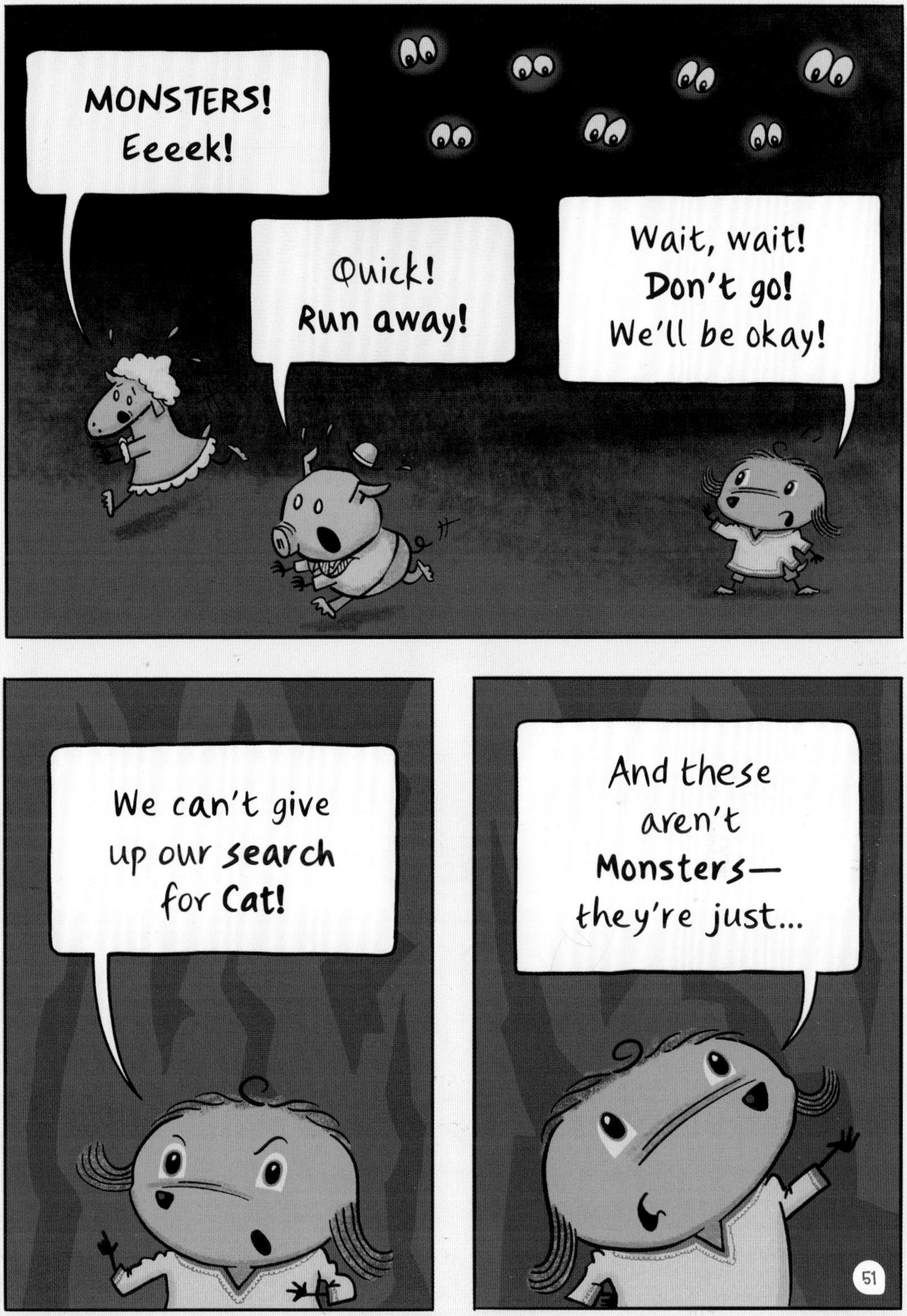
MONSTERS! Eeeek!
Quick! Run away!
Wait, wait! Don't go! We'll be okay!
We can't give up our search for Cat!
And these aren't Monsters— they're just...

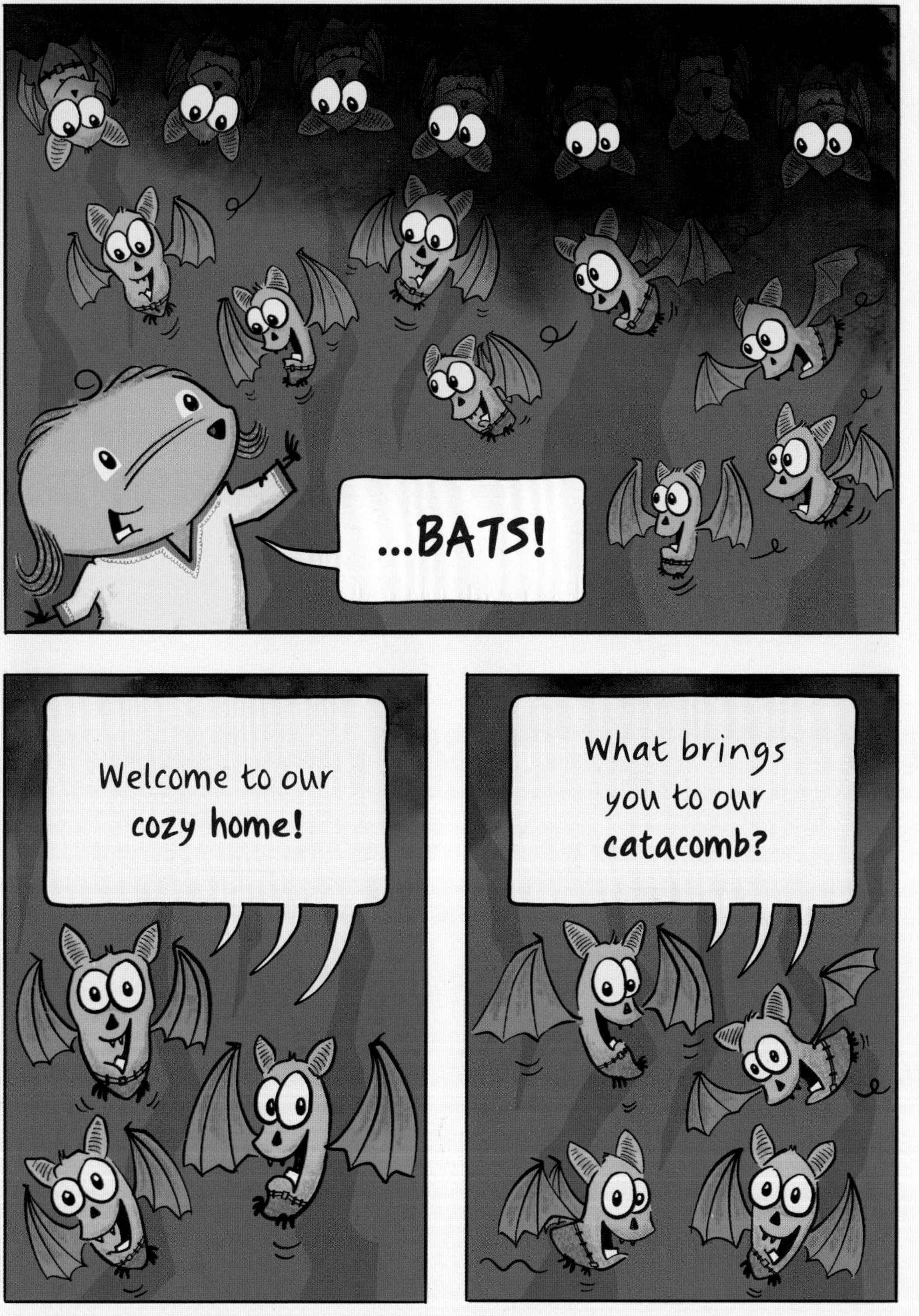
...BATS!
Welcome to our cozy home!
What brings you to our catacomb?

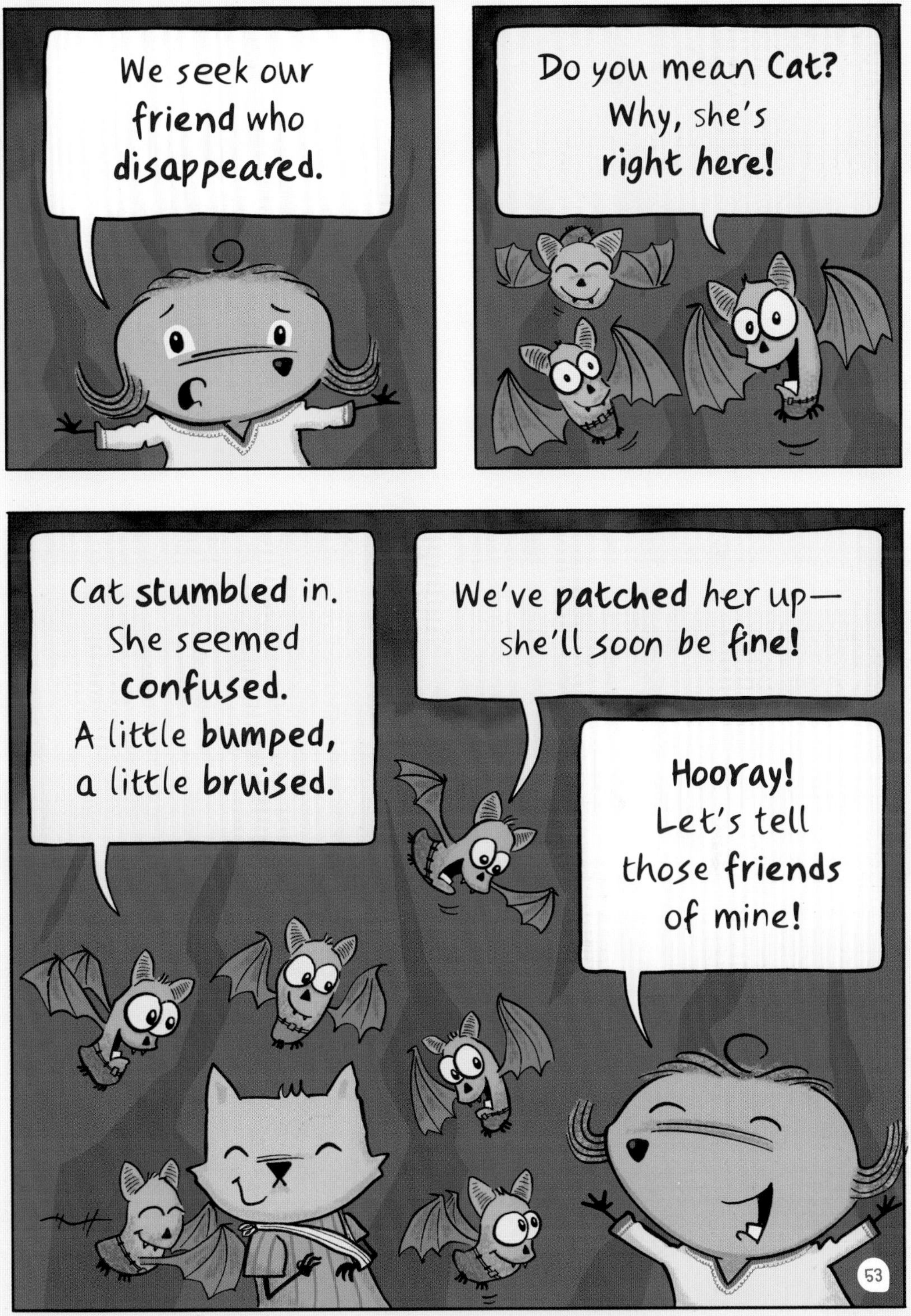
We seek our friend who disappeared.
Do you mean Cat? Why, she's right here!
Cat stumbled in. She seemed confused. A little bumped, a little bruised.
We've patched her up— she'll soon be fine!
Hooray! Let's tell those friends of mine!

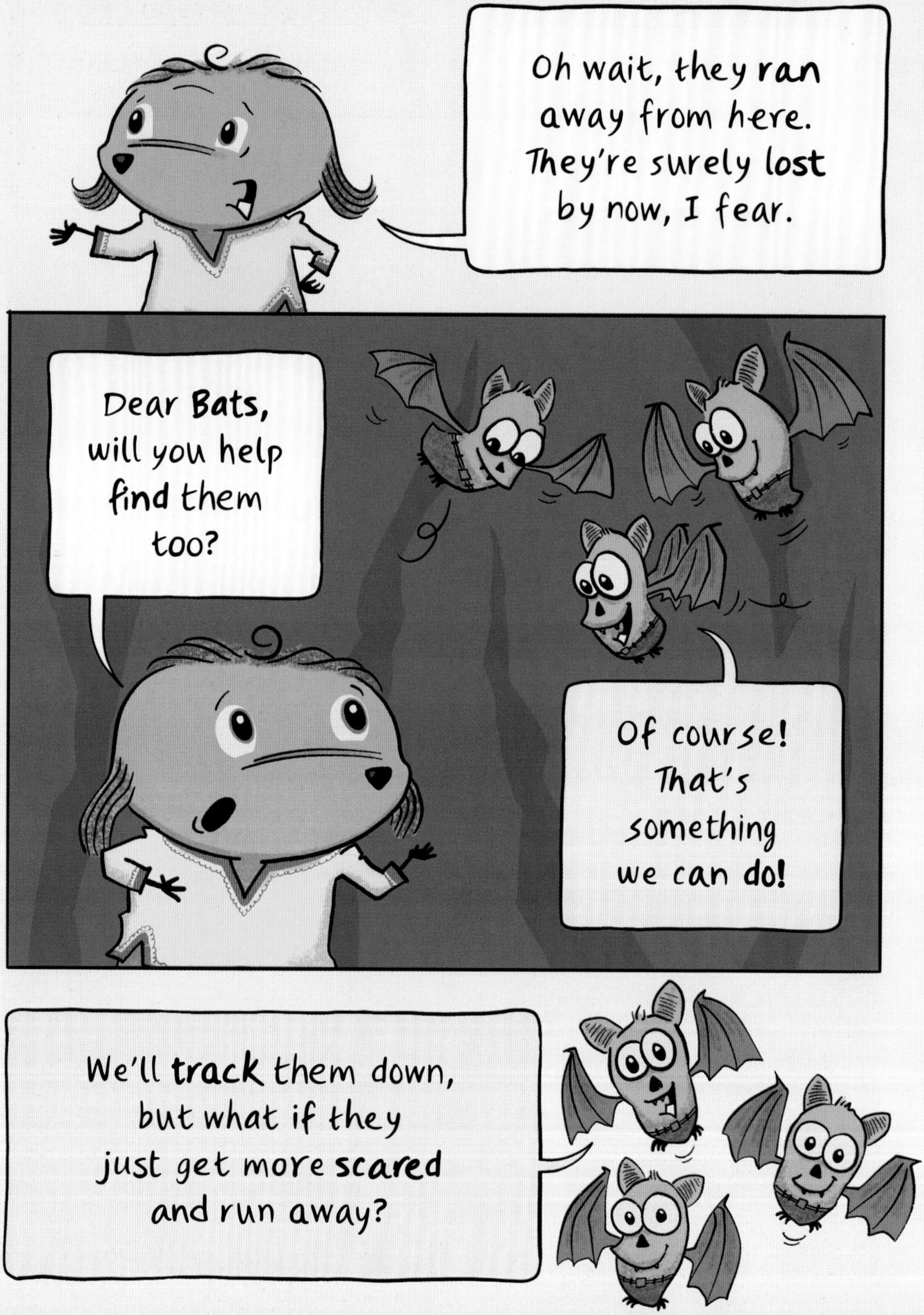
Oh wait, they **ran** away from here. They're surely **lost** by now, I fear.
Dear **Bats**, will you help **find** them too?
Of course! That's something we can **do**!
We'll **track** them down, but what if they just get more **scared** and run away?

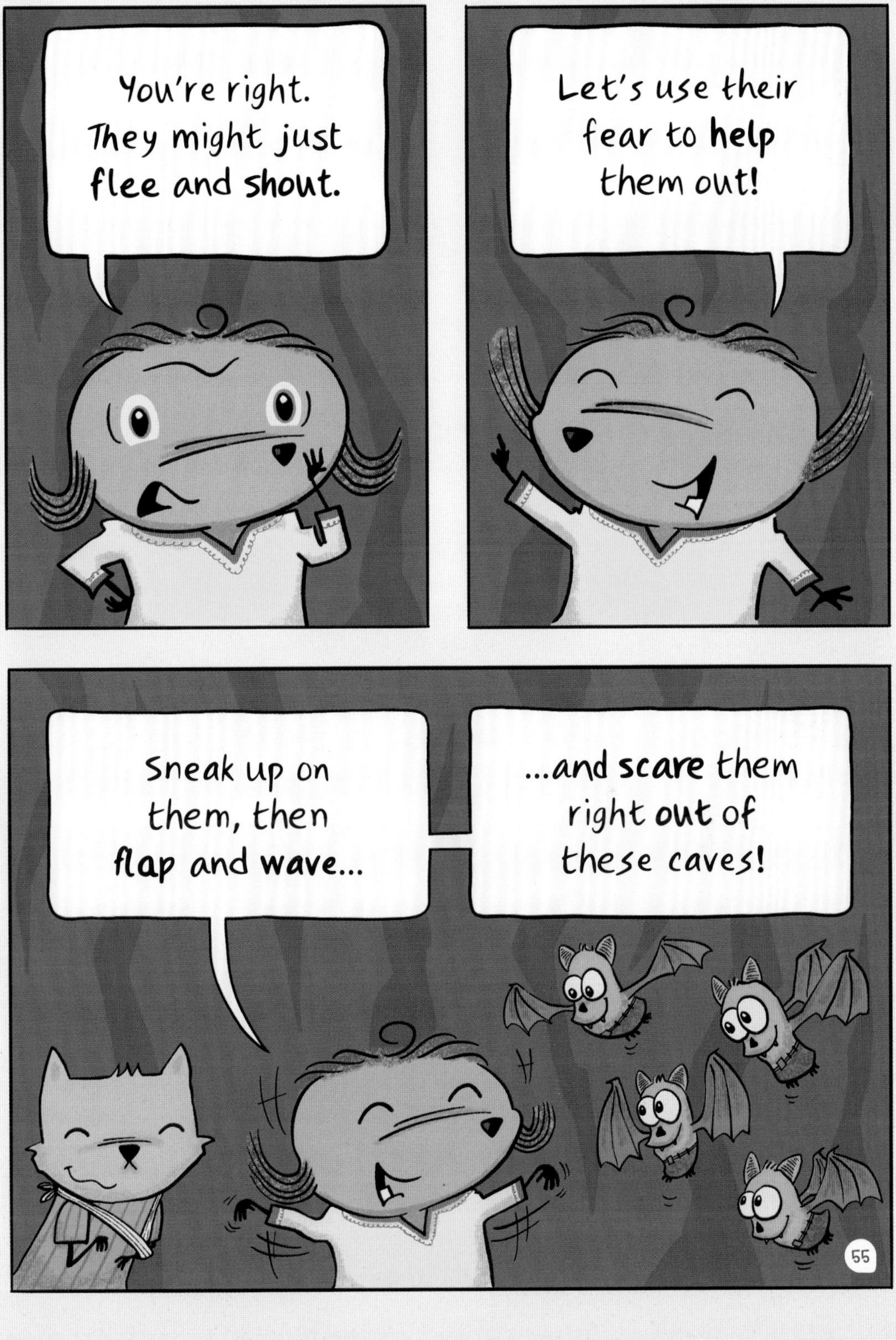
You're right. They might just **flee** and **shout.**
Let's use their fear to **help** them out!
Sneak up on them, then **flap** and **wave**...
...and **scare** them right **out** of these caves!

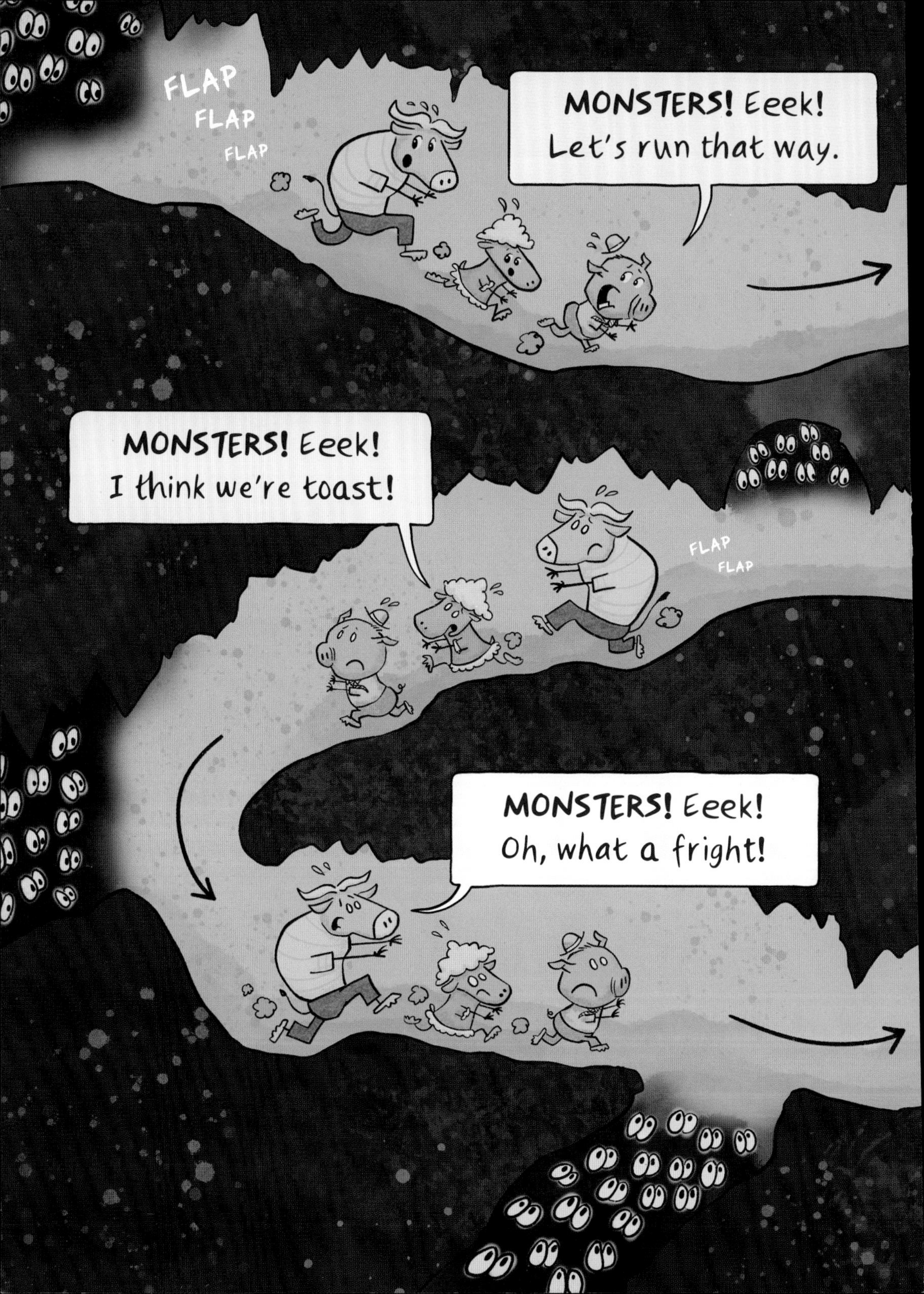
FLAP
FLAP
FLAP
MONSTERS! Eeek!
Let's run that way.
MONSTERS! Eeek!
I think we're toast!
FLAP
FLAP
MONSTERS! Eeek!
Oh, what a fright!

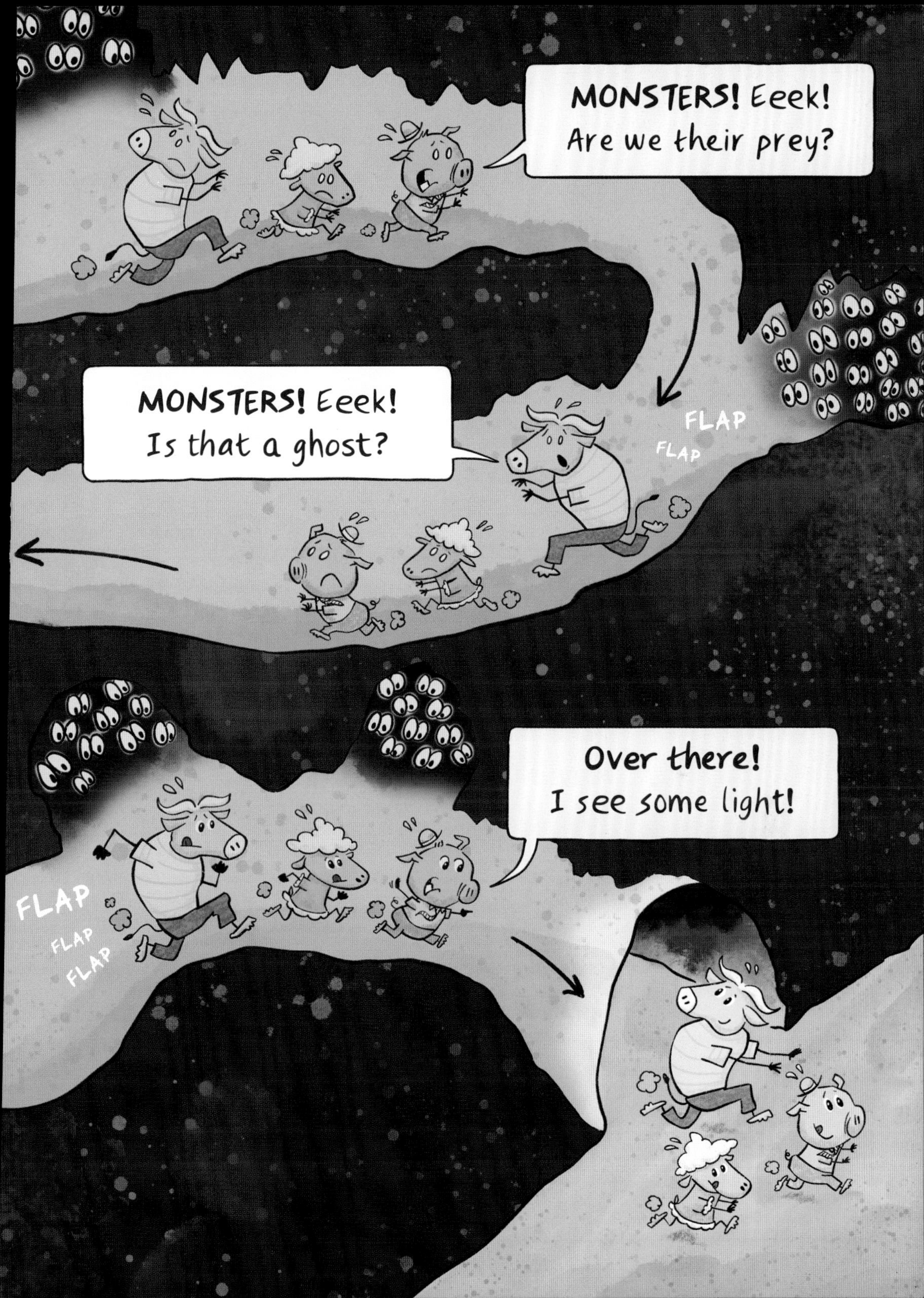
MONSTERS! Eeek!
Are we their prey?
MONSTERS! Eeek!
Is that a ghost?
FLAP
FLAP
Over there!
I see some light!
FLAP
FLAP
FLAP

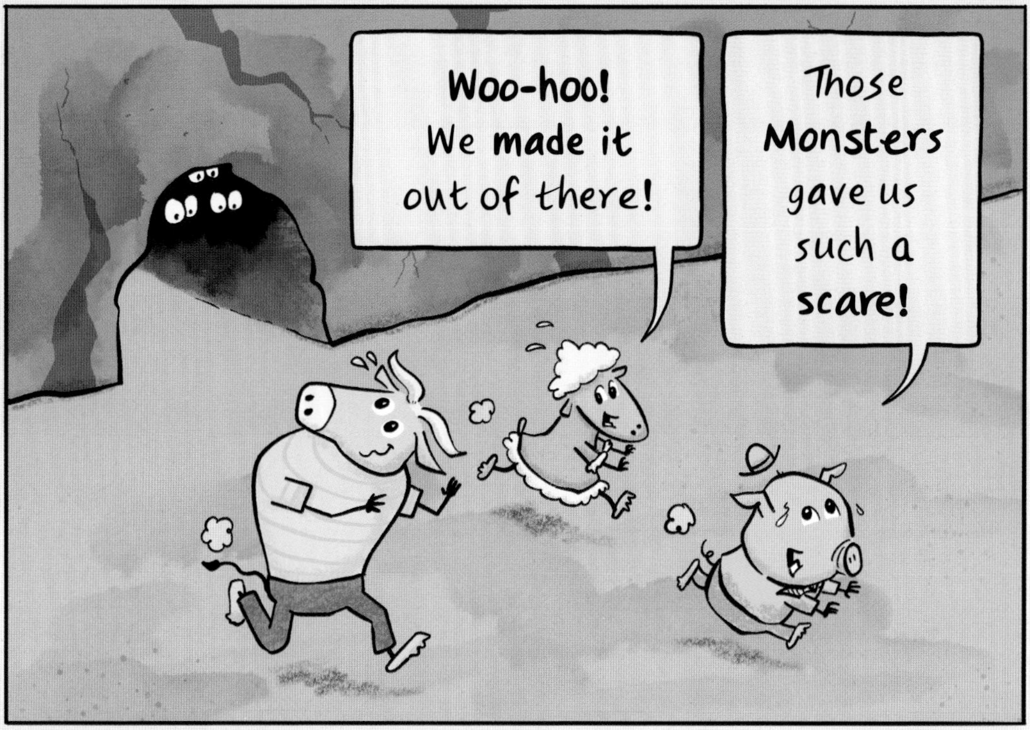
Woo-hoo! We made it out of there!
Those Monsters gave us such a scare!

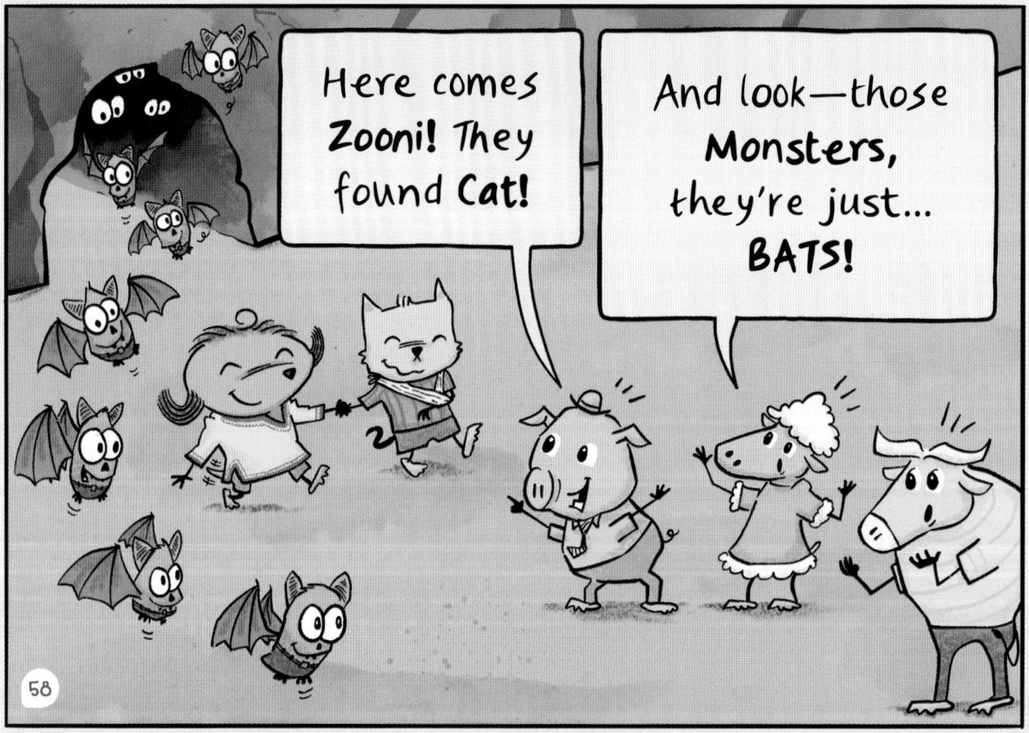
Here comes Zooni! They found Cat!
And look—those Monsters, they're just... BATS!

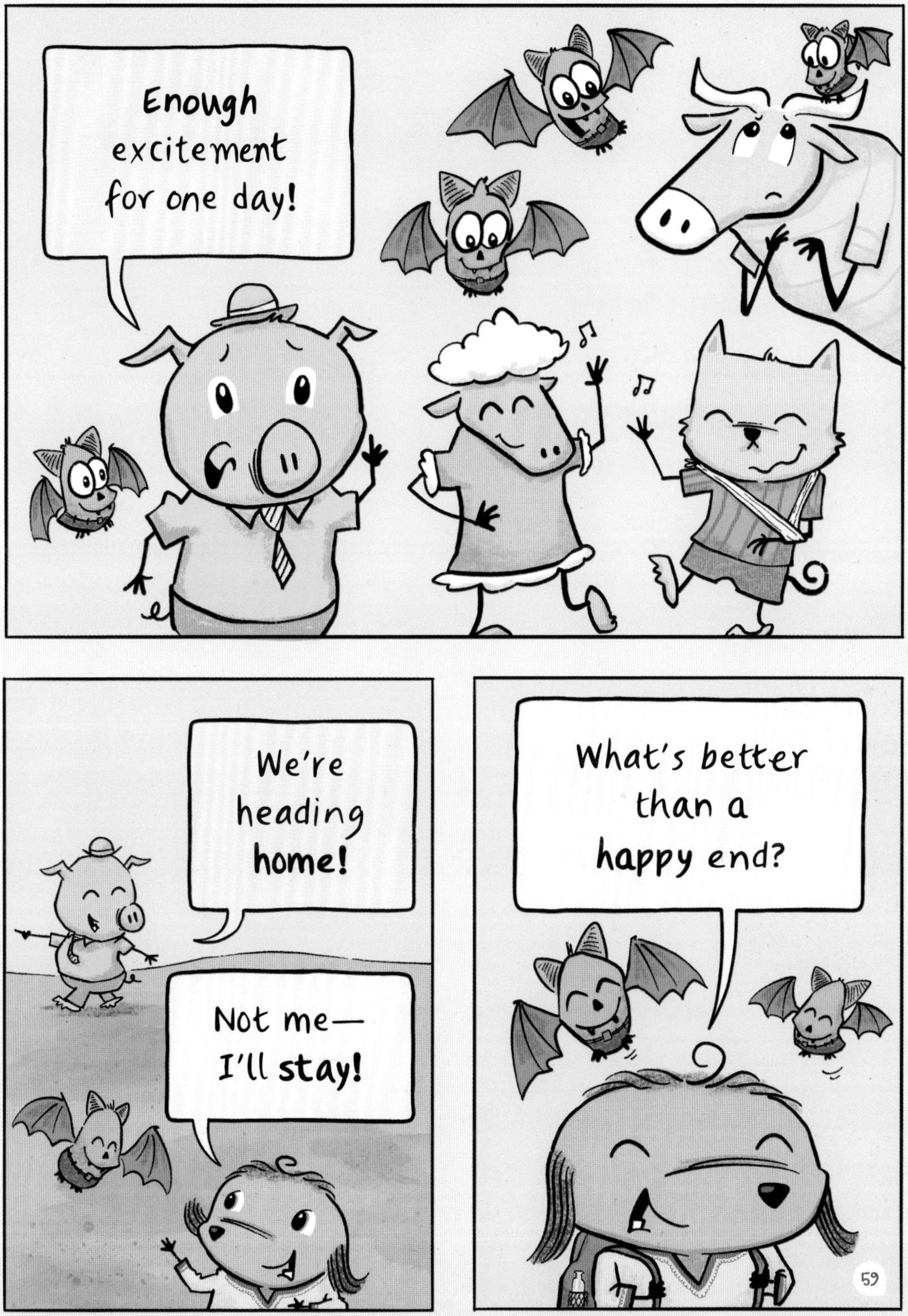
Enough excitement for one day!
We're heading home!
Not me—I'll stay!
What's better than a happy end?

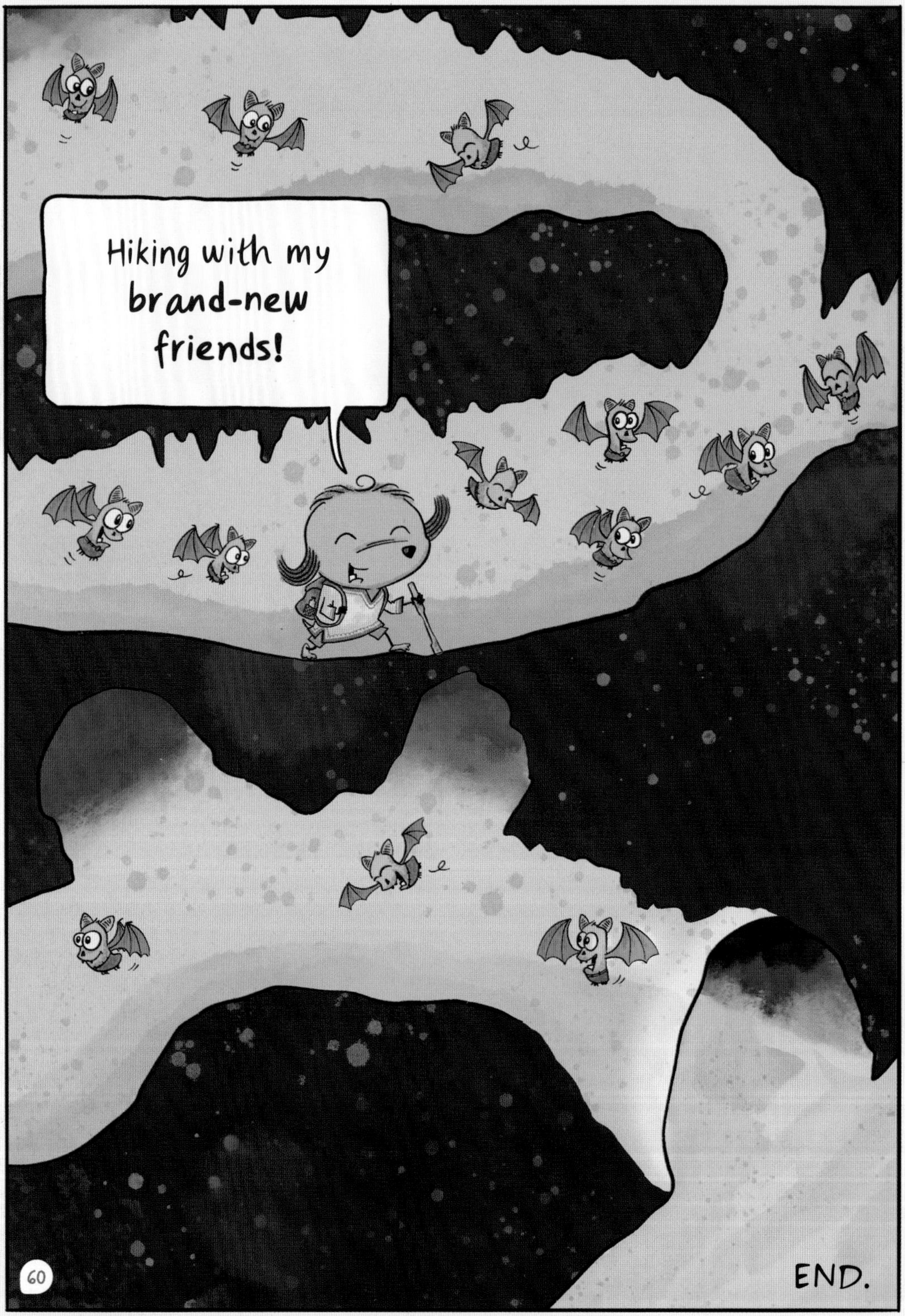
Hiking with my brand-new friends!
END.

ZOONI LOVES... PANCAKES

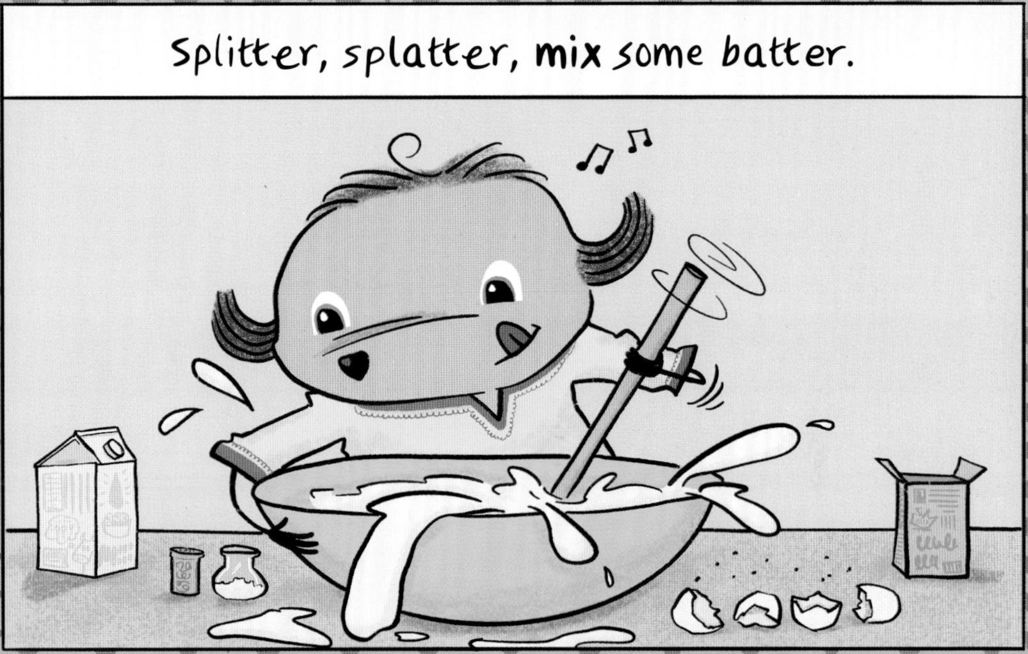
Splitter, splatter, mix some batter.

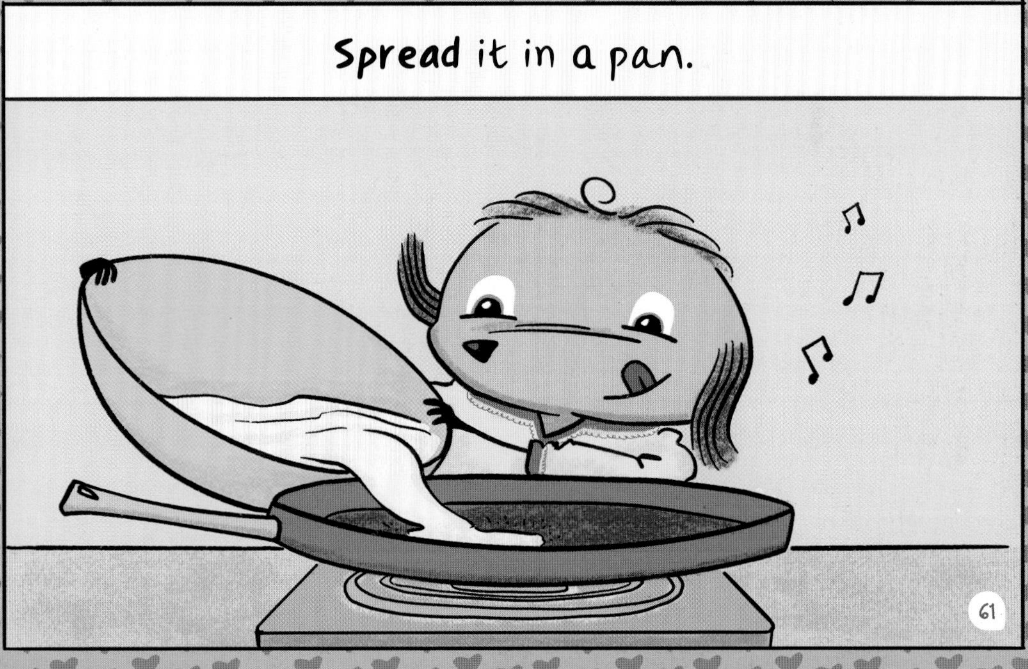
Spread it in a pan.

Cook it, tip it, try to flip it,
any way you can.

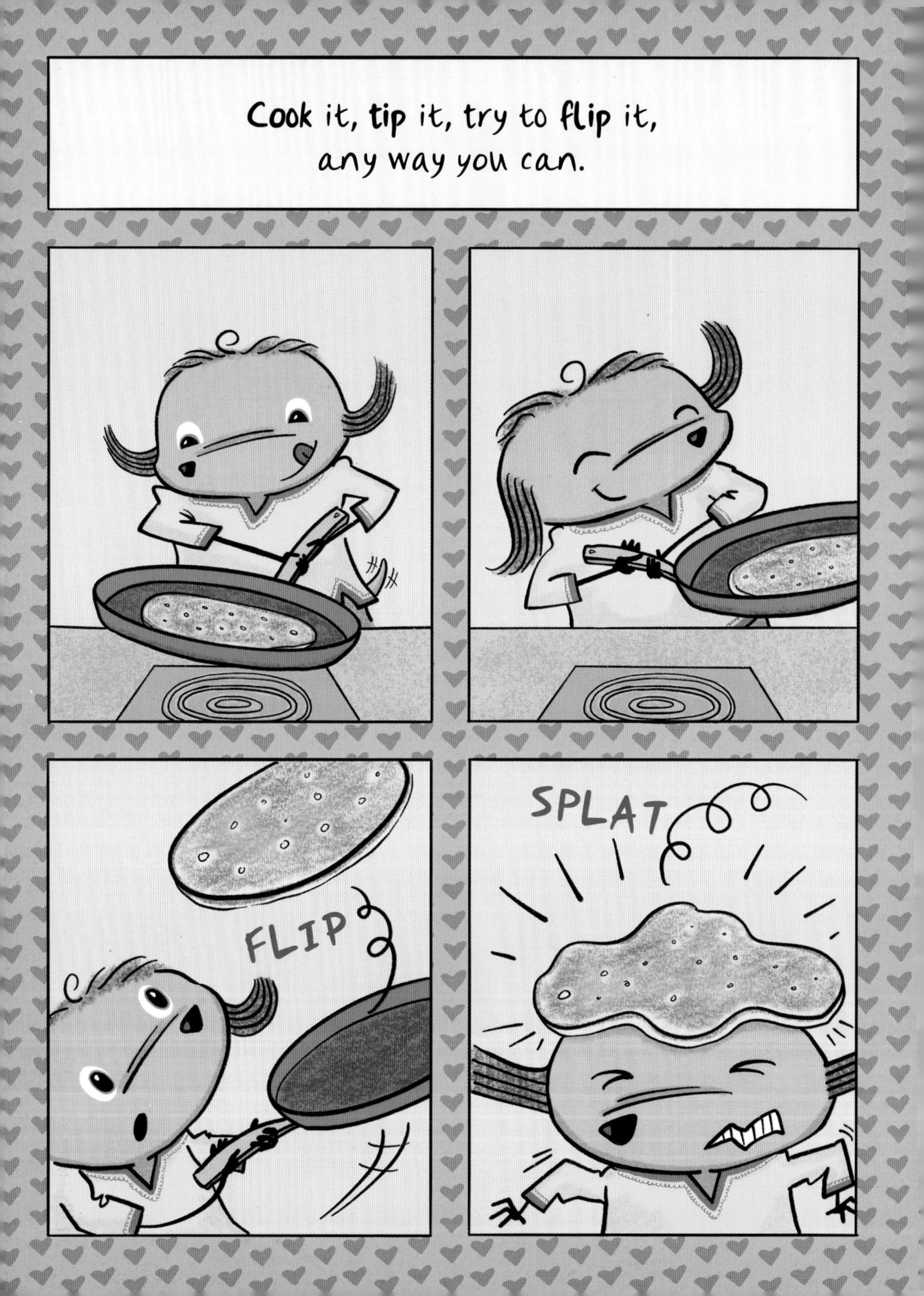
FLIP
SPLAT

Add some **cherries**, mix in **berries**,
pour some **syrup** too!

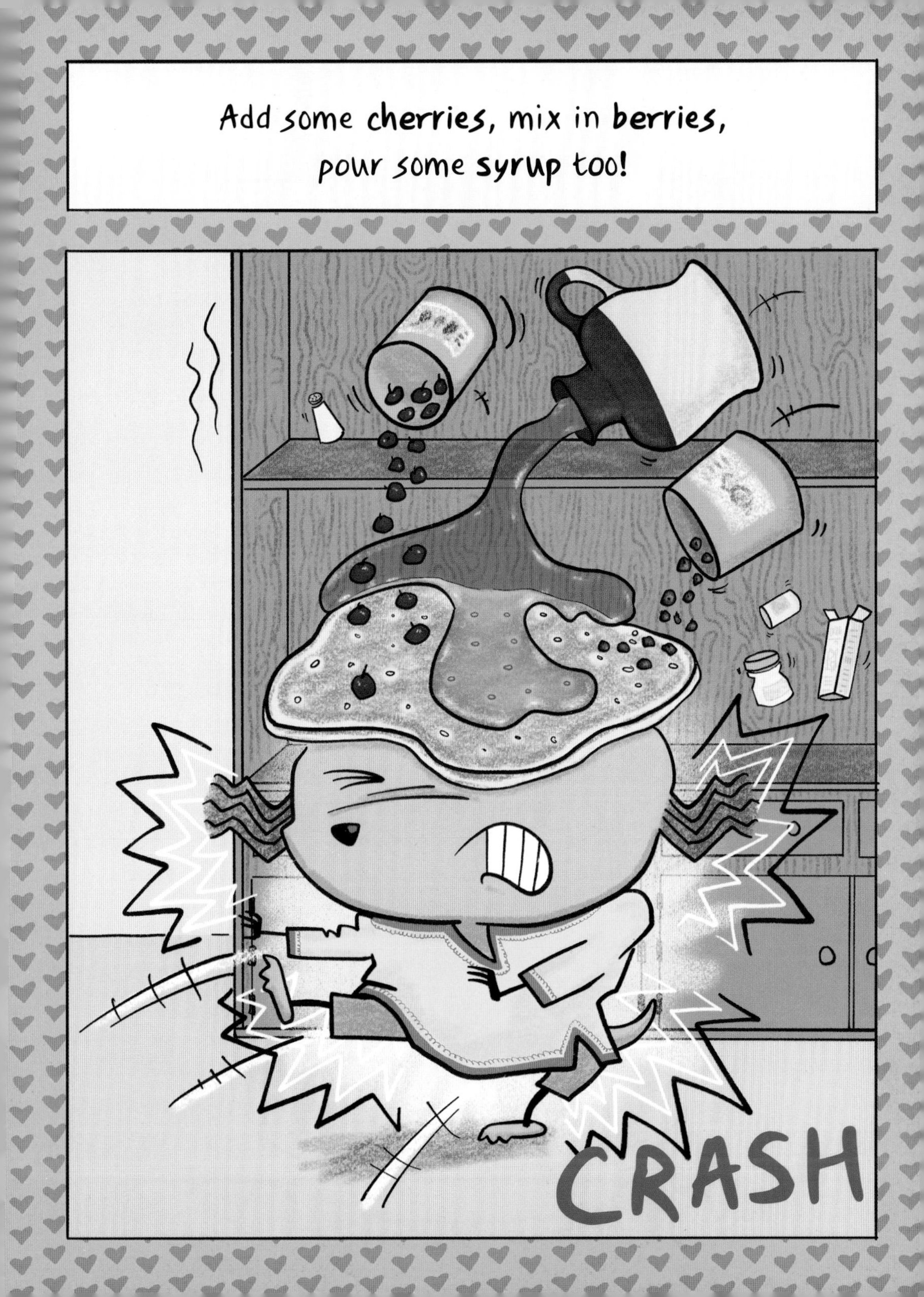
CRASH

Looks so **yummy**, call your **chummies**, **pancake** for the crew!

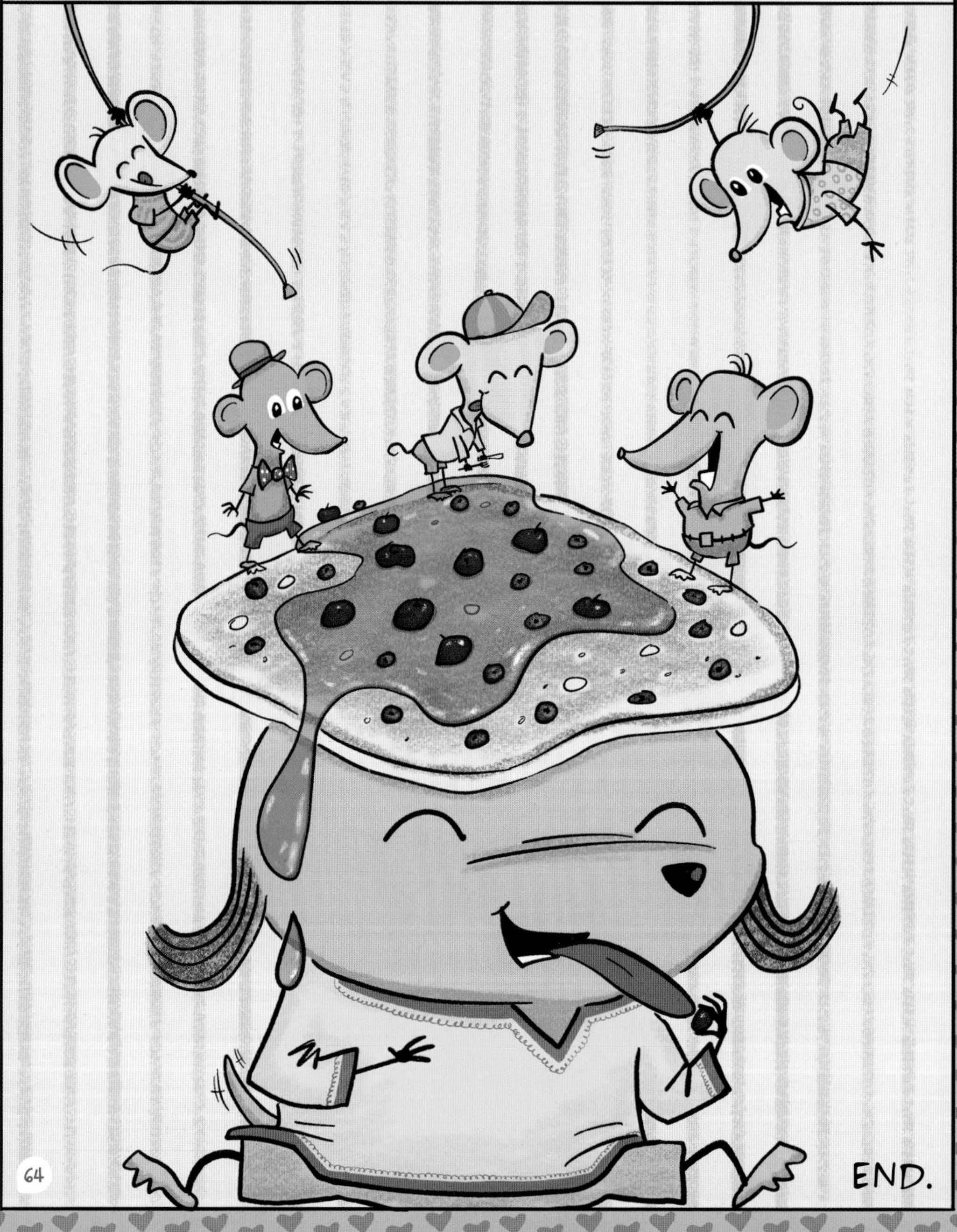
END.

BOATING DAY

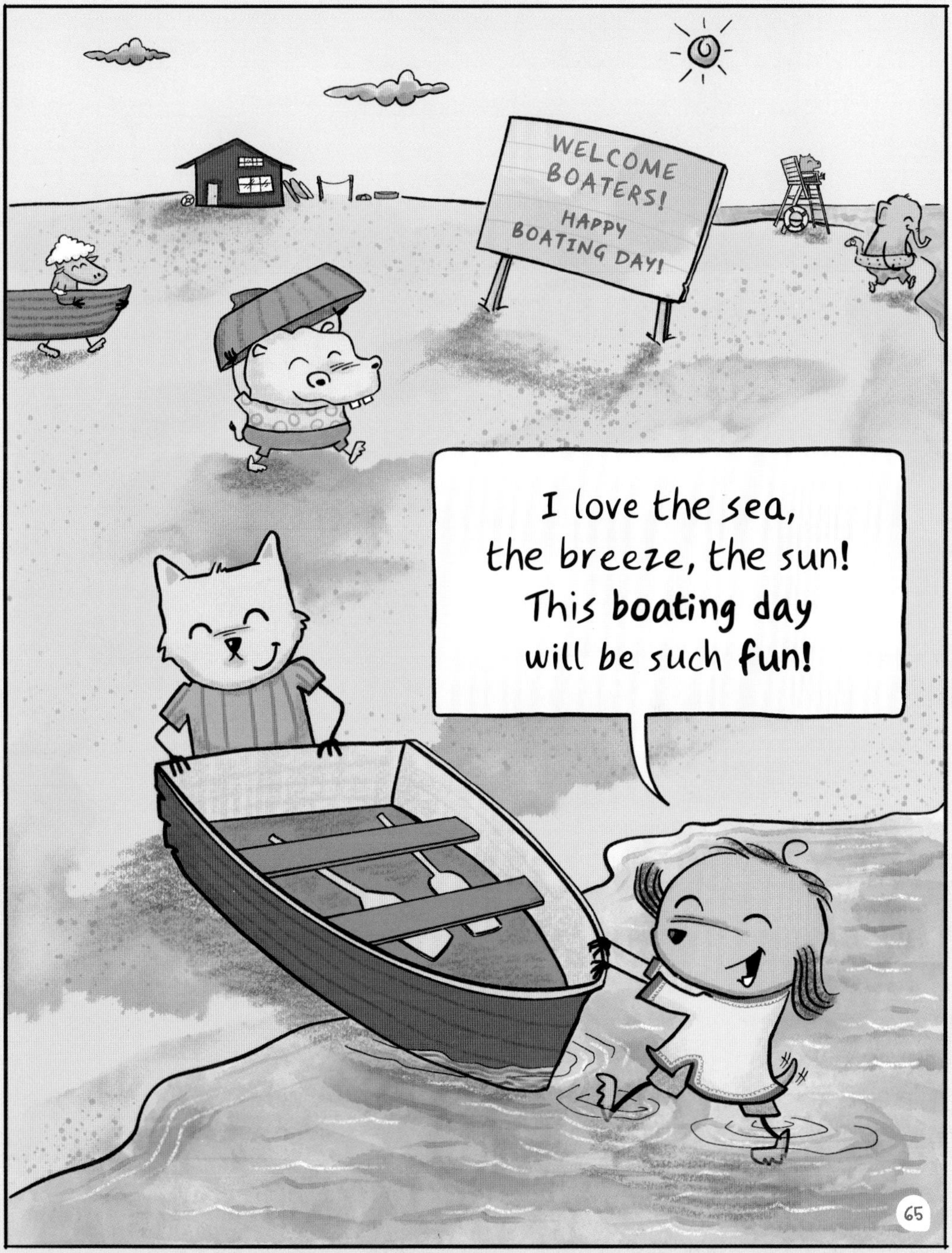
WELCOME BOATERS!
HAPPY BOATING DAY!
I love the sea, the breeze, the sun! This **boating day** will be such **fun!**

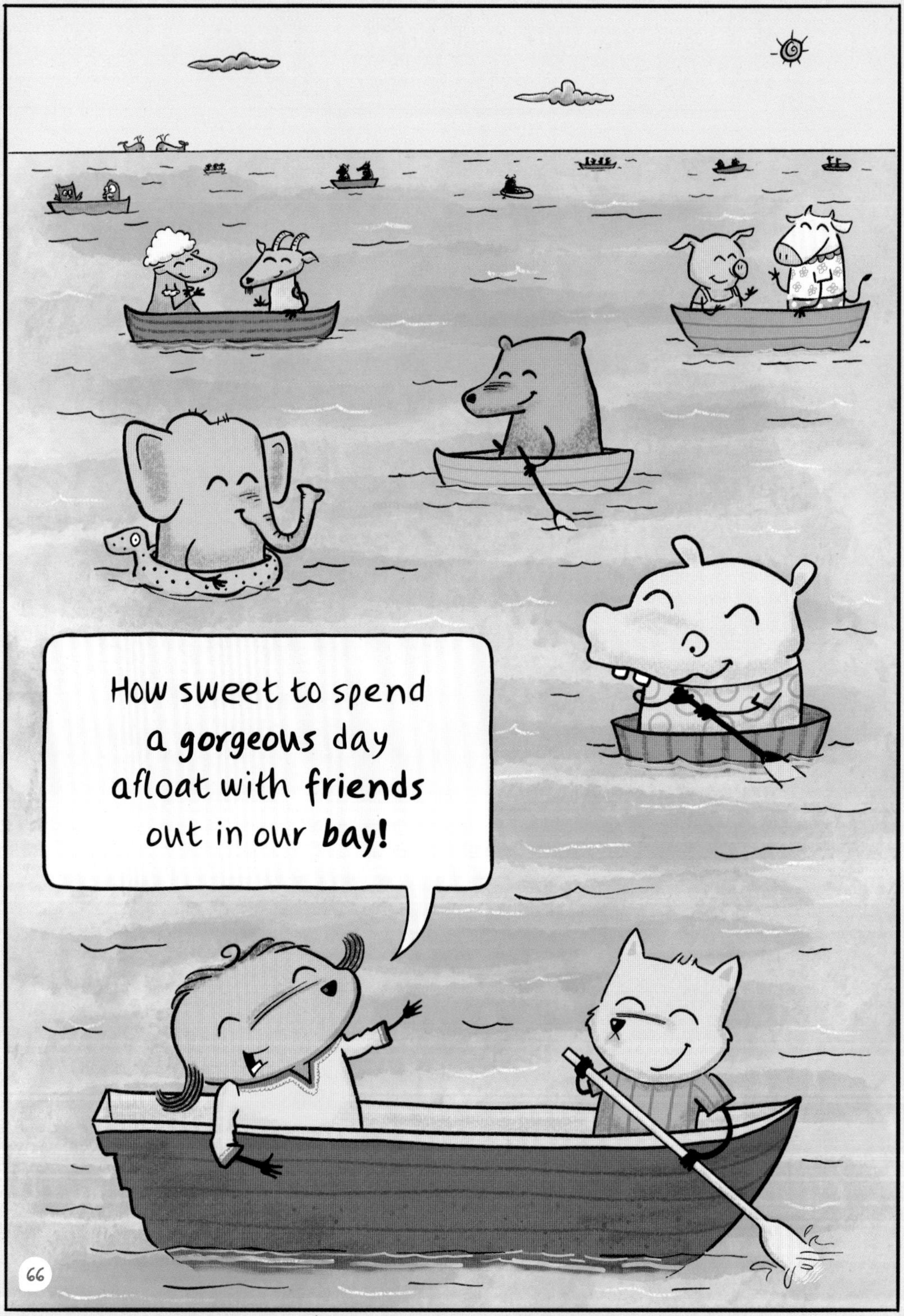
How sweet to spend a gorgeous day afloat with friends out in our bay!

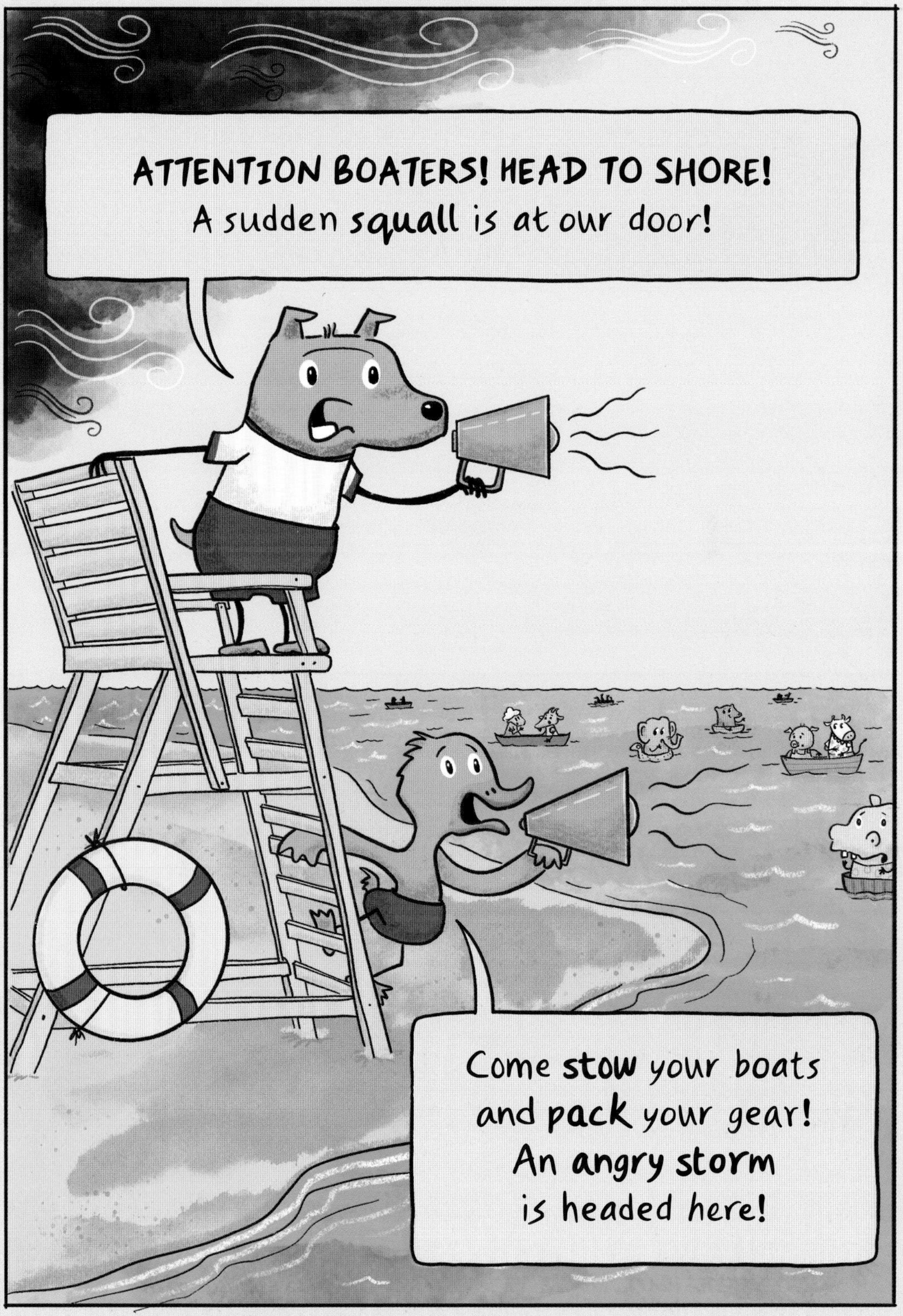
ATTENTION BOATERS! HEAD TO SHORE! A sudden squall is at our door!
Come stow your boats and pack your gear! An angry storm is headed here!

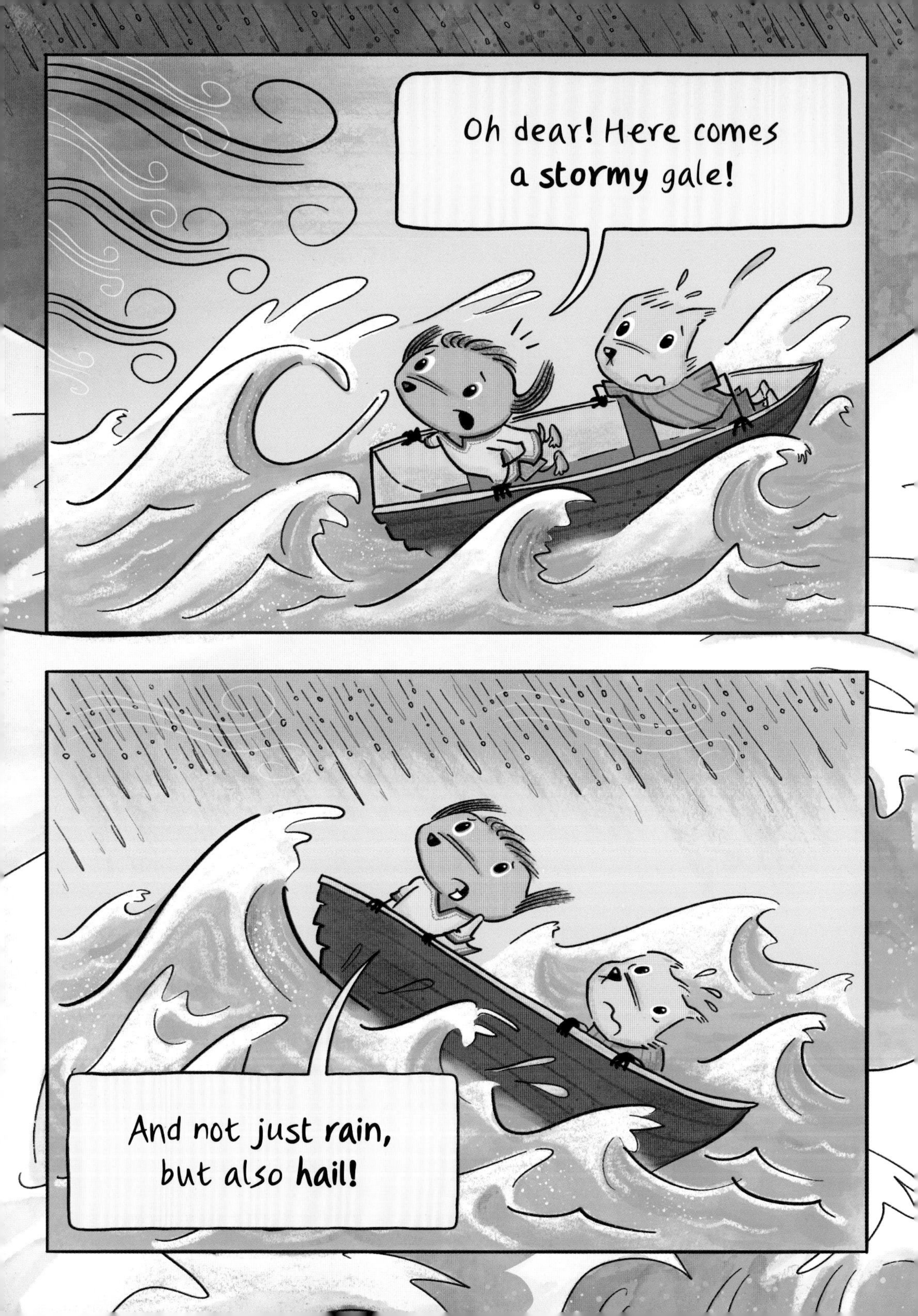
Oh dear! Here comes a stormy gale!
And not just rain, but also hail!

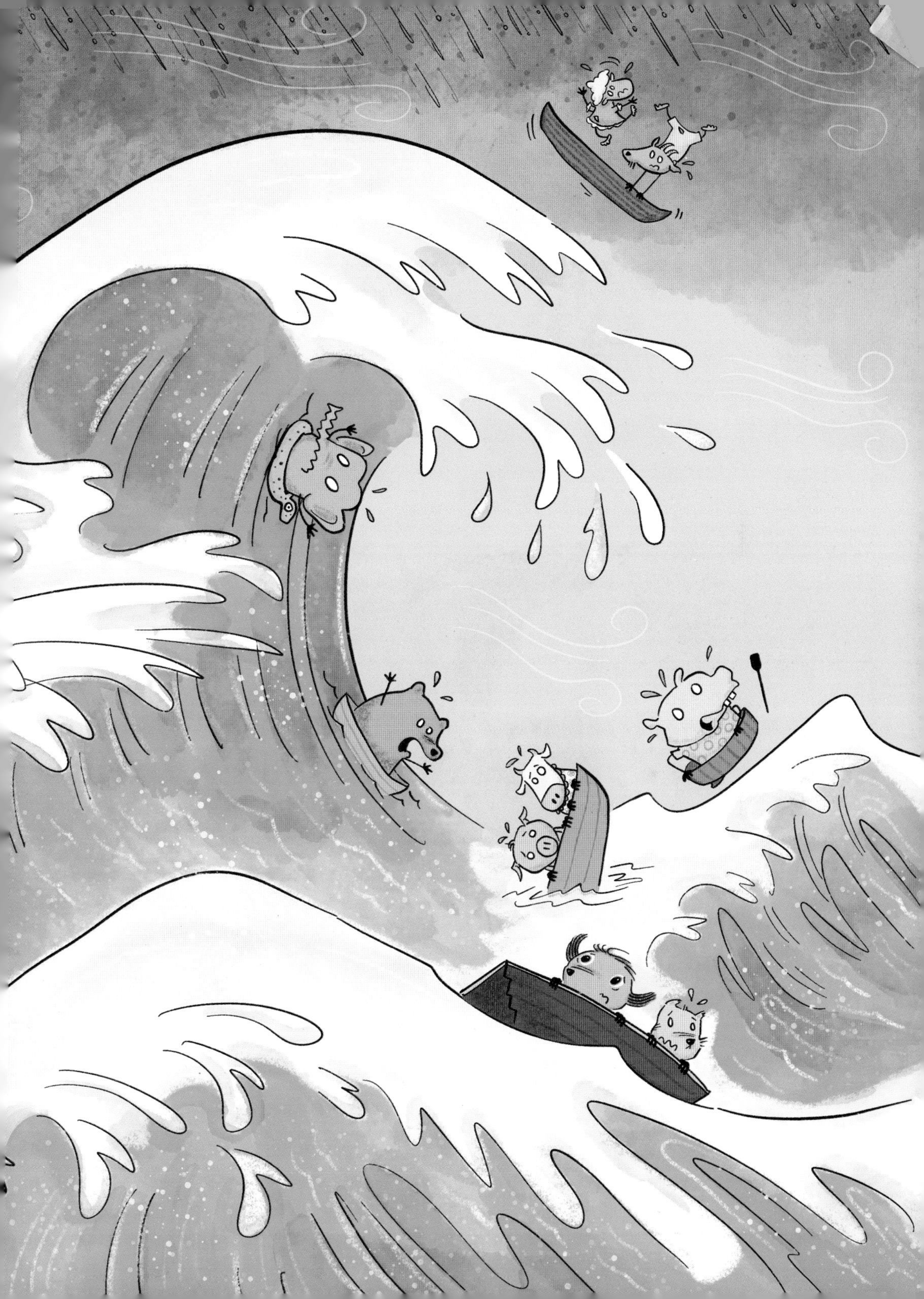

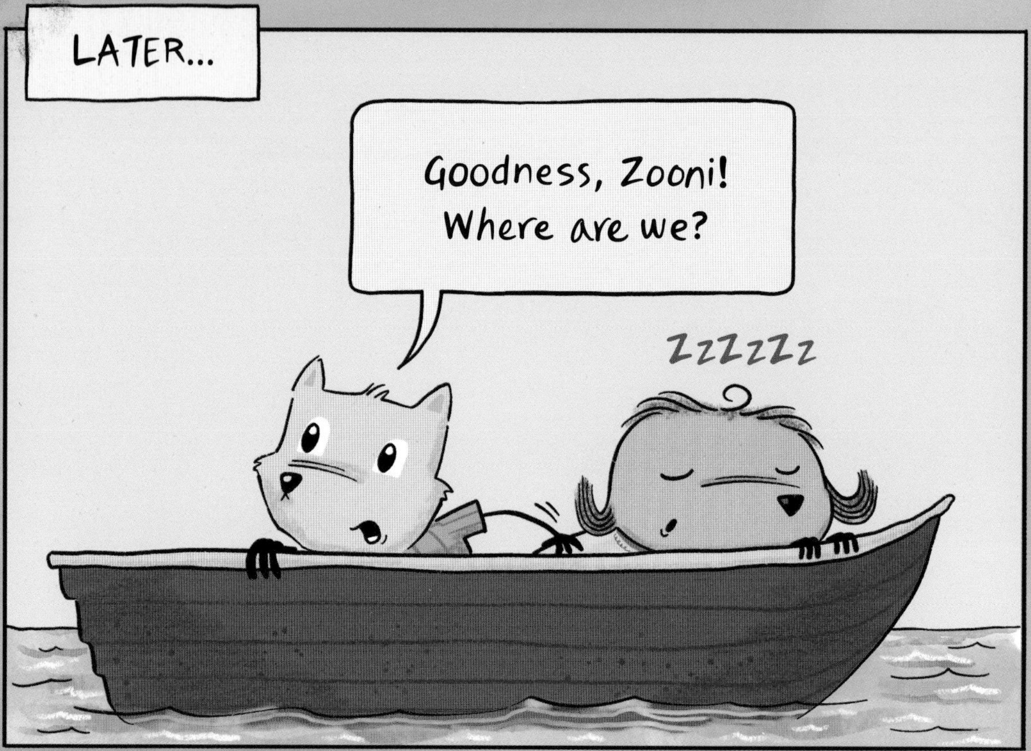
LATER...
Goodness, Zooni! Where are we?
ZzZzZz

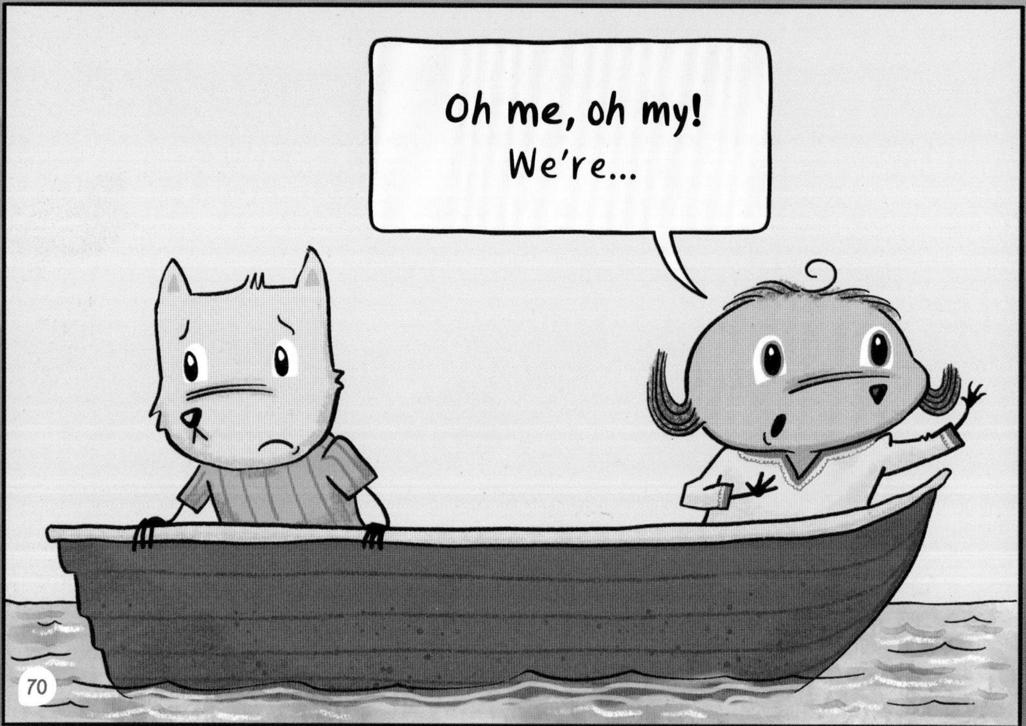
Oh me, oh my! We're...

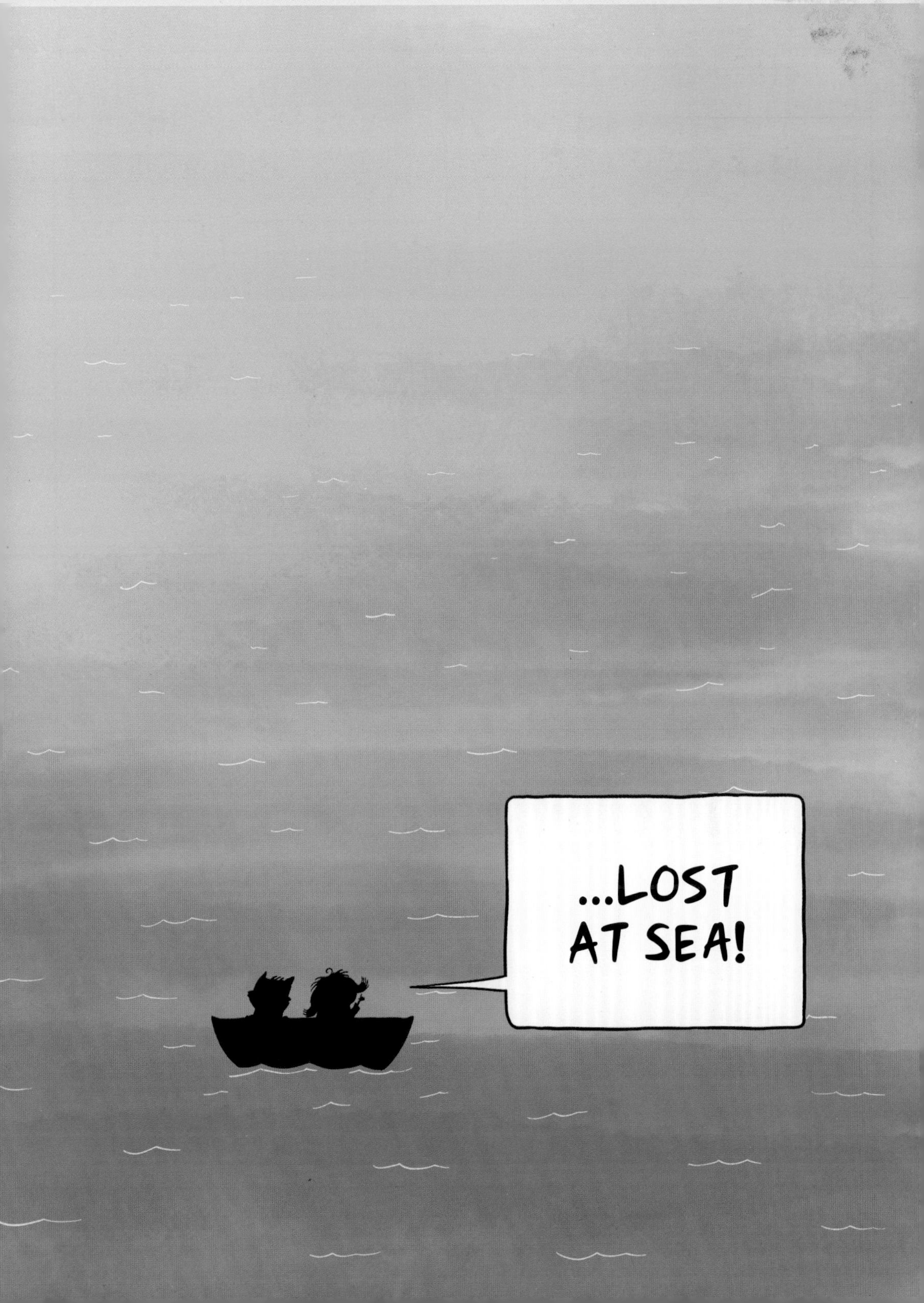
...LOST AT SEA!

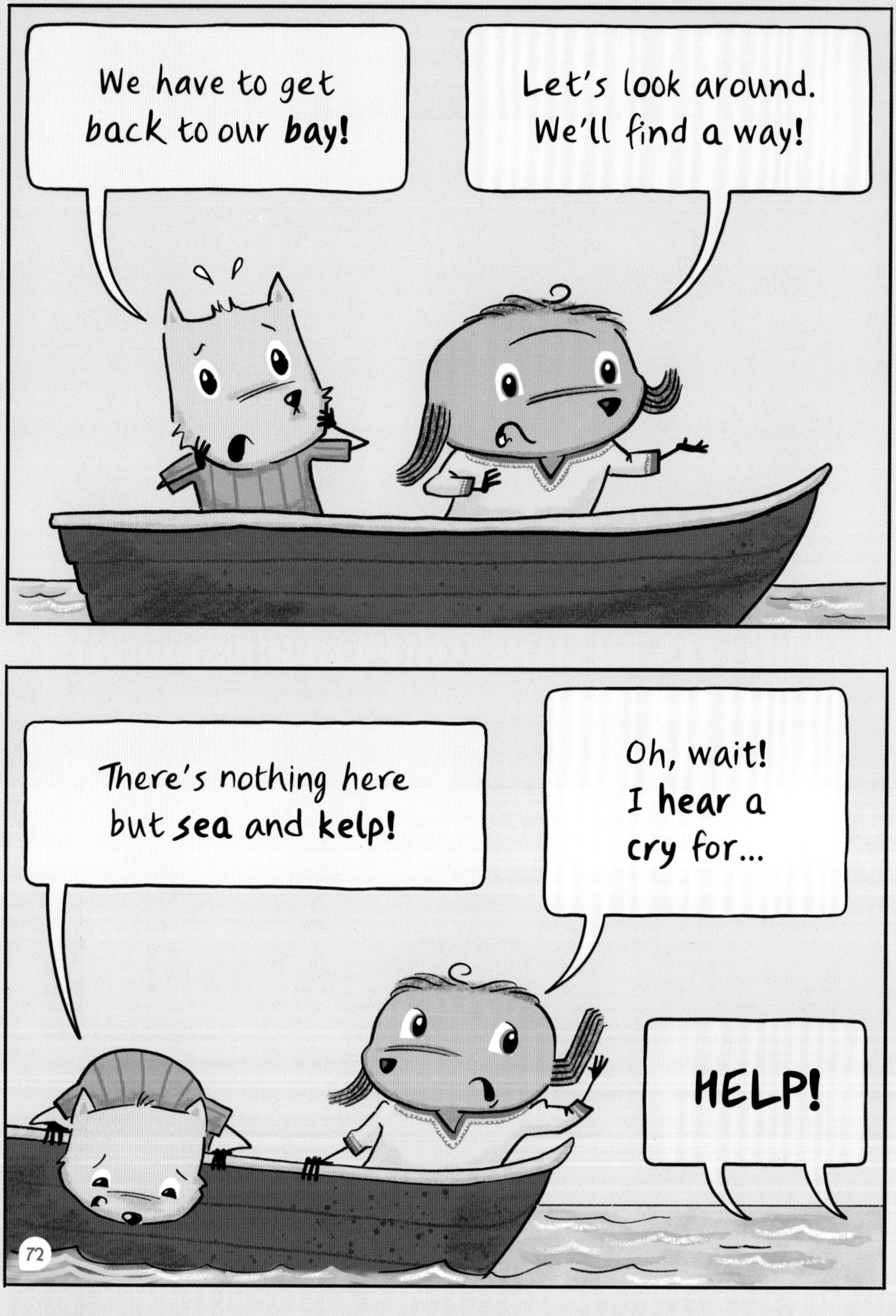
We have to get back to our bay!
Let's look around. We'll find a way!
There's nothing here but sea and kelp!
Oh, wait! I hear a cry for...
HELP!

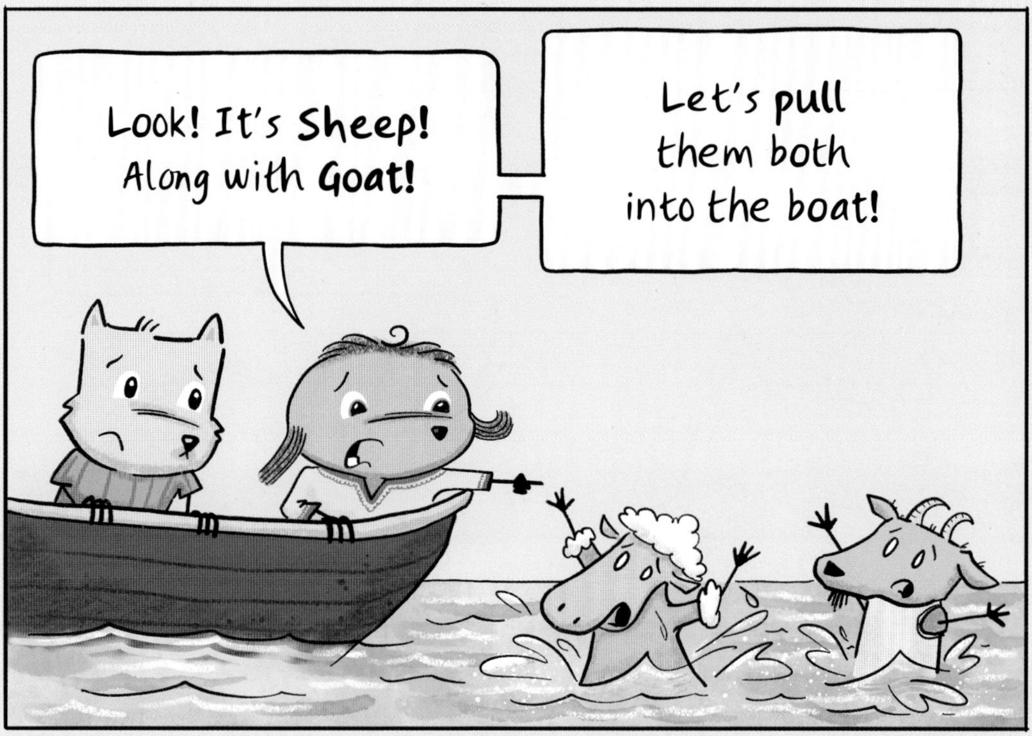
Look! It's Sheep! Along with Goat!
Let's pull them both into the boat!

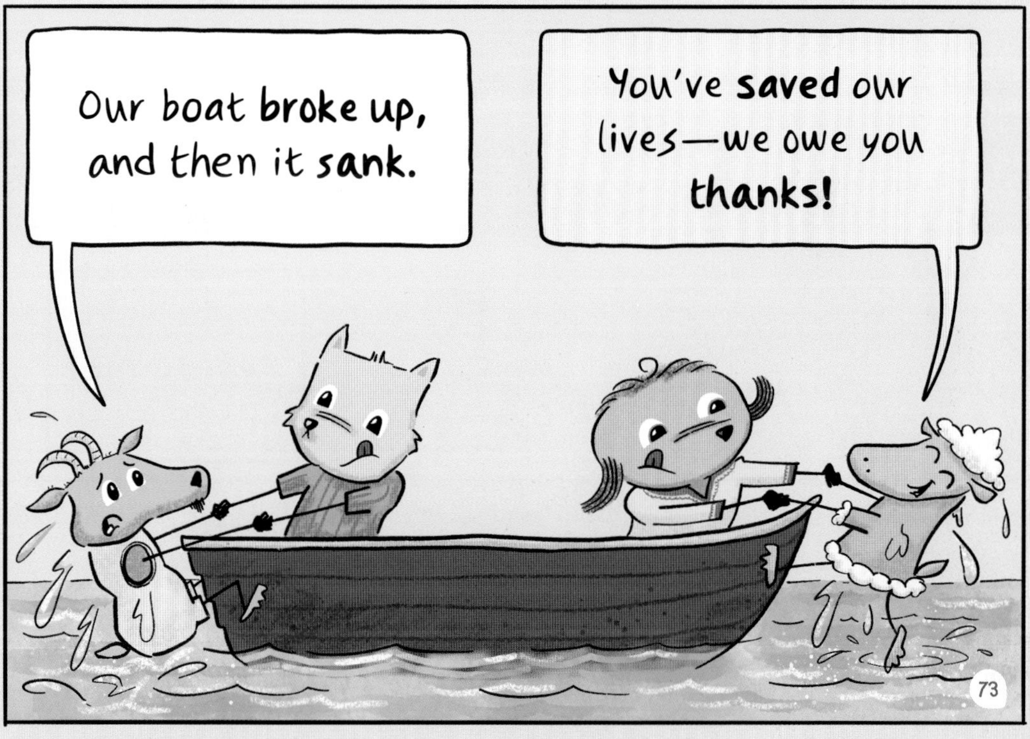
Our boat broke up, and then it sank.
You've saved our lives—we owe you thanks!

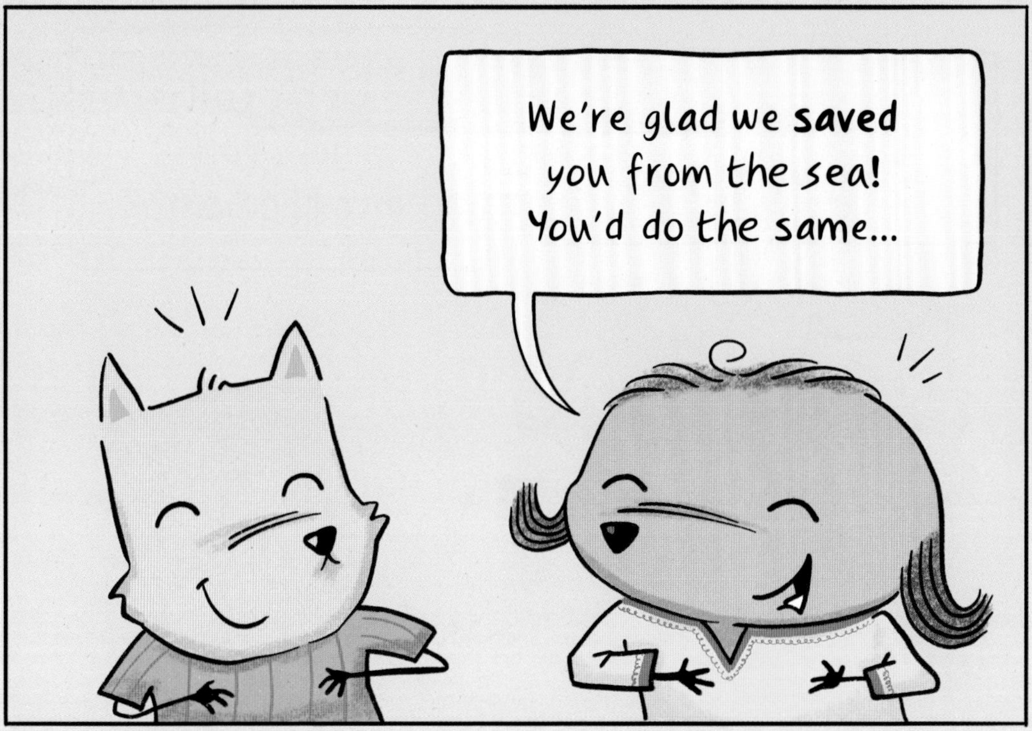
We're glad we **saved** you from the sea! You'd do the same...

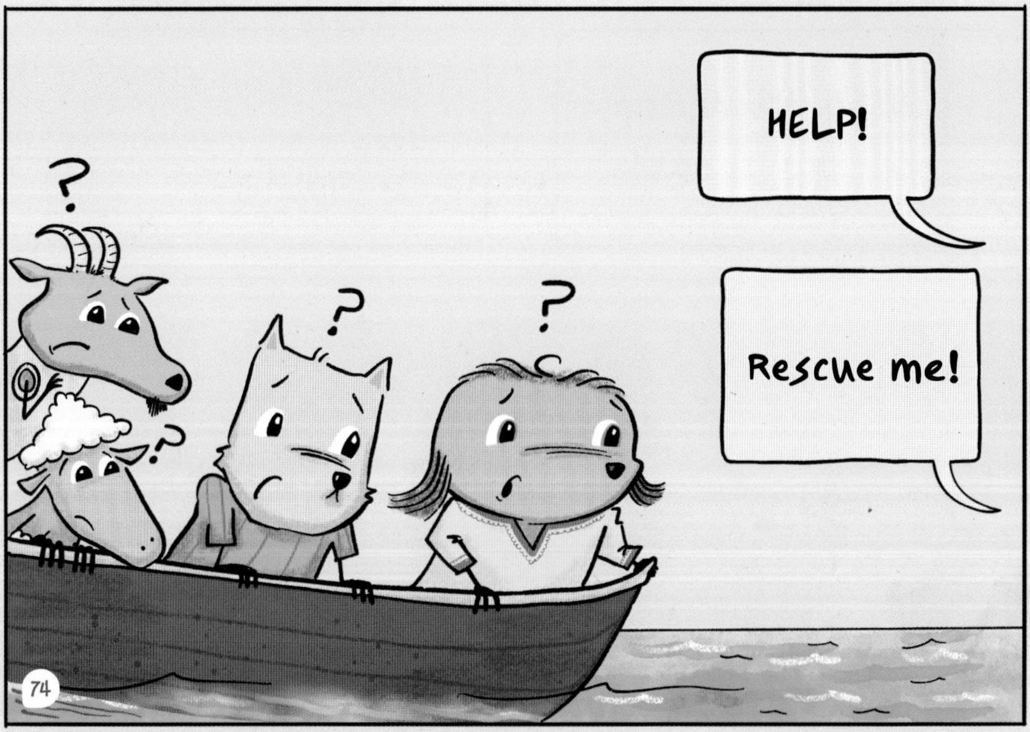
?
?
?
?
HELP!
Rescue me!
74

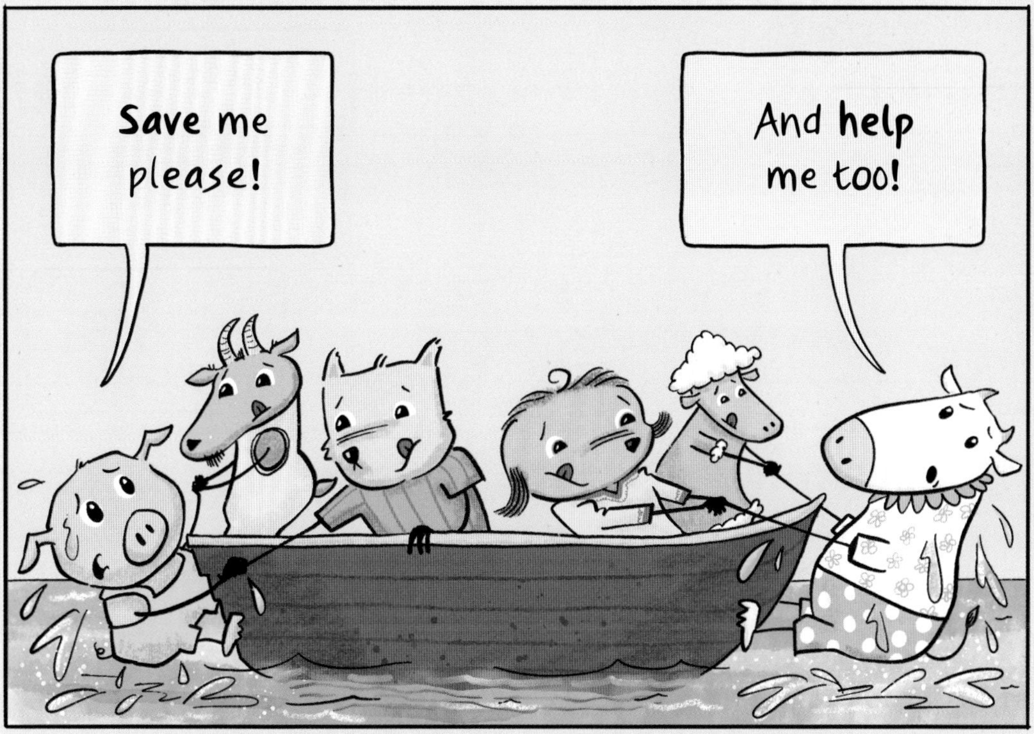
Save me please!
And help me too!

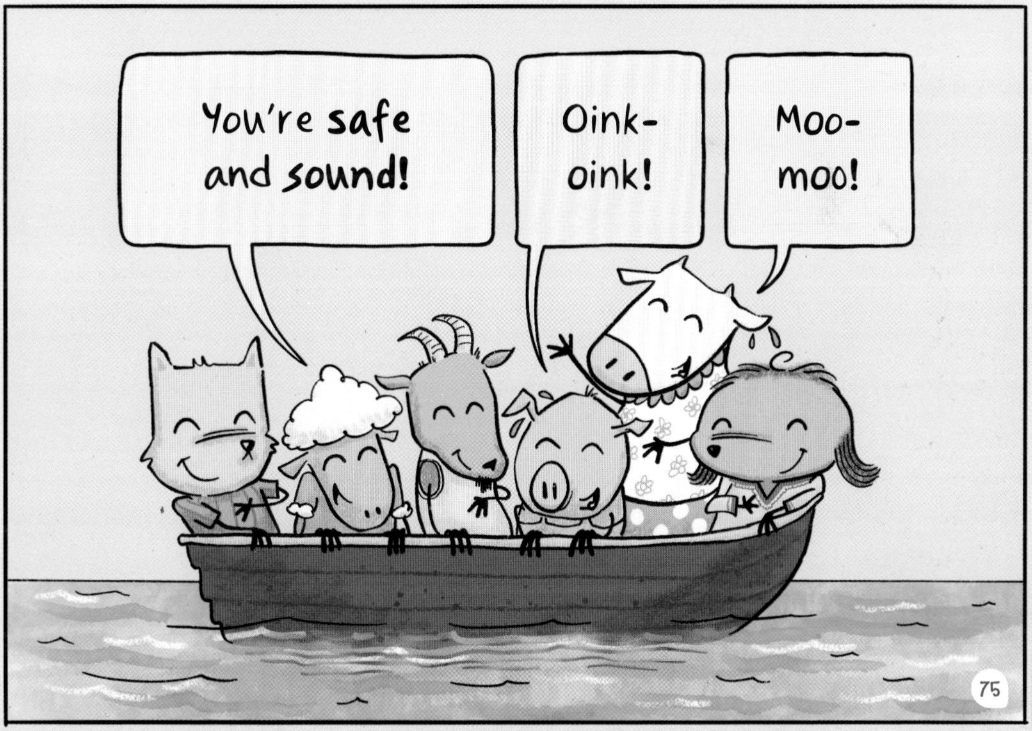
You're safe and sound!
Oink-oink!
Moo-moo!

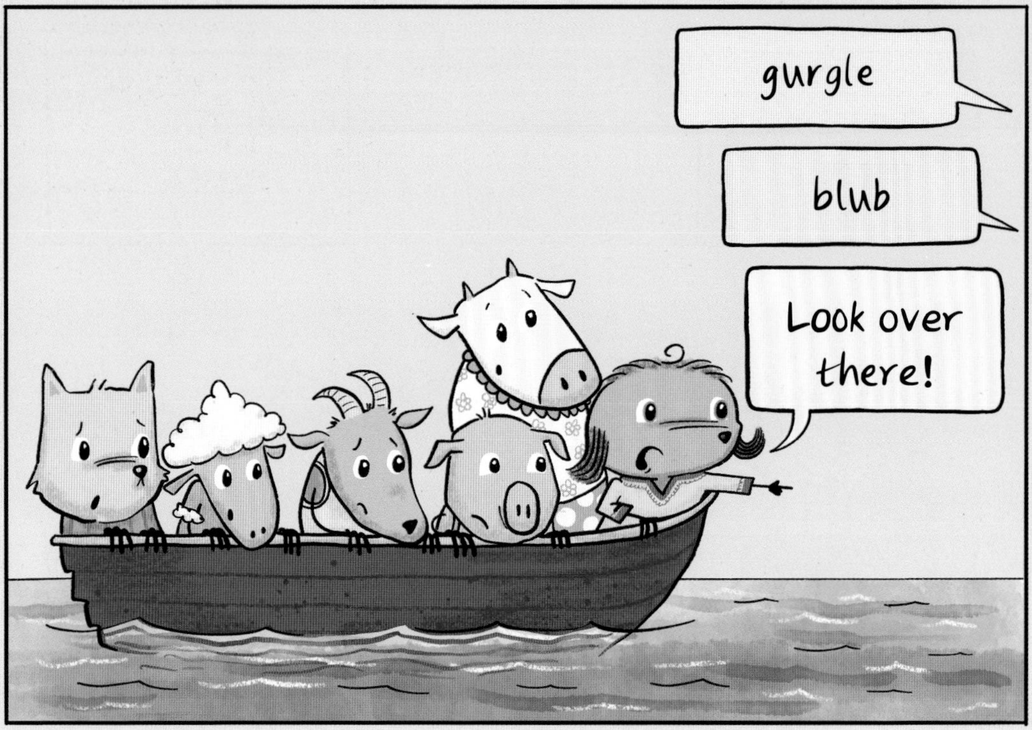
gurgle
blub
Look over there!

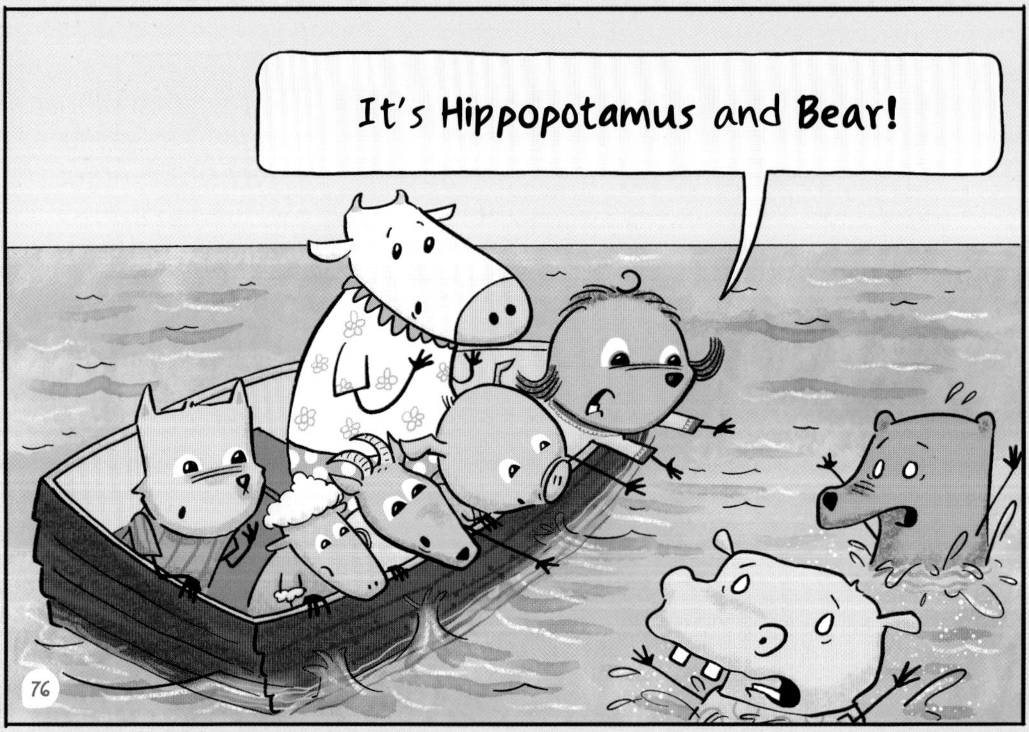
It's Hippopotamus and Bear!

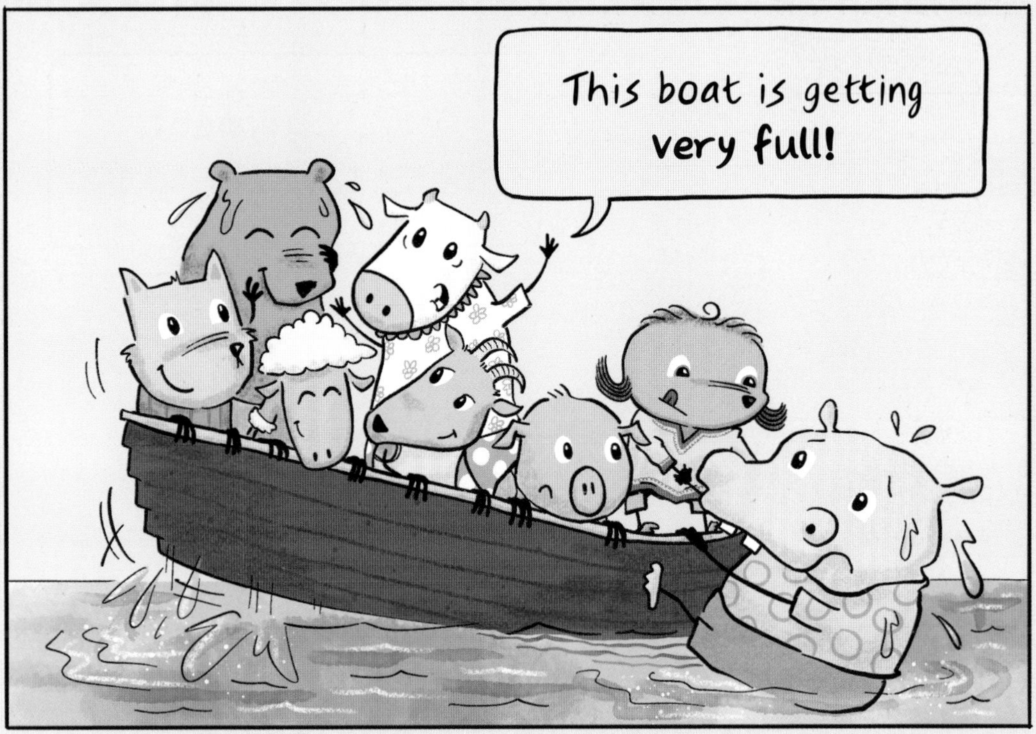
This boat is getting **very full!**

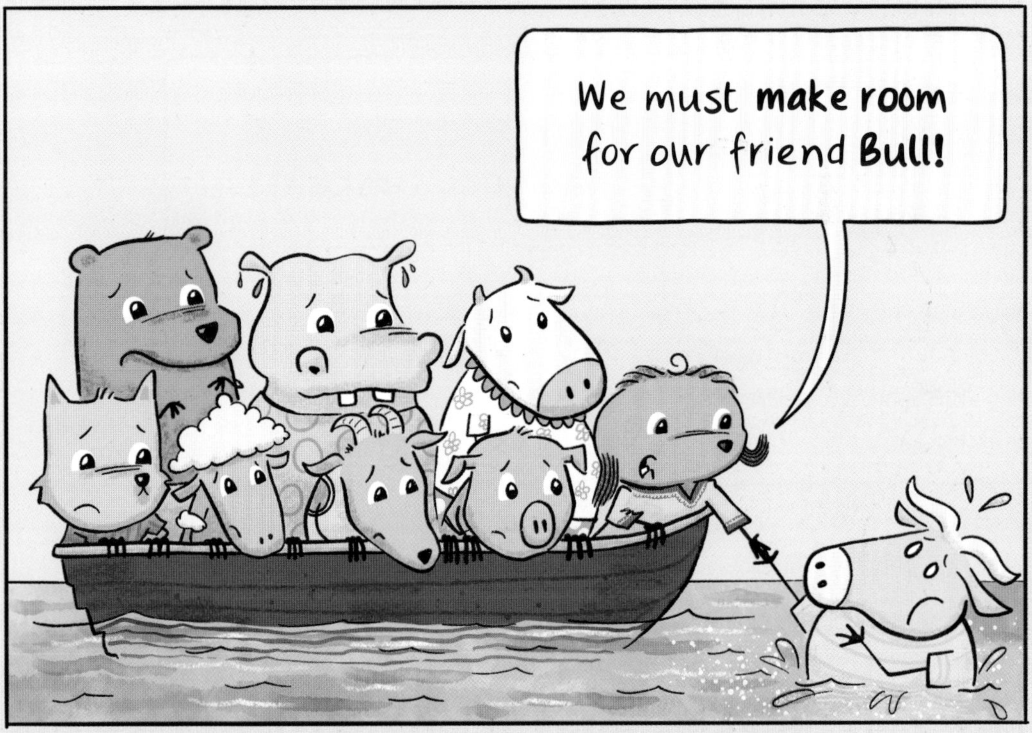
We must **make room** for our friend **Bull!**

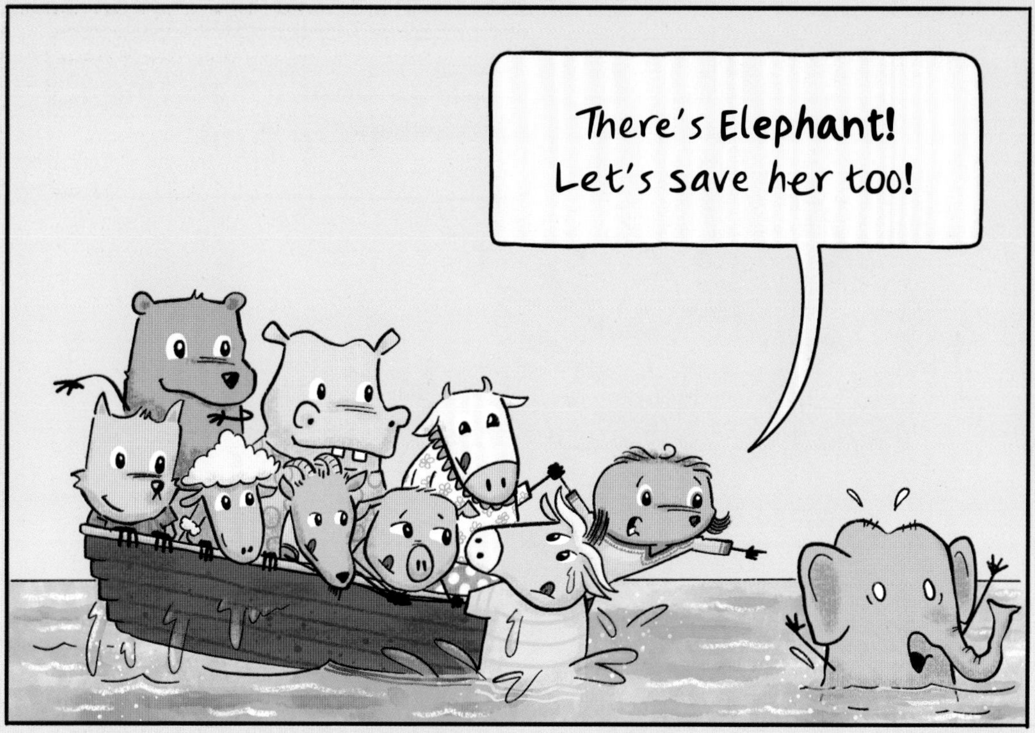
There's Elephant! Let's save her too!

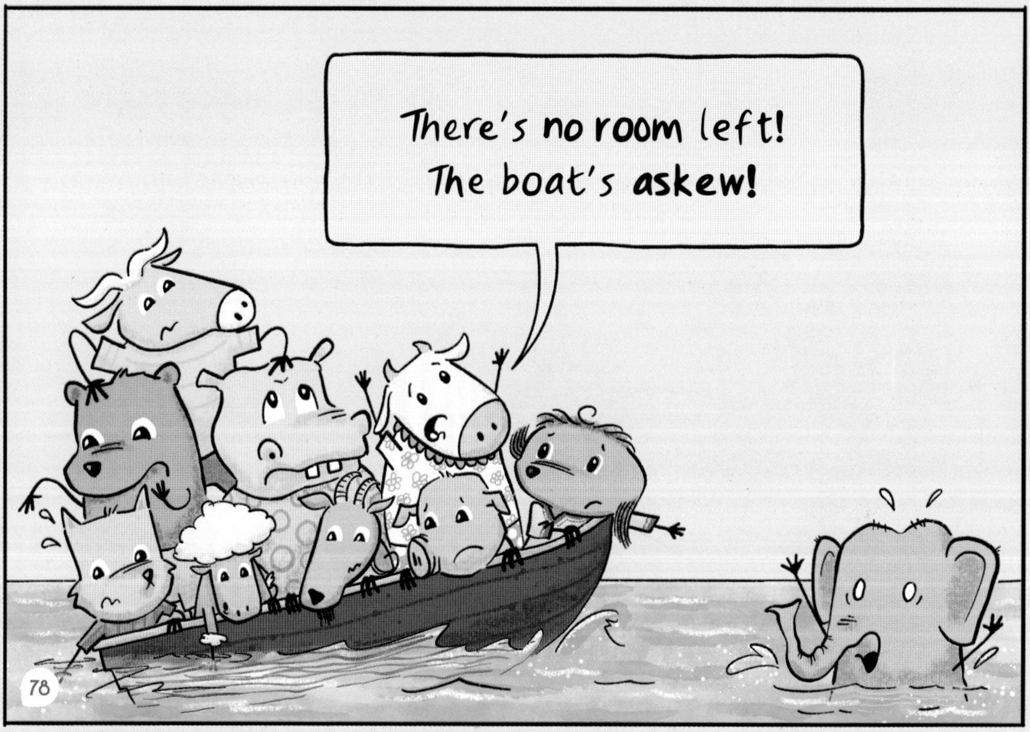
There's no room left! The boat's askew!

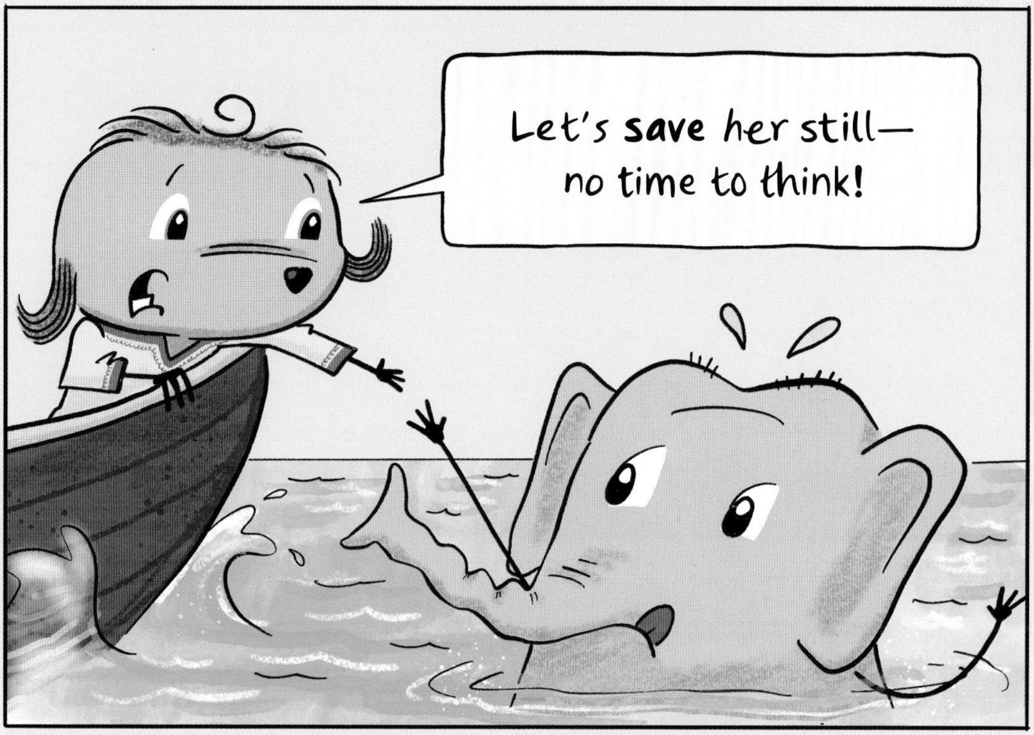
Let's **save** her still—
no time to think!

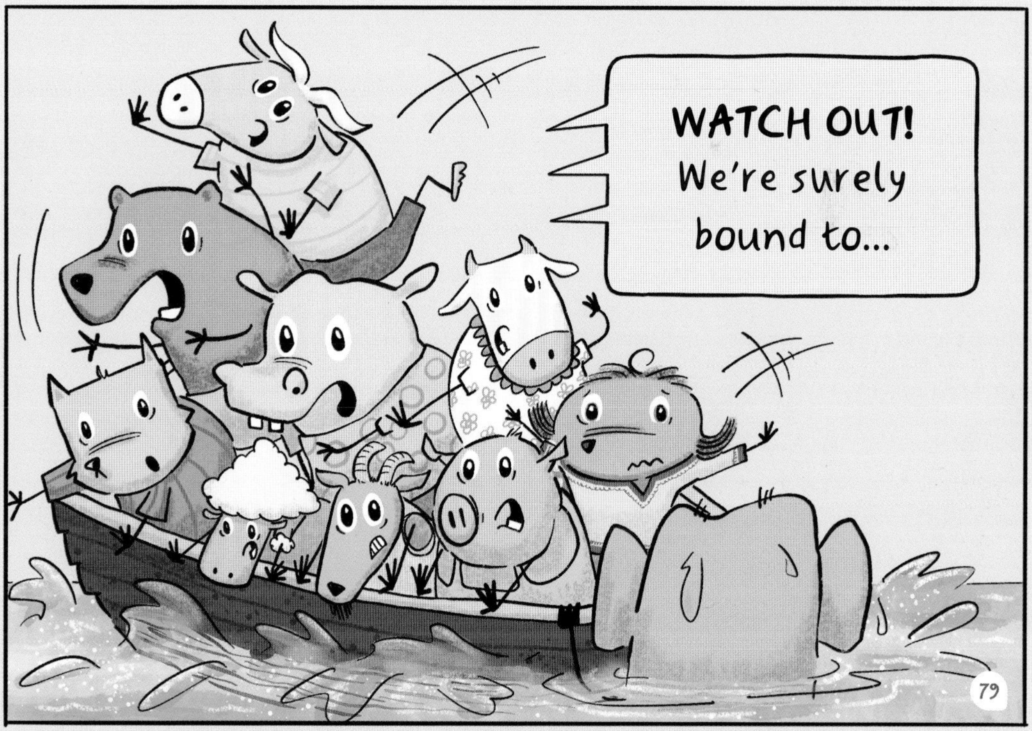
WATCH OUT!
We're surely
bound to...

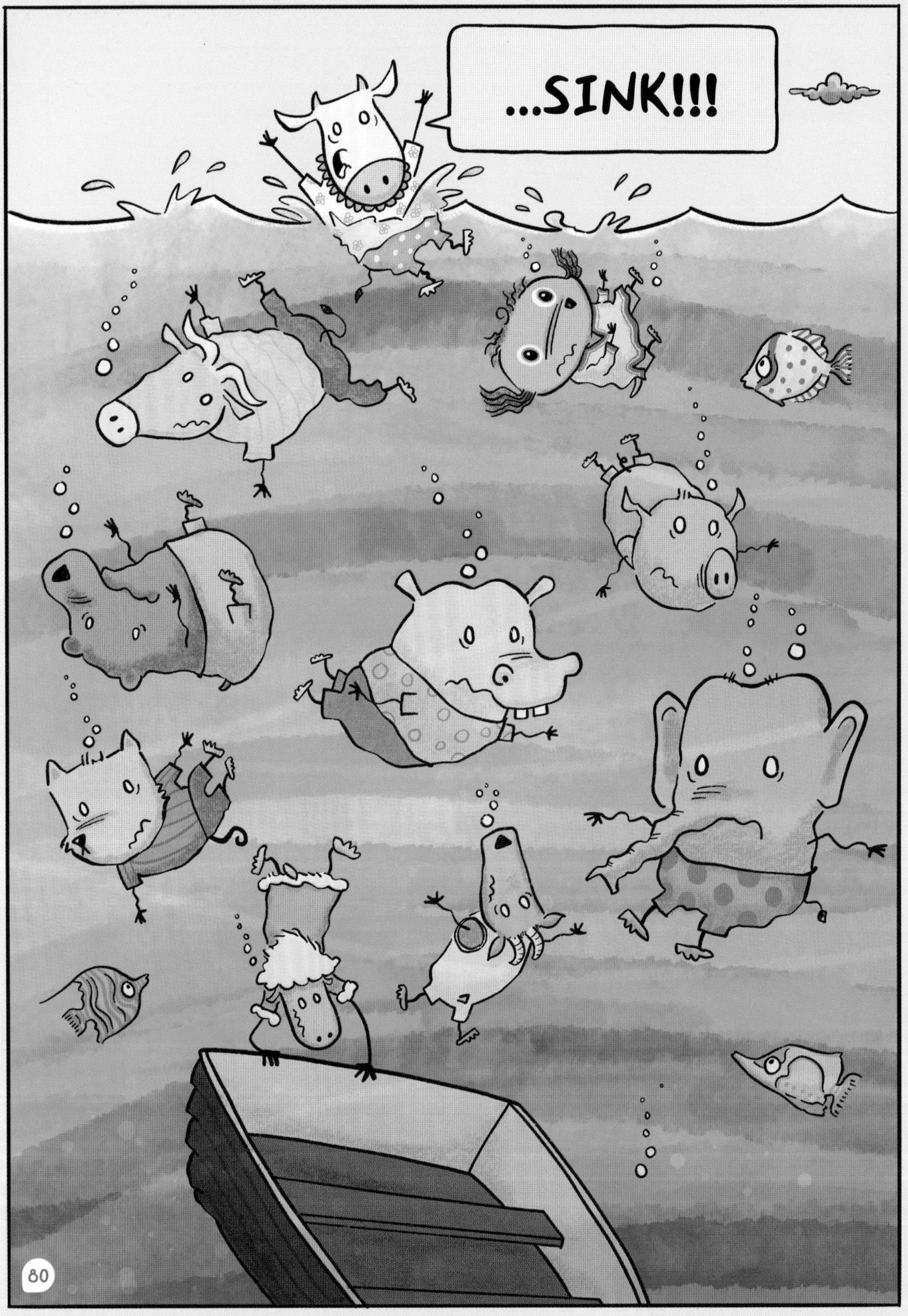
...SINK!!!

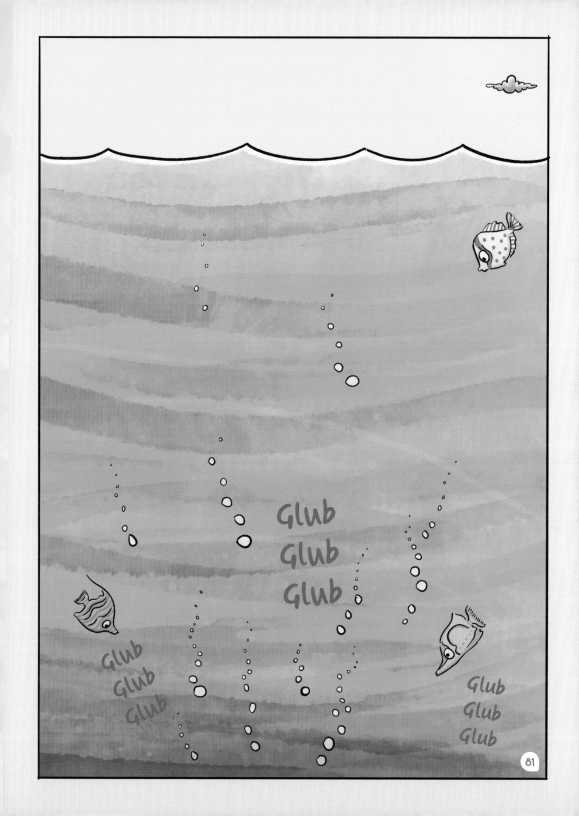

Glub
Glub
Glub

Glub
Glub
Glub

Glub
Glub
Glub

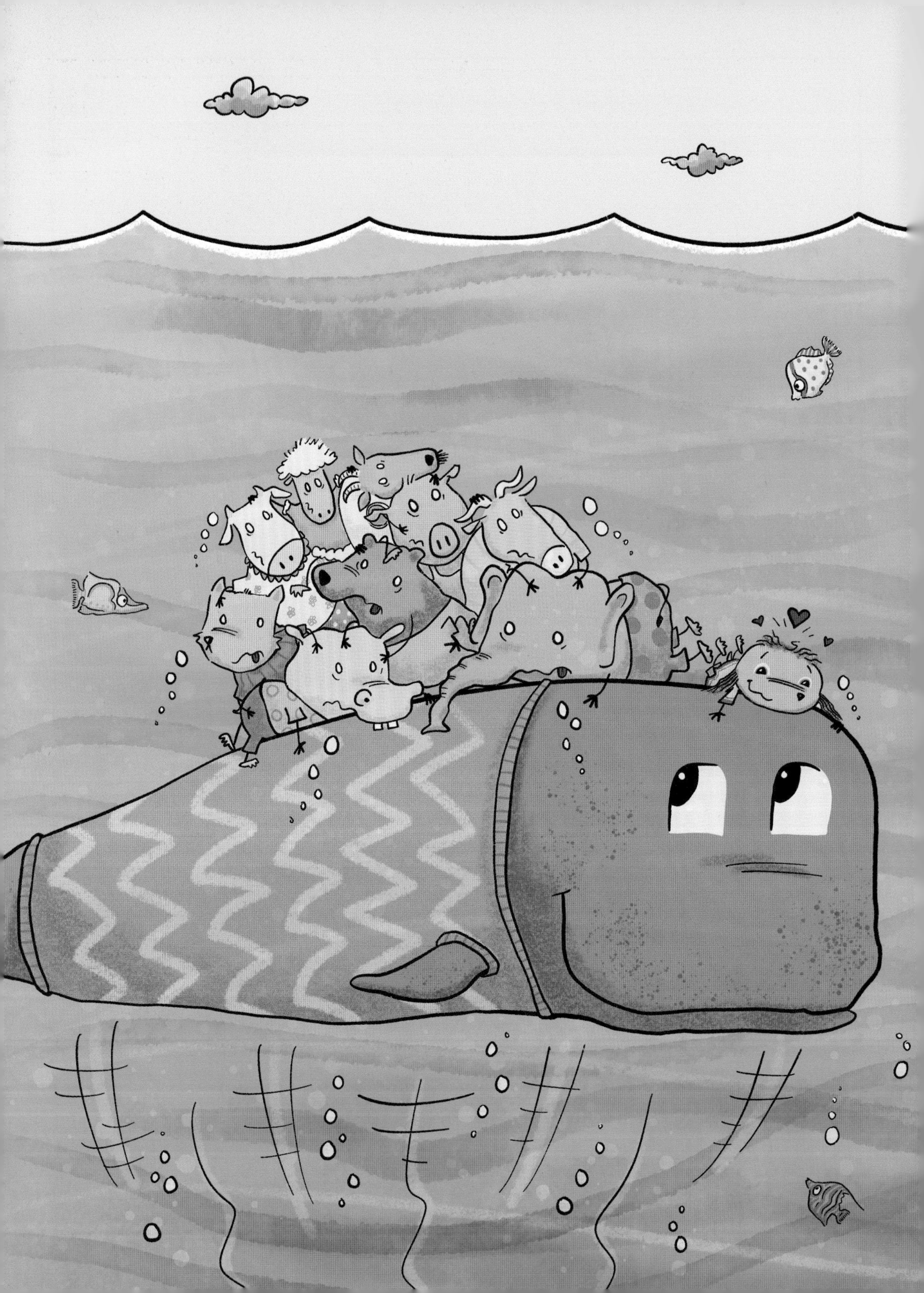

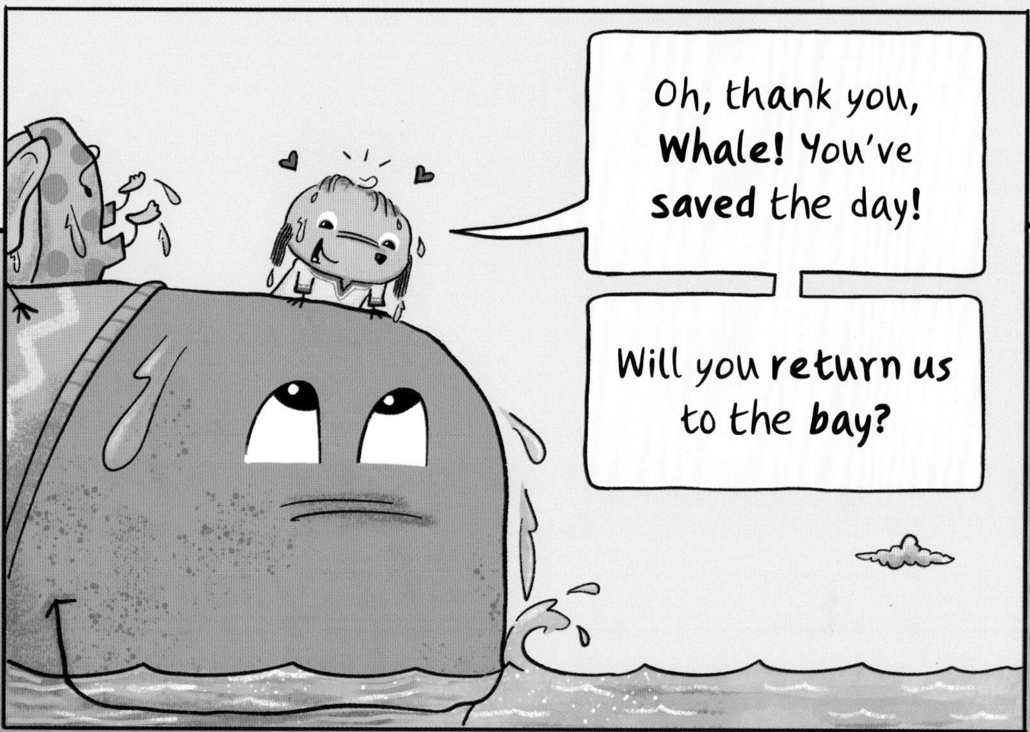
Oh, thank you, **Whale!** You've **saved** the day!
Will you **return us** to the **bay?**

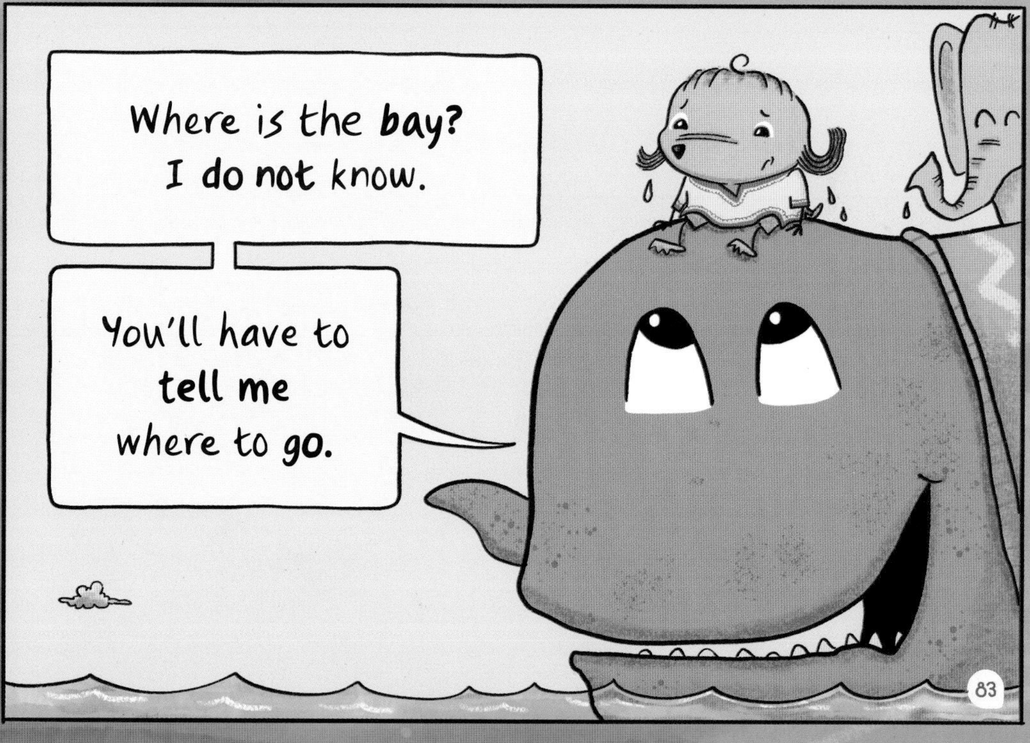
Where is the **bay?** I **do not** know.
You'll have to **tell me** where to **go.**

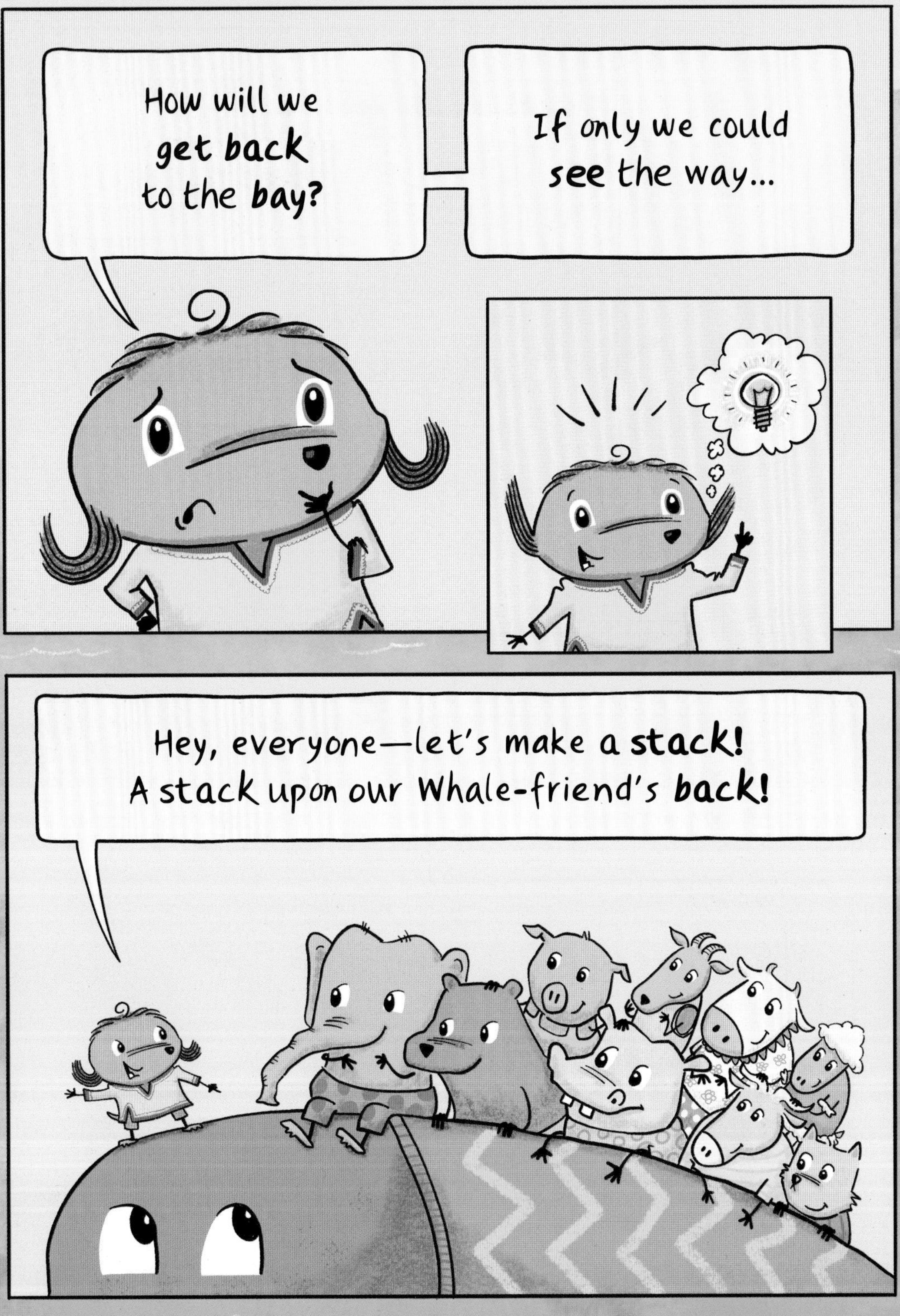
How will we get back to the bay?
If only we could see the way...
Hey, everyone—let's make a stack! A stack upon our Whale-friend's back!

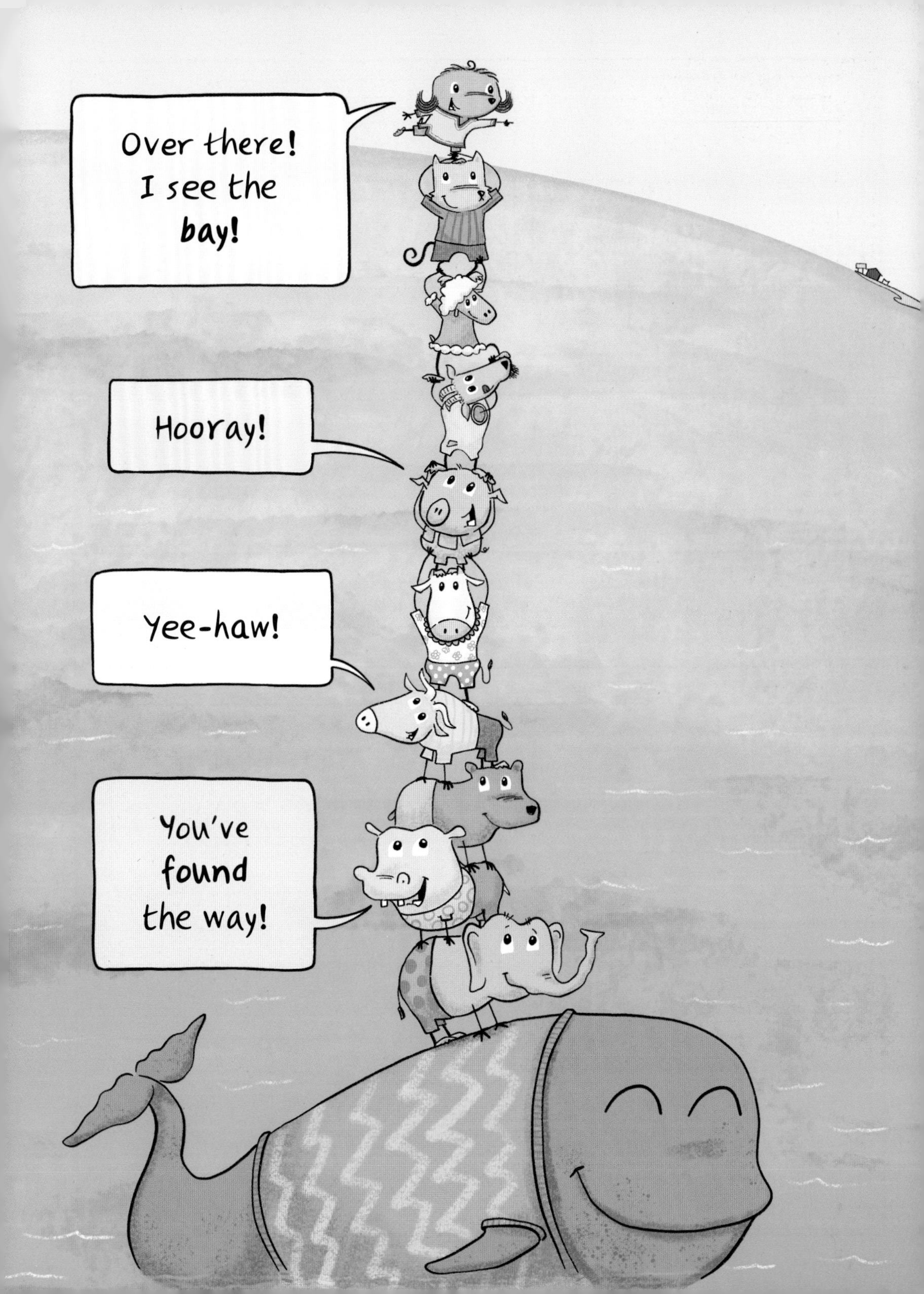
Over there! I see the **bay**!
Hooray!
Yee-haw!
You've **found** the way!

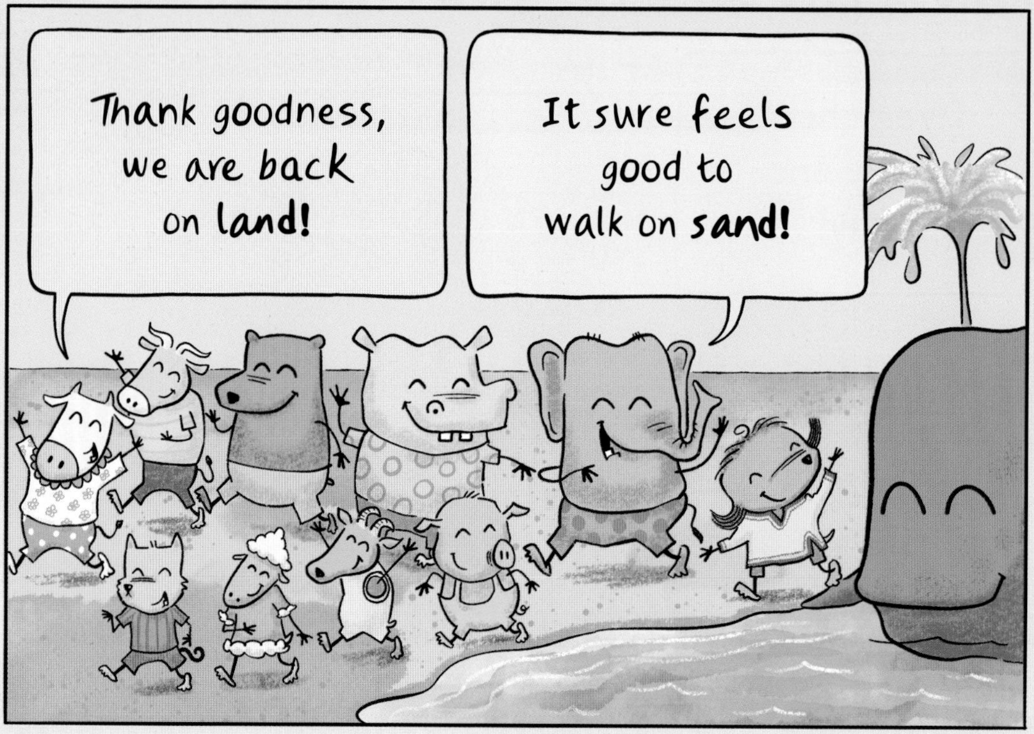
Thank goodness, we are back on **land!**
It sure feels good to walk on **sand!**

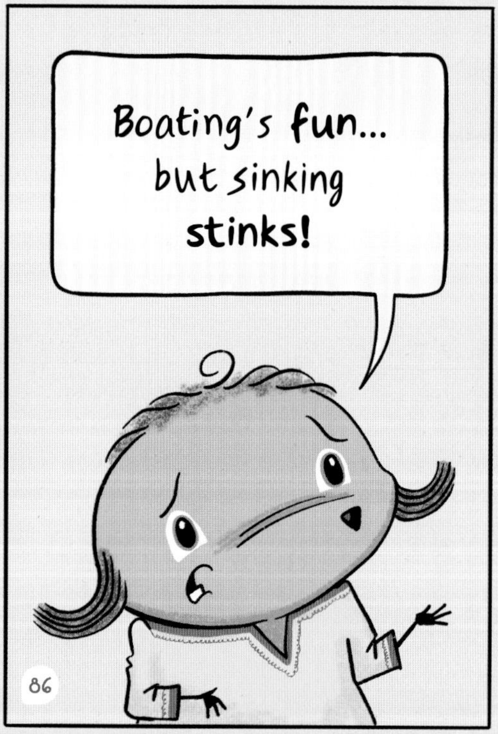
Boating's **fun...** but sinking **stinks!**

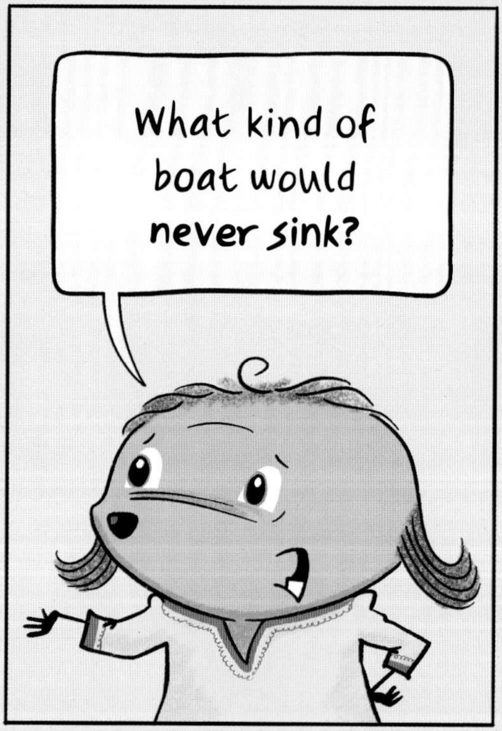
What kind of boat would **never sink?**

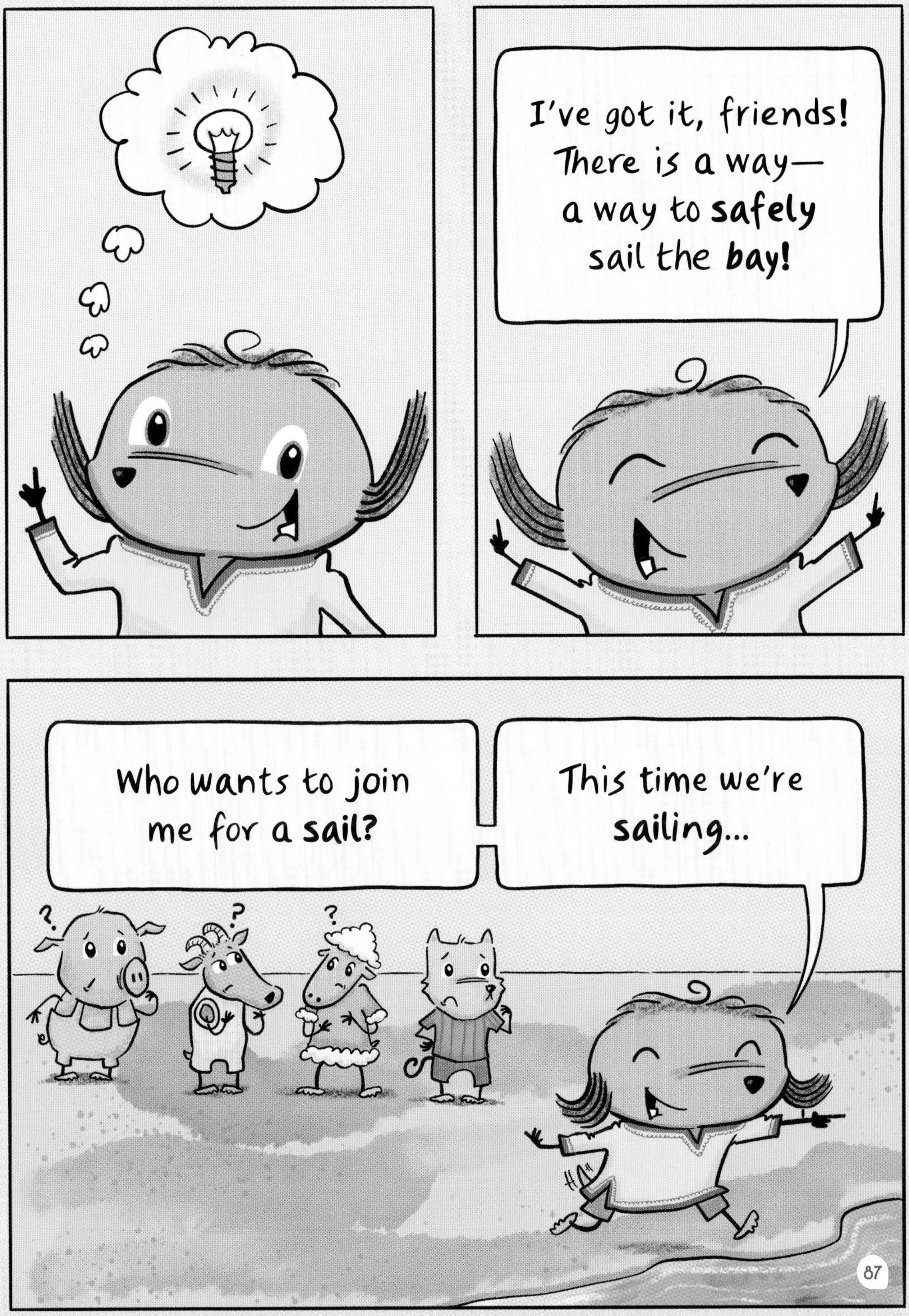
I've got it, friends! There is a way— a way to safely sail the bay!
Who wants to join me for a sail?
This time we're sailing...
?
?
?

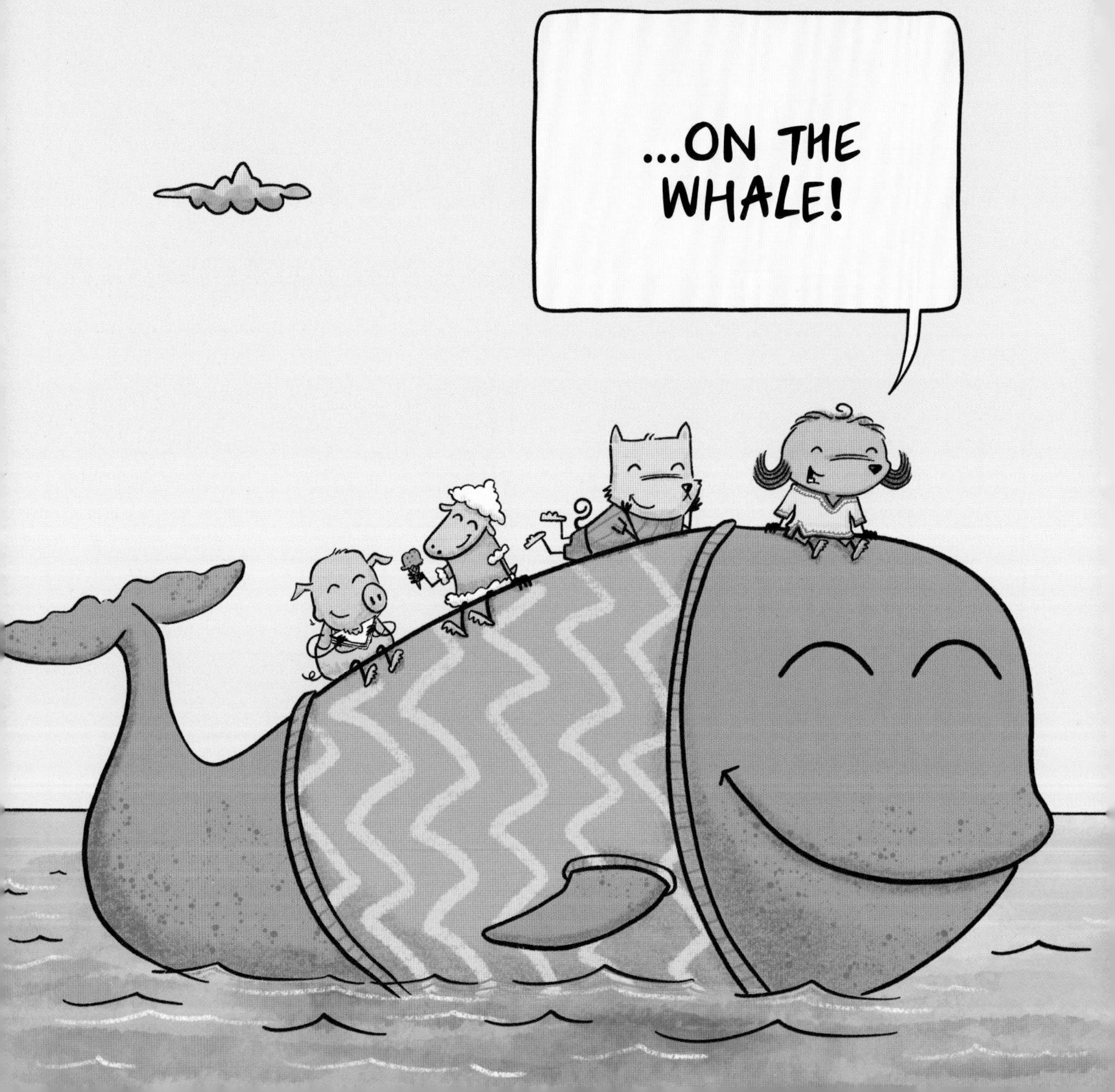
...ON THE WHALE!

END.

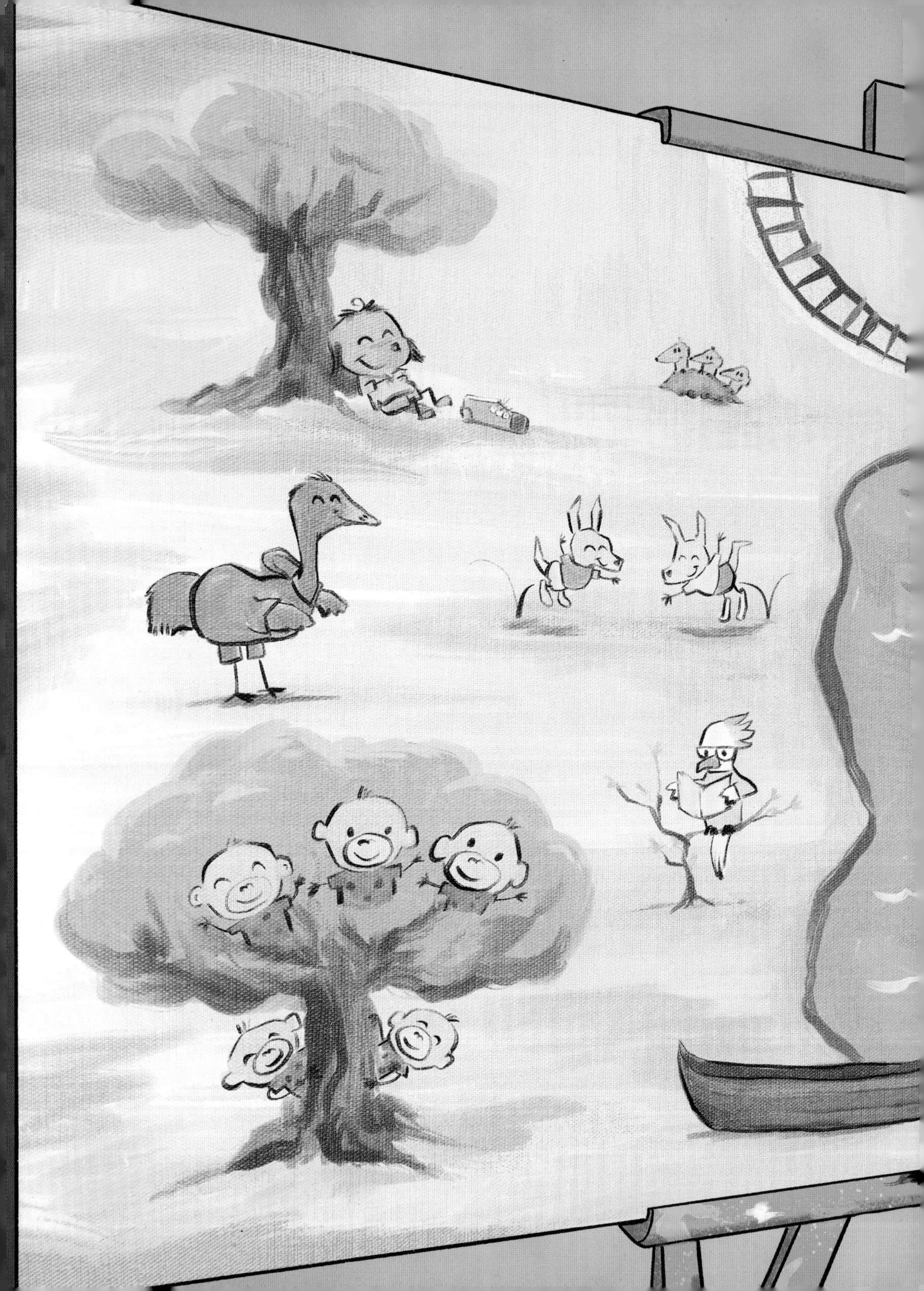

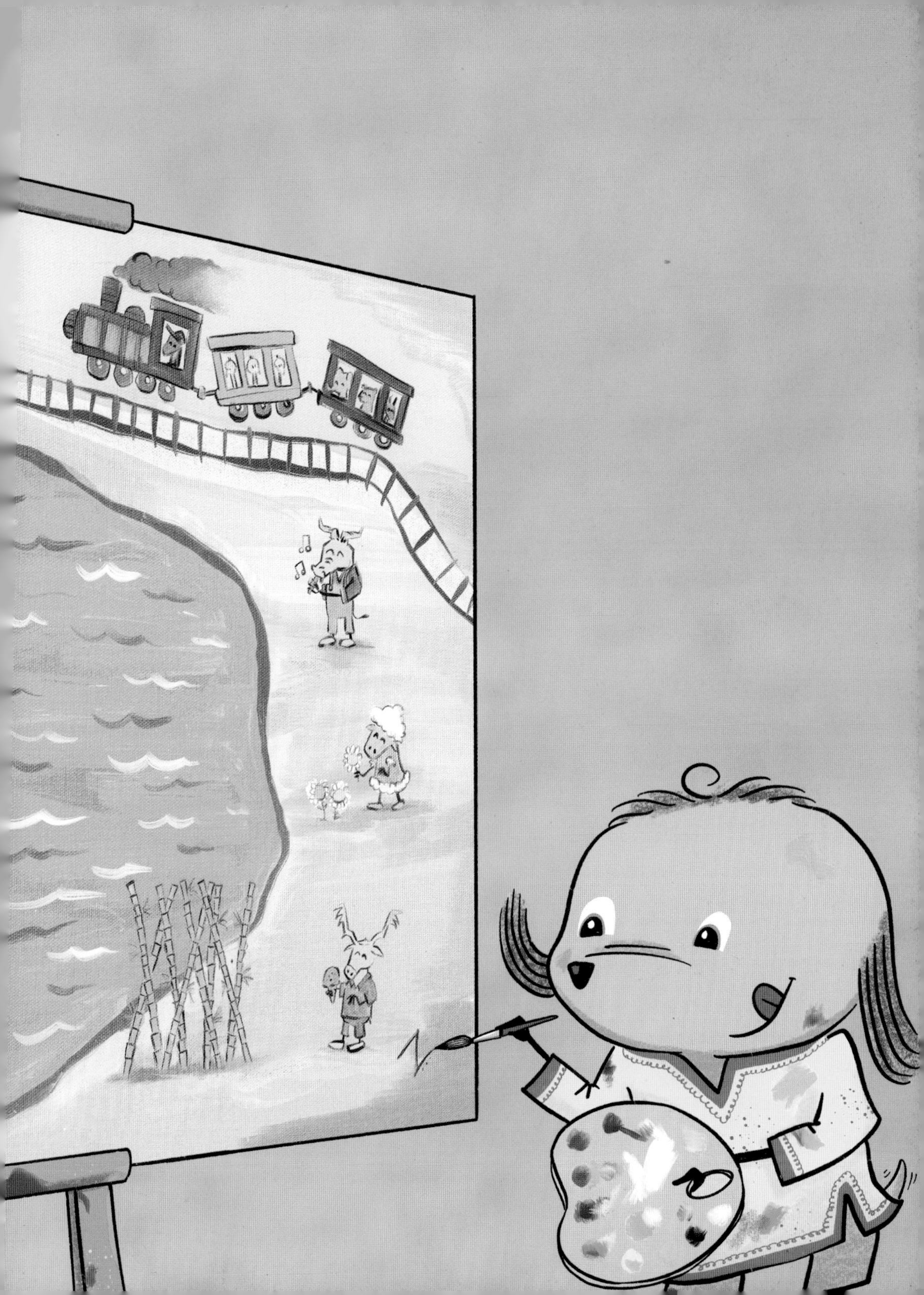